THE SWORD IN THE STONE

Terence Hanbury White was born in 1906, the son of a District Superintendent of Police in India, and, like virtually all children of servants of the British Empire, he was educated at boarding school in England. He then went to Cambridge, where he achieved a first class degree in English, and became a schoolmaster, soon rising in his profession to be Head of English at Stowe School in Buckinghamshire. By this time he was already writing and publishing novels, and after a short time he resigned from his job to become a full-time author – just before *The Sword in the Stone* was published. It turned out to be the first of four books he would write about King Arthur; the completed series had the title *The Once and Future King*, and it was eventually turned into a Broadway and Hollywood musical called *Camelot*; and *The Sword in the Stone* was made into a Walt Disney animated film. By the time White died in 1964, he had thousands of devoted admirers all round the world.

Collins Modern Classics

The Sword in the Stone

by

T. H. White

Illustrated by
Robert Shadbolt

 Collins

An imprint of HarperCollinsPublishers

First published in Britain by William Collins Sons & Co Ltd 1938
First published as a Collins Modern Classic 1998

5 7 9 10 8 6

Collins Modern Classics is an imprint of
HarperCollins*Publishers* Ltd, 77-85 Fulham Palace Road,
Hammersmith, London W6 8JB

The HarperCollins website address is
www.**fire**and**water**.com

ISBN 0 00 675399 X

Printed and bound in Great Britain by
Omnia Books Limited, Glasgow

Contents

For
Sir Thomas Maleore
Knight
★

"I pray you all, gentlemen and gentlewomen that readeth this book, from the beginning to the ending, pray for me while I am on live, that God send me good deliverance, and when I am dead, I pray you all pray for my soul."

Sir Thomas Maleore, Knight.
July 31st, 1485.

CHAPTER ONE

ON MONDAYS, WEDNESDAYS, and Fridays it was Court Hand and Summulae Logicales, while the rest of the week it was the Organon, Repetition and Astrology. The governess was always getting muddled with her astrolabe, and when she got specially muddled she would take it out of the Wart by rapping his knuckles. She did not rap Kay's knuckles because when Kay grew older he would be Sir Kay, and the master of the estate. The Wart was called the Wart because it rhymed with Art, which was short for his real name. Kay had given him the nickname. Kay was not called anything but Kay, because he was too dignified to have a nickname and would have flown into a passion if anybody had tried to give him one. The governess had red hair and some mysterious wound from which she derived a lot of prestige by showing it to all the women of the castle, behind closed doors. It was believed to be where she sat down, and to have been caused by sitting on a broken bottle at a picnic by mistake. Eventually she offered to show it to Sir Ector, who was Kay's father, had hysterics and was sent away. They found out afterwards that she had been in a lunatic hospital for three years.

In the afternoons the programme was: Mondays and Fridays, tilting and horsemanship; Tuesdays, hawking; Wednesdays, fencing; Thursdays, archery; Saturdays, the theory of chivalry, with the proper measures to be blown on all occasions, terminology of the chase and hunting etiquette. If you did the wrong thing at the mort or the undoing, for instance, you were bent over the body of the dead beast and smacked with the flat side of a sword. This was called being bladed. It was horseplay, a sort of joke like being shaved when crossing the line. Kay was not bladed, although he often went wrong.

After they had got rid of the governess, Sir Ector said, "After all, damn it all, we can't have the boys runnin' about all day like hooligans, after all, can we, damn it all? Ought to be havin' a first-rate eddication, at their age. When I was their age I was doin' all this Latin and stuff at five o'clock every mornin'. Happiest time of my life. Pass the port."

Sir Grummore Grummursum, who was staying the night because he had been benighted out questin' after a specially long run, said that when he was their age he was swished every mornin' because he would go hawkin' instead of learnin'. He attributed to this weakness the fact that he could never get beyond the Future Simple of Utor. It was a third of the way down the left-hand page, he said. He thought it was page ninety-seven. He passed the port.

Sir Ector said, "Had a good quest today?"

Sir Grummore said, "Oh, not so bad. Rattlin' good day, in fact. Found a chap called Sir Bruce Saunce Pité choppin' off a maiden's head in Weedon Bushes, ran him to Mixbury Plantation in the Bicester, where he doubled back, and lost him in Wicken Wood. Must have been a good twenty-five miles as he ran."

"A straight-necked 'un," said Sir Ector.

"But about these boys and all this Latin and that," added Sir Ector. "Amo, amas, you know, and runnin' about like hooligans: what would you advise?"

"Ah," said Sir Grummore, laying his finger by his nose and winking at the port, "that takes a deal of thinkin' about, if you don't mind my sayin' so."

"Don't mind at all," said Sir Ector. "Very kind of you to say anythin'. Much obliged, I'm sure. Help yourself to port."

"Good port this," said Sir Grummore.

"Get it from a friend of mine," said Sir Ector.

"But about these boys," said Sir Grummore. "How many of them are there, do you know?"

"Two," said Sir Ector, "counting them both, that is."

"Couldn't send them to Eton, I suppose?" inquired Sir Grummore cautiously. "Long way and all that, we know."

"Isn't so much the distance," said Sir Ector, "but that giant What's-'is-name is in the way. Have to pass through his country, you understand."

"What is his name?"

"Can't recollect it at the moment, not for the life of me. Fellow that lives by the burbly water."

"Ah, Galapas," said Sir Grummore.

"That's the very chap."

"The only other thing," said Sir Grummore, "is to have a tutor."

"You mean a fellow who teaches you," said Sir Ector wisely.

"That's it," said Sir Grummore. "A tutor, you know, a fellow who teaches you."

"Have some more port," said Sir Ector. "You need it after all this questin'."

"Splendid day," said Sir Grummore. "Only they never seem to kill nowadays. Run twenty-five miles and then mark to ground or lose him altogether. The worst is when you start a fresh quest."

"We kill all our giants cubbin'," said Sir Ector. "After that they give you a fine run, but get away."

"Run out of scent," said Sir Grummore, "I dare say. It's always the same with these big giants in a big country. They run out of scent."

"But even if you were to have a tutor," said Sir Ector. "I don't see how you would get him."

"Advertise," said Sir Grummore.

"I have advertised," said Sir Ector. "I put it in the *Humberland News and Cardoile Advertiser.*"

"The only other way," said Sir Grummore, "is to start a quest."

"You mean a quest for a tutor," explained Sir Ector.

"That's it," said Sir Grummore.

"Hic, Hac, Hoc," said Sir Ector. "Have some more port."

"Hunc," said Sir Grummore.

So it was decided. When Sir Grummore Grummursum had gone away next day, Sir Ector tied a knot in his handkerchief to remember to start a quest for a tutor as soon as he had time, and, as he was not quite sure how to set about it, he told the boys what Sir Grummore had suggested and warned them not to be hooligans meanwhile. Then they went haymaking.

It was July, and every able-bodied man and woman on the estate worked all that month in the field, under Sir Ector's direction. In any case the boys would have been excused from being eddicated just then.

Sir Ector's castle stood in an enormous clearing in a still more enormous forest. It had a big green courtyard and a moat with pike in it. The moat was crossed by a strongly-fortified stone bridge which ended halfway across it: the other half was covered by a wooden drawbridge which was wound up every night. As soon as you had crossed the draw-bridge you were at the top of the village street – it had only one street – and this extended for about half a mile, with little white thatched houses of mud on either side of it. The street divided the clearing into two huge fields, that on the left being cultivated in hundreds of long narrow strips, while that on the right ran down to a little river and was used as pasture. Half of the right-hand field was fenced off for hay.

It was July, and real July weather, such as they only had in old England. Everybody went bright brown like Red Indians with startling teeth and flashing eyes. The dogs moved about with their tongues hanging out, or lay panting in bits of shade, while the farm horses sweated through their coats and flicked their tails and tried to kick the horseflies off their bellies with their great hind hoofs. In the pasture field the cows were on the gad, and could be seen galloping about with their tails in the air, which made Sir Ector angry.

Sir Ector stood on the top of a rick, whence he could see what everybody was doing, and shouted commands all over the two-hundred-acre field, and grew purple in the face. The best mowers mowed away in a line where the grass was still uncut, their scythes roaring all together in the strong sunlight. The women raked the dry hay together in long lines, with wooden rakes, and two boys with pitchforks followed up on either side of the line turning the hay inwards so that it lay well for picking up. Then the great carts followed, rumbling with their spiked wooden wheels, and drawn by horses or slow white oxen. One man stood on top of the cart to receive the hay and direct operations, while one man walked on either side picking up what the boys had prepared and throwing it to him with a fork. The cart was led down the lane between two lines of hay, and was loaded in strict rotation from the front poles to the back, the man on top calling out in a stern voice where he wanted each fork to be pitched. The loaders grumbled at the boys for not having laid the hay properly and threatened to tan them when they caught them, if they got left behind.

Chapter One

When the waggon was loaded, it was drawn to Sir Ector's rick and pitched to him. It came up easily because it had been loaded systematically – not like modern hay – and Sir Ector scrambled about on top, getting in the way of the two assistants, who did all the real work, and stamping and perspiring and scratching about with his fork and trying to make the rick grow straight and shouting that it would all fall down as soon as the west winds came.

The Wart loved haymaking, and was good at it. Kay, who was two years older, generally stood on the edge of the bundle of hay which he was trying to pick up, with the result that he worked twice as hard as the Wart for only half the result. But he hated to be beaten by anybody at anything and used to fight away with the wretched hay – which he loathed like poison – until he was quite sick.

The day after Sir Grummore's visit was hot, sweltering for the men who toiled from milking to milking and then again till sunset in their battle with the sultry element. For the hay was an element to them, like sea or air, in which they bathed and plunged themselves and which they even breathed in. The seeds and small scraps stuck in their hair, their mouths, their nostrils, and worked, tickling, inside their clothes. They did not wear many clothes, and the shadows between their sliding muscles were blue on the nut-brown skins. Those who feared thunder had felt ill that morning.

In the afternoon a terrible storm came. Sir Ector kept them at it till the great flashes were right overhead, and then, with the sky as dark as night, the rain came hurling against them so that they were drenched at once and could not see a hundred yards. The boys lay crouched under the waggons, wrapped in hay to keep their wet bodies warm against the now cold wind, and all joked with one another while heaven fell. Kay was shivering, though not with cold, but he joked like the others because he would not show he was afraid. At the last and greatest thunderbolt every man startled involuntarily, and each saw the other startle, until they all laughed away their shame.

But that was the end of the haymaking for them and the beginning of play. The boys were sent home to change their clothes. The old dame who had been their nurse fetched dry jerkins out of a press, and scolded them for catching their deaths, and denounced Sir Ector for keeping them on so long. Then they slipped their heads into the laundered shirts, and ran out into the refreshed and sparkling court.

"I vote we take Cully and see if we can get some rabbits in the chase," cried the Wart.

"The rabbits won't be out in this wet," said Kay sarcastically, delighted to have caught him out over natural history.

"Oh, come on," said the Wart. "It'll soon dry."

"I must carry Cully, then."

Kay insisted on carrying the goshawk and flying her, when they went out together. This he had a right to do, not only because he was older than the Wart but also because he was Sir Ector's proper son. The Wart was not a proper son. He did not understand about this, but it made him feel unhappy, because Kay seemed to regard it as making him inferior in some way. Also it was different not having a father and mother, and Kay had taught him that being different was necessarily wrong. Nobody talked to him about it, but he thought about it when he was alone, and was distressed. He did not like people to bring it up, and since the other boy always did bring it up when a question of precedence arose, he had got into the habit of giving in at once before it could be mentioned. Besides, he admired Kay and was a born follower. He was a hero-worshipper.

"Come on, then," cried the Wart, and they scampered off towards the mews, turning a few cartwheels on the way.

The mews was one of the most important parts of the castle, next to the stables and the kennels. It was opposite to the solar and faced south. The outside windows had to be small, for reasons of fortification, but the windows which looked inwards to the courtyard were big and sunny. All the windows had close vertical slats nailed down them, but no horizontal ones. There was no glass, but to keep the hawks from draughts there was horn in the small windows. At one end of the mews there was a little fireplace and a kind of snuggery, like the place in a saddle-room where the grooms sit to clean their tack on wet winter nights after hunting. Here there were a couple of stools, a cauldron, a bench with all sorts of small knives and surgical instruments, and some shelves with pots on them. The pots were labelled Cardamum, Ginger, Barley Sugar, Wrangle, For a Snurt, For the Craye, Vertigo, etc. There were leather skins hanging up, which had been snipped about as pieces were cut out of them for jesses, hoods or leashes. On the neat row of nails there were Indian bells and swivels and silver varvels each with Ector cut on. A special shelf, and the most beautiful of all, held the hoods: very old cracked rufter hoods which had been made for birds before Kay was born, tiny hoods for the merlins, small hoods for tiercels, splendid new hoods which had been knocked up to pass away the long winter evenings. All the hoods, except the rufters, were made in Sir Ector's colours: white leather with red baize at the sides and a bunch of blue grey plumes on top, made out of the hackle feathers of herons. On the bench there was a jumble of oddments such as are to be found in every workshop, bits of cord, wire, metal, tools, some bread, and cheese which the mice had been at, a leather bottle, some frayed gauntlets for the left hand, nails, bits of sacking, a couple of lures and some rough tallies scratched on the wood. These read: Conays IIIIIIII, Harn III, etc. They were not spelt very well.

Right down the length of the room, with the afternoon sun shining full on them, there ran the screen perches to which the birds were tied. There were two little merlins which had only just been taken up from hacking, an old peregrine who was not much use in this wooded country but who was kept for appearances, a kestrel on which the boys had learnt the rudiments of falconry, a spar-hawk which Sir Ector was kind enough to keep for the parson, and caged off in a special apartment of his own at the far end, there was the tiercel goshawk Cully.

The Mews was neatly kept, with sawdust on the floor to

absorb the mutes, and the castings taken up every day. Sir Ector visited the mews each morning at seven o'clock and the two austringers stood at attention outside the door. If they had forgotten to brush their hair he confined them to barracks. They took no notice.

Kay put on one of the left-handed gauntlets and called Cully from the perch; but Cully, with all his feathers close-set and malevolent, glared at him with a mad marigold eye and refused to come. So Kay took him up.

"Do you think we ought to fly him?" asked the Wart doubtfully. "Deep in the moult like this?"

"Of course we can fly him, yon ninny," said Kay. "He only wants to be carried a bit, that's all."

So they went out across the hay-field, noting how the carefully-raked hay was now sodden again and losing its goodness, into the chase where the trees began to grow, far apart as yet and parklike, but gradually crowding into the forest shade. The conies had hundreds of buries under these trees, so close together that the problem was not to find a rabbit, but find a rabbit far enough away from its hole.

"Hob says that we mustn't fly Cully till he has roused at least twice," said the Wart.

"Hob doesn't know anything about it," said the other boy. "Nobody can tell whether a hawk is fit to fly except the man who is carrying it.

"Hob is only a villein anyway," added Kay, and began to undo the leash and swivel from the jesses.

When he felt the trappings being taken off him, so that he

was in hunting order, Cully did make some movements as if to rouse. He raised his crest, his shoulders coverts and the soft feathers of his thighs, but at the last moment he thought better or worse of it and subsided without the rattle. This movement of the hawk's made the Wart itch to carry him, so that he yearned to take him away from Kay and set him to rights himself. He felt certain that he could get Cully into a good temper by scratching his feet and softly teasing his breast feathers upwards, if only he were allowed to do it himself, instead of having to plod along behind with the stupid lure; but he knew how annoying it must be for Kay to be continually subjected to advice, and so he held his peace. Just as in modern shooting you must never offer criticism to the man in command, so in hawking it was important that no outside advice should be allowed to disturb the judgement of the actual austringer.

"So-ho!" cried Kay, throwing his arms upwards to give the hawk a better take-off, and a rabbit was scooting across the close-nibbled turf in front of them, and Cully was in the air. The movement had surprised the Wart, the rabbit and the hawk, all three, and all three hung a moment in surprise. Then the great wings of the aerial assassin began to row the air, but reluctantly and undecided, the rabbit vanished in a hidden hole, and up went the hawk, swooping like a child flung high in a swing, until the wings folded and he was sitting in a tree. Cully looked down at his masters, opened his beak in an angry pant of failure, and remained motionless. The two hearts stood still.

CHAPTER TWO

A GOOD WHILE after that, when they had been whistling and luring and following the disturbed and sulky hawk from tree to tree, Kay lost his temper.

"Let him go, then," said Kay. "He's no use anyway."

"Oh, we couldn't leave him," cried the Wart. "What would Hob say?"

"It's my hawk, not Hob's," exclaimed Kay furiously. "What does it matter what Hob says? He is my servant."

"But Hob made Cully. It's all right for us to lose him, for we didn't have to sit up with him three nights and carry him all day and all that. We can't lose Hob's hawk. It would be beastly."

"Serve him right, then. He's a fool and it's a rotten hawk. Who wants a rotten, stupid hawk? You'd better stay yourself, if you're so keen on it. I'm going home."

"I'll stay," said the Wart sadly, "if you'll send Hob when

you get back."

Kay began walking off in the wrong direction, raging in his heart because he knew that he had flown the bird when he was not properly in yarak, and the Wart had to shout after him the right way. Then he sat down under the tree and looked up at Cully like a cat watching a sparrow, but with his heart beating fast.

It was all right for Kay, who was not really keen on hawking except in so far as it was the proper occupation for a boy in his station of life, but the Wart had some of the falconer's feelings and knew that a lost hawk was the greatest possible calamity. He knew that Hob had worked on Cully for fourteen hours a day, over a period of months, in order to teach him his trade, and that his work had been like Jacob's struggle with the angel. When Cully was lost a part of Hob was lost too. The Wart did not dare to face the look of reproach which would be in Hob's eye, after all that he had tried to teach them.

What was he to do? He had better sit still, leaving the lure on the ground, so that Cully could settle down and come in his own time. But Cully had no intention of doing this. He had been given a generous crop the night before, so that he was not hungry: the hot day had put him in a bad temper: the waving and whistling of the boys below him, and their pursuit of him from tree to tree, had disturbed his never very powerful brains. Now he did not quite know what he wanted to do, but it was not what anybody else wanted. He thought perhaps it would be nice to kill something, just from spite.

A long time after that, the Wart was on the verge of the true forest, and Cully inside it. In a series of infuriating removes they had come nearer and nearer, till they were further from the castle than the Wart had ever been, and now they had reached it quite.

Wart would not have been frightened of a forest nowadays, but the great jungle of old England was a different thing. It was not only that there were wild boars in it, whose sounders would at this season be furiously rooting about, nor that one of the surviving wolves might be slinking behind any tree, with pale eyes and slavering chops. The man and wicked animals were not the only inhabitants of the crowded gloom. When men themselves became mad and wicked they took refuge there, outlaws cunning and bloody as the gorecrow, and as persecuted. The Wart thought particularly of a man named Wat, whose name the cottagers used to frighten their children with. He had once lived in Sir Ector's village and the Wart could remember him. He squinted, had no nose, and was weak in his wits. The children threw stones at him. One day he turned on the children and caught one and made a snarly noise and bit off his nose too. Then he ran away into the forest. They threw stones at the child with no nose, now, but Wat was supposed to be in the forest still, running on all fours and dressed in skins.

There were magicians in the forest also in those days, as well as strange animals not known to modern works of natural history. There were regular bands of outlaws, not like Wat, who lived together and wore green and shot with arrows which never missed. There were even a few dragons, though they were rather small ones, which lived under stones and could hiss like a kettle.

Added to this, there was the fact that it was getting dark. The forest was trackless and nobody in the village knew what was on the other side. The evening hush had fallen, and all the high trees stood looking at the Wart without a sound.

He felt that it would be safer to go home, while he still knew where he was; but he had a stout heart, and did not want to give in. He understood that once Cully had slept in freedom for a whole night he would be wild again and irreclaimable. Cully was a passager. But if the poor Wart could only make him to roost, and if Hob would only arrive then with a dark lantern, they might still take him that night by climbing the tree, while he was sleepy and muddled with the light. He could see more or less where the hawk had perched, about a hundred yards within the thick trees, because the home-going rooks of evening were mobbing that place.

Wart made a mark on one of the trees outside the forest, hoping that it might help him to find his way back, and then began to fight his way into the undergrowth as best he might. He heard by the rooks that Cully had immediately moved further off.

The night fell still as the small boy struggled with the brambles; but he went on doggedly, listening with all his ears, and Cully's evasions became sleepier and shorter until at last, before the utter darkness fell, he could see the hunched shoulders in a tree above him against the sky. Wart sat down under the tree, so as not to disturb the bird any further as it went to sleep, and Cully, standing on one leg, ignored his existence.

"Perhaps," said the Wart to himself, "even if Hob doesn't come, and I don't see how he can very well follow me in this trackless forest now, I shall be able to climb up by myself at about midnight because he ought to be deep in sleep then. I could speak to him softly by name, so that he thought it was just the usual person coming to take him up while hooded. I shall have to climb very quietly. Then, if I do get him, I shall have to find my way home, and the drawbridge will be up. But perhaps somebody will wait for me, for Kay will have told them I am out. I wonder which way it was? I wish Kay had not gone."

He snuggled down between the roots of the tree, trying to find a comfortable place where the hard wood did not stick into his shoulder blades.

"I think the way was behind that big spruce with the spiky top. I ought to try to remember which side of me the sun is setting, so that when it rises I may keep it on the same side going home. Did something move under that spruce tree, I wonder? Oh, I wish I may not meet that old wild Wat and have my nose bitten off. How aggravating Cully looks, standing there on one leg as if there was nothing the matter."

At this there was a quick whirr and a smack, and the Wart found an arrow sticking in the tree wood between the fingers of his right hand. He snatched his hand away, thinking he had been stung by something, before he noticed it was an arrow. Then everything went slow. He had time to notice quite carefully what sort of an arrow it was, and how it had driven three inches into the solid wood. It was a black arrow with yellow bands round it, like a horrible wasp, and its cock feather was yellow. The two others were black. They were goose feathers.

The Wart found that, although he was frightened of the danger of the forest before it happened, once he was in it he was not frightened any more. He got up quickly, but it seemed to him slowly, and went behind the other side of the tree. As he did this, another arrow came whirr and tock, but this one buried all except its feathers in the grass, and stayed there still, as if it had never moved.

On the other side of the tree he found a waste of bracken, six foot high. This was splendid cover, but it betrayed his whereabouts by rustling. He heard another arrow hiss through the fronds, and what seemed to be a man's voice cursing, but it was not very near. Then he heard the man, or whatever it was, running about in the bracken. It was reluctant to fire any more arrows because they were valuable things and would certainly get lost in the undergrowth. Wart went like a snake, like a coney, like a silent owl. He was small and the creature had no chance against him in this game. In five minutes he was safe.

The assassin searched for his arrows and went away grumbling; but the Wart realized that, even if he was safe, he had lost his way and his hawk. He had not the faintest idea where he was. He lay down for half an hour, pressed under the fallen tree where he had hidden to give time for the thing to go right away and for his own heart to cease its thundering. It had begun beating like this as soon as he knew he had got away from the outlaw.

"Oh," thought the Wart, "now I am truly lost, and now there is almost no alternative except to have my nose bitten off, or to be pierced right through with one of those waspy arrows, or to be eaten by a hissing dragon or a wolf or a wild boar or a magician – if magicians do eat boys, which I expect they do. Now I may well wish that I had been a good boy, and not angered the governess when she got muddled with her astrolabe, and had loved my dear guardian Sir Ector as much as he deserved."

At these melancholy thoughts, and especially at the recollections of kind Sir Ector with his pitchfork and his big red nose, the poor Wart's eyes became full of tears and he lay most desolate beneath the tree.

The sun finished the last rays of its lingering goodbye, and the moon rose in awful majesty over the silver treetops, before he dared to rise. Then he got up, and dusted the twigs out of his jerkin, and wandered off forlornly, taking the easiest way always and trusting himself to God. He had been walking like this for about half an hour, and sometimes sighing to himself and sometimes feeling more cheerful – because it really was very cool and lovely in the summer forest by moonlight – when he came upon the most beautiful thing that he had ever seen in his short life.

There was a clearing in the forest, a wide sward of moonlit grass, and the white rays shone full upon the tree trunks on the opposite side. These trees were beeches, whose trunks are always most beautiful in a pearly light, and among the beeches there was the smallest movement and a silvery clink. Before the clink there were just beeches, but immediately afterwards there was a Knight in full armour, standing still, and silent and unearthly, among the majestic trunks. He was mounted on an enormous white horse that stood as rapt as its master, and he carried in his right hand, with its butt resting on the stirrup, a high, smooth jousting lance, which stood up among the tree stumps, higher and higher, till it was outlined against the velvet sky. All was moonlit, all silver, too beautiful to describe.

The Wart did not know what to do. He did not know whether it would be safe to go up to this Knight, for there were so many terrible things in the forest that even the Knight might be a ghost. Most ghostly he looked, too, as he hoved meditating on the confines of the gloom. Eventually the Wart made up his mind that even if it was a ghost, it would be the ghost of a Knight, and Knights were bound by their vows to help people in distress.

"Excuse me," said the Wart, when he was right under the mysterious figure, "but can you tell me the way back to Sir Ector's castle?"

At this the ghost jumped violently, so that it nearly fell off its horse, and gave out a muffled baaaing noise through its visor, like a flock of sheep.

"Excuse me," began the Wart again, and stopped, terrified, in the middle of his speech.

For the ghost lifted up its visor, revealing two enormous eyes frosted like ice; exclaimed in an anxious voice, "What, what?"; took off its eyes — which turned out to be horn-rimmed spectacles, completely fogged by being inside the helmet; tried to wipe them on the horse's mane – which only made them worse; lifted both hands above its head and tried to wipe them on its plume; dropped its lance; dropped the spectacles, got off the horse to search for them – the visor shutting in the process; lifted its visor; bent down for the spectacles; stood up again as the visor shut once more, and exclaimed in a plaintive voice, "Deah, deah!"

The Wart found the spectacles, wiped them, and gave them to the ghost, who immediately put them on (the visor shut again at once) and began scrambling back on the horse for dear life. When it was there it held out its hand for the lance, which the Wart handed up, and, feeling all secure, opened its visor with its left hand and held it open. It peered at the Wart with one hand up, like a lost mariner searching for land, and exclaimed, "Ah – hah; whom have we heah, what what?"

"Please," said the Wart, "I am a boy whose guardian is Sir Ector."

"Charming fellah," said the Knight. "Charming fellah. Never met him in my life."

"Can you tell me the way back to his castle?"

"Faintest ideah," said the Knight. "Faintest ideah. Stranger in these parts meself."

"I have got lost," said the Wart.

"Funny thing that. Funny thing that, what? Now Ay have been lost for seventeen years.

"Name of King Pellinore," continued the Knight. "May have heard of me, what?" Here the visor shut with a pop, like an echo to the What, but was opened again immediately.

"Seventeen years ago, come Michaelmas, and been after the Questing Beast ever since. Boring, very."

"I should think it would be," said the Wart, who had never heard of King Pellinore, or the Questing Beast, but felt that this was the safest thing to say in the circumstances.

"It is the burden of the Pellinores," said the Knight proudly. "Only a Pellinore can catch it; that is, of course, or his next of kin. Train all the Pellinores with that ideah in mind. Limited eddication, rather. Fewmets, and all that."

"I know what fewmets are," said the Wart with interest. "They are the droppings of the beast pursued. The harbourer keeps them in his horn, to show to his master, and can tell by them whether it is a warrantable beast or otherwise, and what state it is in."

"Intelligent child," remarked King Pellinore. "Very. Now Ay carry fewmets about with me practically all the time.

"Insanitary habit," added the King, beginning to look rather dejected, "and quite pointless. Only one Questing Beast, you know, what, so there can't be any question whether it is warrantable or not."

Here his visor began to droop so much that the Wart decided he had better forget his own troubles and try to cheer his companion up, by asking questions on the one subject about which King Pellinore seemed qualified to speak. Even talking to a lost royalty was better than being alone in the wood.

"What does the Questing Beast look like?"

"Ah, we call it the Beast Glatisant, you know," replied the monarch, assuming a learned air and beginning to speak quite volubly. "Now the Beast Glatisant, or, as we say in English, the Questing Beast – you may call it either," he added graciously, – "this Beast has the head of a serpent, ah, and the body of a libbard, the haunches of a lion, and he is footed like a hart. Wherever this beast goes he makes a noise in his belly as it had been the noise of thirty couples of hounds questing.

"Except when he is drinking, of course," added the King severely, as if he had rather shocked himself by leaving this out.

"It must be a dreadful kind of monster," said the Wart, looking at him anxiously.

"A dreadful monster," repeated the other complacently. "It is the Beast Glatisant, you know."

"And how do you follow it?"

This seemed to be the wrong kind of question, for King Pellinore immediately began to look much more depressed than ever, and glanced over his shoulder so hurriedly that his visor shut down altogether.

"Ay have a brachet," said King Pellinore sadly, as soon as he had restored himself. "There she is, over theah."

The Wart looked in the direction which had been indicated with a despondent thumb, and saw a lot of rope wound round a tree. The other end of the rope was tied to King Pellinore's saddle.

"I don't see her very well."

"Wound herself round the other side of the tree, Ay dare say," said the King, without looking round. "She always goes the opposite way to me."

The Wart went over to the tree and found a large white

dog scratching herself for fleas. As soon as she saw the Wart, she began wagging her whole body, grinning vacuously, and panting in her efforts to lick his face in spite of the cord. She was too tangled up to move.

"It's quite a good brachet," said King Pellinore, "only it pants so, and gets wound round things, and goes the opposite way. What with that and the visor, what, Ay sometimes don't know which way to turn."

"Why don't you let her loose?" asked the Wart. "She would follow the Beast just as well like that."

"She just goes right away then, you know, and Ay don't see her sometimes for a week.

"Gets a bit lonely without her," added the King wistfully, "following this Beast about, what, and never knowing where one is. Makes a bit of company, you know."

"She seems to have a friendly nature," said the Wart.

"Too friendly. Sometimes Ay doubt whether she is really after the Beast at all."

"What does she do when she sees it?"

"Nothing," said King Pellinore.

"Oh, well," said the Wart, "I dare say she will get to be interested in it after a time."

"It's eight months anyway since Ay saw the Beast at all."

King Pellinore's voice had got sadder and sadder since the beginning of the conversation, and now he definitely began to sniffle. "It's the curse of the Pellinores," he exclaimed. "Always mollocking about after that beastly Beast. What on earth use is it, anyway? First you have to stop to unwind the brachet, then your visor falls down, then you can't see through your spectacles. Nowhere to sleep, never know where you are. Rheumatism in the winter, sunstroke in the summer. All this beastly armour takes hours to put on. When it is on it's either frying or freezing, and it gets rusty. You have to sit up all night polishing the stuff. Oh, how Ay do wish Ay had a nice house of my own to live in, a house with beds in it and real pillows and sheets. If Ay was rich that's what Ay would buy. A nice bed with a nice pillow and a nice sheet that you could lie in, and then Ay would put this beastly horse in a meadow and tell that beastly brachet to run away and play, and throw all this beastly armour out of the window, and let the beastly Beast go and chase itself, that Ay would."

"If you could only show me the way home," said the Wart craftily, "I am sure Sir Ector would put you up in a bed for the night."

"Do you really mean it?" cried King Pellinore. "In a bed?"

"A feather bed," said the Wart firmly.

King Pellinore's eyes grew as round as saucers.

"A feather bed!" he repeated slowly. "Would it have pillows?"

"Down pillows."

"Down pillows!" whispered the King, holding his breath. And then, letting it all out in a rush. "What a lovely house your guardian must have!"

"I don't think it is more than two hours away," said the Wart, following up his advantage.

"And did this gentleman really send you out to invite me in?" inquired the King wonderingly. (He had forgotten all about the Wart being lost.) "How nice of him, how very nice of him, Ay do think, what?"

"He will be very pleased to see us," said the Wart, quite truthfully.

"Oh, how *nice* of him," exclaimed the King again, beginning to bustle about his various trappings. "And what a lovely gentleman he must be, to have a feather bed!

"Ay suppose Ay should have to share it with somebody?" he added doubtfully.

"You could have one of your very own."

"A feather bed of one's very own," exclaimed King Pellinore, "with sheets and a pillow – perhaps even two pillows, or a pillow and a bolster – and no need to get up in time for breakfast!

"Does your guardian get up in time for breakfast?" inquired the King, a momentary doubt striking him.

"Never," said the Wart.

"Fleas in the bed?" asked the King suspiciously.

"Not one."

"Well!" said King Pellinore. "It does sound too nice for words, Ay must say. A feather bed and none of those beastly fewmets for ever so long. How long did you say it would take us to get there?"

"Two hours," said the Wart; but he had to shout the second of these words, for the sounds were drowned in his mouth by a dreadful noise which had that moment arisen close beside them.

"What was that?" exclaimed the Wart.

"Hark!" cried the King.

"Oh, mercy!" wailed the Wart.

"It's the Beast!" shouted the King.

And immediately the loving huntsman had forgotten everything else, but was busied about his task. He wiped his spectacles upon the seat of his trousers, the only accessible piece of cloth about him, while the belling and bloody cry arose all round; balanced them on the end of his long nose, just before the visor automatically clapped to; clutched his jousting lance in his right hand, and galloped off in the direction of the noise. He was brought up short by the rope which was wound round the tree – the vacuous brachet meanwhile giving a melancholy yelp – and fell off his horse with a tremendous clang. In a second he was up again – the Wart was convinced that his spectacles must be broken – and hopping round the white horse with one foot in the stirrup. The girths stood the test and he was in the saddle somehow, with his jousting lance between his legs, and then he was galloping round and round the tree, in the opposite direction to that in which the brachet had wound herself up. He went round three times too often, the brachet meanwhile running and yelping in the opposite direction, and then, after four or five back casts, they were both free of the obstruction. "Yoicks, what!" cried King Pellinore, waving his lance in the air, and swaying excitedly in the saddle. Then he disappeared completely into the gloom of the forest, with the unfortunate brachet trailing and howling behind him at the other end of the string.

CHAPTER THREE

THE WART SLEPT well in the woodland nest where he had laid himself down, in that kind of thin but refreshing sleep which people have when they first lie out of doors. At first he only dipped below the surface of sleep, and skimmed along like a salmon in shallow water, so close to the surface that he fancied himself in the air. He thought himself awake when he was already asleep. He saw the stars above his face, whirling round on their silent and sleepless axis, and the leaves of the trees rustling against them, and heard small changes in the grass. These little noises of footsteps and soft-fringed wing-beats and stealthy bellies drawn over the grass blades or rattling against the bracken at first frightened or interested him, so that he moved to see what they were (but never saw), then soothed him, so that he no longer cared to see what they were but trusted them to be themselves, and finally left him altogether as he swam down deeper and deeper, nuzzling his nose into the scented turf, into the warm ground, into the unending waters under the earth.

It had been difficult to go to sleep in the bright summer moonlight, but once he was there it was not difficult to stay. The sun came early, causing him to turn over in protest, but in going to sleep he had learnt to vanquish light, and now the light could not rewake him. It was nine o'clock, five hours after daylight, before he rolled over, opened his eyes, and was awake at once. He was hungry.

The Wart had heard about people who lived on berries, but this did not seem practical at the moment because it was July, and there were none. He found two wild strawberries and ate them greedily. They tasted nicer than anything, so he wished there were more. Then he wished it was April, so that he could find some birds' eggs and eat those, or that he had not lost his goshawk Cully, so that the bird could catch him a rabbit which he would cook by rubbing two sticks together like the base Indian. But he had lost Cully, or he would not have lost himself, and probably the sticks would not have lit in any case. He decided that he could not have gone more than three or four miles from home, so the best thing he could do would be to sit still and listen. Then he might hear the noise of the haymakers, if he was lucky with the wind, and could hearken his way home by that.

What he did hear was a faint clanking noise, which made him think that King Pellinore must be after the Questing Beast again, close by. Only the noise was so regular and single in intention that it made him think of King Pellinore doing some special action with great patience and concentration, trying to scratch his back without taking off his armour, for instance. He went towards the noise.

There was a clearing in the forest, and in this clearing there was a snug little cottage built of stone. It was a cottage, although the Wart could not notice this at the time, which was divided into two bits. The main bit was the hall or every-purpose room, which was high because it extended from floor to roof, and this room had a fire on the floor whose smoke issued eventually out of a hole in the thatch of the roof. The other half of the cottage was divided into two rooms by a horizontal floor which made the top half into a bedroom and study, while the bottom half served for a larder, store-room, stable and barn. A white donkey lived in this downstairs room, and a ladder led to the one upstairs.

There was a well in front of the cottage, and the metallic noise which the Wart had heard was caused by a very old gentleman who was drawing water out of it by means of a handle and chain.

Clank, clank, clank, said the chain, until the bucket hit the lip of the well, and "Oh, drat the whole thing," said the old gentleman. You would think that after all these years of study one could do better for oneself than a by-our-lady well with a by-our-lady bucket, whatever the by-our-lady cost.

"I wish to goodness," added the old gentleman, heaving his bucket out of the well with a malevolent glance, "that I was only on the electric light and company's water, drat it."

Chapter Three

The old gentleman that the Wart saw was a singular spectacle. He was dressed in a flowing gown with fur tippets which had the signs of the zodiac embroidered all over it, together with various cabalistic signs, as of triangles with eyes in them, queer crosses, leaves of trees, bones and birds and animals and a planetarium whose stars shone like bits of looking glass with the sun on them. He had a pointed hat like a dunce's cap, or like the headgear worn by ladies of that time, except that the ladies were accustomed to have a bit of veil floating from the top of it. He also had a wand of lignum vitae, which he had laid down in the grass beside him, and a pair of horn-rimmed spectacles like those of King Pellinore. They were extraordinary spectacles, being without earpieces, but shaped rather like scissors or the the antennae of the tarantula wasp.

"Excuse me, sir," said the Wart, "but can you tell me the way to Sir Ector's castle, if you don't mind?"

The aged gentleman put down his bucket and looked at the Wart.

"Your name would be Wart," he said.

"Yes, sir, please, sir," said the Wart.

"My name," said the aged gentleman, "is Merlyn."

"How do you do?" said the Wart.

"How do you do?" said Merlyn. "It is clement weather, is it not?"

"It is," said the Wart, "for the time of the year."

When these formalities had been concluded, the Wart had leisure to examine his new acquaintance more closely. The aged gentleman was staring at him with a kind of unwinking and benevolent curiosity which made him feel that it would not be at all rude to stare back, no ruder than it would be to stare at one of his guardian's cows who happened to be ruminating his personality as she leant her head over a gate.

Merlyn had a long white beard and long white moustache which hung down on either side of it, and close inspection showed that he was far from clean. It was not that he had dirty finger-nails or anything like that, but some large bird seemed to have been nesting in his hair. The Wart was familiar with the nests of spar-hawk and gos, those crazy conglomerations of sticks and oddments which had been taken over from squirrels and crows, and he knew how the twigs and the tree foot were splashed with white mutes, old bones, muddy feathers and castings. This was the impression which he gathered from Merlyn. The old gentleman was streaked with droppings over his shoulders, among the stars and triangles of his gown, and a large spider was slowly lowering itself from the tip of his hat, as he gazed and slowly blinked at the little boy in front of him. He had a faintly worried expression, as though he were trying to remember some name which began with Chol but which was pronounced in quite a different way, possibly Menzies or was it Dalziel? His mild blue eyes, very big and round under the tarantula spectacles, gradually filmed and clouded over as he gazed at the boy, and then he turned his head away with a resigned expression, as though it was all too much for him after all.

"Do you like peaches?" asked the old gentleman.

"Very much indeed," answered the Wart, and his mouth

began to water so that it was full of sweet, soft liquid.

"It is only July, you know," said the old man reprovingly, and walked off in the direction of the cottage without looking round.

The Wart followed after him, since this was the simplest thing to do, and offered to carry the bucket (which seemed to please the old gentleman, who gave it to him) and waited while he counted his keys, and muttered and mislaid them and dropped them in the grass. Finally, when they had got their way into the black and white cottage with as much trouble as if they were burglaring it, he climbed up the ladder after his host and found himself in the upstairs room.

It was the most marvellous room that the Wart had ever been in.

There was a real corkindrill hanging from the rafters, very lifelike and horrible with glass eyes and scaly tail stretched out behind it. When its master came into the room it winked one eye in salutation, although it was stuffed. There were hundreds of thousands of brown books in leather bindings, some chained to the bookshelves and others propped up against each other as if they had had too much spirits to drink and did not really trust themselves. These gave out a smell of must and solid brownness which was most secure. Then there were stuffed birds, popinjays, and maggot-pies, and kingfishers, and peacocks with all their feathers but two, and tiny birds like beetles, and a reputed phoenix which smelt of incense and cinnamon. It could not have been a real phoenix, because there is only one of these at a time. Over the mantelpiece there was a fox's mask,

with GRAFTON. BUCKINGHAM TO DAVENTRY, 2 HRS 20 MINS
written under it, and also a forty-pound salmon with AWE, 43
MIN., BULLDOG written under it, and a very life-like basilisk
with CROWHURST OTTER HOUNDS in Roman print. There
were several boars' tusks and the claws of tigers and libbards
mounted in symmetrical patterns, and a big head of Ovis Poli,
six live grass snakes in a kind of aquarium, some nests of the
solitary wasp nicely set up in a glass cylinder, an ordinary
beehive whose inhabitants went in and out of the window
unmolested, two young hedgehogs in cotton wool, a pair of
badgers which immediately began to cry Yik-Yik-Yik-Yik in
loud voices as soon as the magician appeared, twenty boxes
which contained stick caterpillars and sixths of the puss-moth,
and even an oleander that was worth two and six, all feeding
on the appropriate leaves, a guncase with all sorts of weapons
which would not be invented for half a thousand years, a rod-
box ditto, a lovely chest of drawers full of salmon flies which
had been tied by Merlyn himself, another chest whose drawers
were labelled Mandragora, Mandrake, Old Man's Beard, etc., a
bunch of turkey feathers and goose-quills for making pens, an
astrolabe, twelve pairs of boots, a dozen purse-nets, three dozen
rabbit wires, twelve corkscrews, an ant's nest between two glass
plates, ink-bottles of every possible colour from red to violet,
darning-needles, a gold medal for being the best scholar at
Eton, four or five recorders, a nest of field mice all alive-o, two
skulls, plenty of cut glass, Venetian glass, Bristol glass and a bottle
of Mastic varnish, some satsuma china and some cloisonné, the
fourteenth edition of the *Encyclopaedia Britannica* (marred as it

was by the sensationalism of the popular plates), two paint-boxes (one oil, one water-colour), three globes of the known geographical world, a few fossils, the stuffed head of a camel-leopard, six pismires, some glass retorts with cauldrons, bunsen burners, etc., and the complete set of cigarette cards depicting wildfowl by Peter Scott.

Merlyn took off his pointed hat when he came into this extraordinary chamber, because it was too high for the roof, and immediately there was a little scamper in one of the dark corners and a flap of soft wings, and a young tawny owl was sitting on the black skull-cap which protected the top of his head.

"Oh, what a lovely owl!" cried the Wart.

But when he went up to it and held out his hand, the owl grew half as tall again, stood up as stiff as a poker, closed its eyes so that there was only the smallest slit to peep through, as one is in the habit of doing when told to shut one's eyes at hide-and-seek, and said in a doubtful voice:

"There is no owl."

Then it shut its eyes entirely and looked the other way.

"It's only a boy," said Merlyn.

"There is no boy," said the owl hopefully, without turning round.

The Wart was so startled by finding that the owl could talk that he forgot his manners and came closer still. At this the owl became so nervous that it made a mess on Merlyn's head – the whole room was quite white with droppings – and flew off to perch on the farthest tip of the corkindrill's tail, out of reach.

"We see so little company," explained Merlyn, wiping his head with half a worn-out pair of pyjama tops which he kept for that purpose, "that Archimedes is a little shy of strangers. Come, Archimedes, I want you to meet a friend of mine called Wart."

Here he held out his hand to the owl, who came waddling like a goose along the corkindrill's back – he waddled with this rolling gait so as to keep his tail from being damaged – and hopped down on to Merlyn's finger with every sign of reluctance.

"Hold out your finger," said Merlyn, "and put it behind his legs. No, lift it up under his train."

When the Wart had done this Merlyn moved the owl gently backwards, so that the Wart's finger pressed against its legs from behind, and it either had to step back on the finger or get pushed off its balance altogether. It stepped back. The Wart stood there delighted, while the furry little feet held tight on to his finger and the sharp claws prickled his skin.

"Say how d'you do properly," said Merlyn.

"I won't," said Archimedes, looking the other way and holding very tight.

"Oh, he *is* lovely," said the Wart again. "Have you had him very long?"

"Archimedes has stayed with me since he was quite small, indeed since he had a tiny head like a chicken's."

"I wish he would talk to me," said the Wart.

"Perhaps if you were to give him this mouse here, politely, he might learn to know you better."

Chapter Three

Merlyn took the dead mouse out of his skull-cap — "I always keep them there," he explained, "and worms too, for fishing. I find it most convenient" — and handed it to the Wart, who held it out rather gingerly towards Archimedes. The nutty little curved beak looked as if it were capable of doing damage, but Archimedes looked closely at the mouse, blinked at the Wart, moved nearer on the finger, closed his eyes and leant forward. He stood there with closed eyes and an expression of rapture on his face, as if he were saying grace, and then, with the absurdest little sideways nibble, took the morsel so gently that he would not have broken a soap bubble. He remained leaning forward with closed eyes, with the mouse suspended from his beak, as if he were not sure what to do with it. Then he lifted his right foot — he was right-handed — and took hold of the mouse. He held it up like a boy holding a stick of rock or a constable with his truncheon, looked at it, nibbled its tail. He turned it round so that it was head first, for the Wart had offered it the wrong way round, and gave one gulp. He looked round at the company with the tail hanging out of the corner of his mouth — as much as to say, "I wish you would not all stare at me so" — turned his head away, politely swallowed the tail, scratched his sailor's beard with his left toe, and began to ruffle out his feathers.

"Let him alone," said Merlyn, "now. For perhaps he does not want to be friends with you until he knows what you are like. With owls, it is never easy-come and easy-go."

"Perhaps he will sit on my shoulder," said the Wart, and with that he instinctively lowered his hand, so that the owl, who liked to be as high as possible, ran up the slope and stood shyly beside his ear.

"Now breakfast," said Merlyn.

The Wart saw that the most perfect breakfast was laid out neatly for two, on the table before the window. There were peaches. There were also melons, strawberries and cream, rusks, brown trout piping hot, grilled perch which were much nicer, chicken devilled enough to burn one's mouth out, kidneys and mushrooms on toast, fricassee, curry, and a choice of boiling coffee or best chocolate made with cream in large cups.

"Have some mustard," said Merlyn, when they had got to the kidneys.

The mustard-pot got up and walked over to his plate on thin silver legs that waddled like the owl's. Then it uncurled its handles and one handle lifted its lid with exaggerated courtesy while the other helped him to a generous spoonful.

"Oh, I love the mustard-pot!" cried the Wart. "Where ever did you get it?"

At this the pot beamed all over its face and began to strut a bit; but Merlyn rapped it on the head with a teaspoon, so that it sat down and shut up at once.

"It's not a bad pot," he said grudgingly. "Only it is inclined to give itself airs."

The Wart was so much impressed by the kindness of the old magician, and particularly by all the lovely things which he possessed, that he hardly liked to ask him personal questions. It seemed politer to sit still and speak when he was spoken to. But Merlyn did not speak very much, and when he did speak it was never in questions, so that the Wart had little opportunity for conversation. At last his curiosity got the better of him, and he asked something which had been puzzling him for some time.

"Would you mind if I ask you a question?"

"It is what I am for," said Merlyn sadly.

"How did you know to set the breakfast for two?"

The old gentleman leaned back in his chair and lit an enormous meerschaum pipe – Good gracious, he breathes fire, thought the Wart, who had never heard of tobacco – before he was ready to reply. Then he looked puzzled, took off his skull-cap – three mice fell out – and scratched in the middle of his bald head.

"Have you ever tried to draw in a looking-glass?" asked Merlyn.

"I don't think I have," said the Wart.

"Looking-glass," said the old gentleman, holding out his hand. Immediately there was a tiny lady's vanity-glass in his hand.

"Not that kind, you fool," said Merlyn angrily. "I want one big enough to shave in."

The vanity-glass vanished, and in its place there was a shaving mirror about a foot square. Merlyn then demanded pencil and paper in quick succession; got an unsharpened pencil and the *Morning Post*; sent them back; got a fountain-pen with no ink in it and six reams of brown-paper suitable for parcels; sent them back; flew into a passion in which he said by-our-lady quite often, and ended up with a carbon pencil and some cigarette papers which he said would have to do.

He put one of the papers in front of the glass and made five dots on it like this:

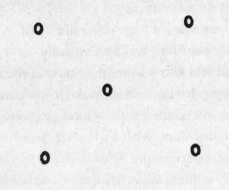

"Now," he said, "I want you to join those five dots up to make a W, looking only in the glass."

The Wart took the pen and tried to do as he was bid, but after a lot of false starts the letter which he produced was this:

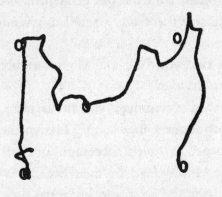

"Well, it isn't bad," said Merlyn doubtfully, "and in a way it does look a bit like an M."

Then he fell into a reverie, stroking his beard, breathing fire, and staring at the paper.

"About the breakfast?" asked the Wart timidly, after he had waited five minutes.

"Ah, yes," said Merlyn. "How did I know to set breakfast for two? That was why I showed you the looking-glass. Now ordinary people are born *forwards* in Time, if you understand what I mean, and nearly everything in the world goes forward too. This makes it quite easy for the ordinary people to live, just as it would be easy to join those five dots into a W if you were allowed to look at them forwards instead of backwards and inside out. But I unfortunately was born at the wrong end of time, and I have to live *backwards* from in front, while surrounded by a lot of people living forwards from behind. Some people call it having second sight."

Merlyn stopped talking and looked at the Wart in an anxious way.

"Have I told you this before?" he inquired suspiciously.

"No," said the Wart. "We only met about half an hour ago."

"So little time to pass as that?" said Merlyn, and a big tear ran down to the end of his nose. He wiped it off with his pyjama tops and added anxiously, "Am I going to tell it you again?"

"I don't know," said the Wart, "unless you haven't finished telling me yet."

"You see," said Merlyn, "one gets confused with Time,

when it is like that. All one's tenses get muddled up, for one thing. If you know what's *going* to happen to people, and not *what* has happened to them, it makes it so difficult to prevent it happening, if you don't want it to have happened, if you see what I mean? Like drawing in a mirror."

The Wart did not quite see, but was just going to say that he was sorry for Merlyn if these things made him unhappy, when he felt a curious sensation at his ear. "Don't jump," said Merlyn, just as he was going to do so, and the Wart sat still. Archimedes, who had been standing forgotten on his shoulder all this time, was gently touching himself against him. His beak was right against the lobe of his ear, which its bristles made to tickle, and suddenly, a soft hoarse little voice whispered, "How d'you do," so that it sounded right inside his head.

"Oh, owl!" cried the Wart, forgetting about Merlyn's troubles instantly. "Look, he has decided to talk to me!"

The Wart gently leant his head against the soft feathers, and the brown owl, taking the rim of his ear in its beak, quickly nibbled right round it with the smallest nibbles.

"I shall call him Archie!" exclaimed the Wart.

"I trust you will do nothing of the sort," cried Merlyn instantly, in a stern and angry voice, and the owl withdrew to the farthest corner of his shoulder.

"Is it wrong?"

"You might as well call me Wol, or Olly," said the owl sourly, "and have done with it.

"Or Bubbles," added the owl in a bitter voice.

Merlyn took the Wart's hand and said kindly, "You are only

young, and do not understand these things. But you will learn that owls are the politest and the most courteous, single-hearted and faithful creatures living. You must never be familiar, rude or vulgar with them, or make them to look ridiculous. Their mother is Athene, the goddess of wisdom, and, though they are often ready to play the buffoon for your amusement, such conduct is the prerogative of the truly wise. No owl can possibly be called Archie."

"I am sorry, owl," said the Wart.

"And I am sorry, boy," said the owl. "I can see that you spoke in ignorance, and I bitterly regret that I should have been so petty as to take offence where none was intended."

The owl really did regret it, and looked so remorseful and upset that Merlyn had to put on a very cheerful manner and change the conversation.

"Well," said he, "now that we have finished breakfast, I think it is high time that we should all three find out way back to Sir Ector."

"Excuse me a moment," he added as an afterthought, and, turning round to the breakfast things, he pointed a knobbly finger at them and said in a stern voice, "Wash up."

At this all the china and cutlery scrambled down off the table, the cloth emptied the crumbs out of the window, and the napkins folded themselves up. All ran off down the ladder, to where Merlyn had left the bucket, and there was such a noise and yelling as if a lot of children had been let out of school. Merlyn went to the door and shouted, "Mind, nobody is to get broken." But his voice was entirely drowned in shrill squeals, splashes, and cries of "My, it is cold," "I shan't stay in long," "Look out, you'll break me," or "Come on, let's duck the teapot."

"Are you really coming all the way home with me?" asked the Wart, who could hardly believe the good news.

"Why not?" said Merlyn. "How else can I be your tutor?"

At this the Wart's eyes grew rounder and rounder, until they were about as big as the owl's who was sitting on his shoulder, and his face got redder and redder, and a big breath seemed to gather itself beneath his heart.

"My!" exclaimed the Wart, while his eyes sparkled with excitement at the discovery. "I must have been on a Quest."

Chapter Four

The Wart started talking before he was halfway over the drawbridge. "Look who I've brought," he said. "Look! I've been on a Quest. I was shot at with three arrows. They had black and yellow stripes. The owl is called Archimedes. I saw King Pellinore. This is my tutor, Merlyn. I went on a Quest for him. He was after the Questing Beast. I mean King Pellinore. It was terrible in the forest. Merlyn made the plates wash up. Hallo, Hob. Look, we have got Cully."

Hob just looked at the Wart, but so proudly that the Wart went quite red. It was such a pleasure to be back home again with all his friends, and everything achieved.

Hob said gruffly, "Ah, master, us shall make an austringer of 'ee yet."

He came for Cully, as if he could not keep his hands off him any longer, but he patted the Wart too, fondling them both because he was not sure which he was gladder to see back. He took Cully on his own fist, reassuming him like a lame man putting on his accustomed wooden leg, after it had been lost.

"Merlyn caught him," said the Wart. "He sent Archimedes to look for him on the way home. Then Archimedes told us that he had been and killed a pigeon and was eating it. We went and frightened him off. After that, Merlyn stuck six of the tail feathers round the pigeon in a circle, and made a loop in a long piece of string to go round the feathers. He tied one end to a stick in the ground, and he went away behind a bush with the other end. He said he wouldn't use magic. He said you couldn't use magic in Great Arts, like it would be unfair to make a great statue by magic. You have to cut it out with a chisel, you see. Then Cully came down to finish the pigeon, and we pulled the string, and the loop slipped over the feathers and caught him round the legs. He was angry. But we gave him the pigeon."

Hob made a duty to Merlyn, who returned it courteously. They looked upon one another with grave affection and eagerness, knowing each other to be masters of the same trade. When they could be alone together they could talk and talk, although each was naturally a silent man. Meanwhile they must wait their time.

"Oh, Kay," cried the Wart, as the latter appeared with their nurse and other delighted welcomers. "Look I have got a magician for our tutor. He has a mustard-pot that walks."

"I am glad you are back," said Kay.

"Alas, where did you sleep, Master Art?" exclaimed the nurse. "Look at your clean jerkin all muddied and torn. Such a turn as you gave us, I really don't know. But look at your poor hair with all them twigs in it. Oh, my own random, wicked little lamb."

Sir Ector came bustling out with his greaves on back to front, and kissed the Wart on both cheeks. "Well, well, well," he exclaimed moistly. "Here we are again, hey? What the devil have you been doin', hey? Settin' the whole household upside down."

But inside him he was proud of the Wart for staying out after a hawk, and prouder still to see that he had got it, for all the while Hob held the bird in the air for everybody to see.

"Oh, sir," said the Wart. "I have been on that Quest you said for a tutor, and I have found him. Please, he is this gentleman here, and he is called Merlyn. He has got some badgers and hedgehogs and mice and things on this white donkey here, because we couldn't leave them behind to starve. He is a great musician, and can make things come out of the air."

"Ah, a magician," said Sir Ector, putting on his glasses and looked closely at Merlyn. "White magic, I hope?"

"Assuredly," said Merlyn, who stood patiently among all this throng with his arms folded in his necromantic gown, and Archimedes sitting very stiff and elongated on the top of his head.

"Ought to have some testimonials, you know," said Sir Ector doubtfully. "It's usual."

"Testimonials," said Merlyn, holding out his hand.

Instantly there were some heavy tablets in it, signed by Aristotle, a parchment signed by Hecate, and some typewritten duplicates signed by the Master of Trinity, who could not remember having met him. All these gave Merlyn an excellent character.

"He had 'em up his sleeve," said Sir Ector wisely. "Can you do anything else?"

"Tree," said Merlyn. At once there was an enormous mulberry growing in the middle of the courtyard, with its luscious blue fruits ready to patter down.

"They do it with mirrors," said Sir Ector.

"Snow," said Merlyn. "And an umbrella," he added hastily.

Before they could turn round the copper sky of summer had assumed a cold and lowering bronze, while the biggest white flakes that were ever seen were floating about them and settling on the battlements. An inch of snow had fallen before they could speak, and all were trembling with the wintry blast. Sir Ector's nose was blue, and had an icicle hanging from the end of it, while all except Merlyn had a ledge of snow upon their shoulders. Merlyn stood in the middle, holding his umbrella high because of the owl.

"It's done by hypnotism," said Sir Ector, with chattering teeth. "Like those wallahs from the Indies.

"But that'll do, you know," he added hastily, "that'll do very well. I'm sure you'll make an excellent tutor for teachin' these boys."

The snow stopped immediately and the sun came out –

"Enough to give a body a pewmonia," said the nurse, "or to frighten the elastic commissioners" – while Merlyn folded up his umbrella and handed it back to the air, which received it.

"Imagine the boy doin' a quest like that all by himself," exclaimed Sir Ector. "Well, well, well. Wonders never cease."

"I don't think much of it as a quest," said Kay. "He only went after the hawk, after all."

"And got the hawk, Master Kay," said Hob reprovingly.

"Oh well," said Kay, "I bet the old man caught it for him."

"Kay," said Merlyn, suddenly terrible, "thou wast ever a proud and ill-tongued speaker, and a misfortunate one. Thy sorrow will come from thine own mouth."

At this everybody felt uncomfortable, and Kay, instead of flying into his usual passion, hung his head. He was not at all an unpleasant person really, but clever, quick, proud, passionate and ambitious. He was one of those people who would be neither a follower or a leader, but only an aspiring heart, impatient in the failing body which imprisoned it. Merlyn repented of his rudeness at once. He made a little silver hunting-knife come out of the air, which he gave him to put things right. The knob of the handle was made of the skull of a stoat, oiled and polished like ivory, and Kay loved it.

CHAPTER FIVE

SIR ECTOR'S HOME was called The Castle of the Forest Sauvage. It was more like a town or a village than any one man's home, and indeed it was the village during all times of danger. Whenever there was a raid or an invasion, everybody on the estate hurried into the castle, driving all the beasts before them into the courts, and there they remained until the danger was over. The little wattle and daub cottages nearly always got burnt, and had to be built again afterwards with much profanity. For this reason it was not worth while troubling to have a village church, as it would constantly be having to be replaced. The villagers went to church in the chapel of the castle. They wore their best clothes and trooped up the street with their most respectable gait on Sundays, looking with vague and dignified looks in all directions, as if reluctant to disclose their destination, and on weekdays they came to mass and vespers in their ordinary clothes, walking much more cheerfully. Everybody went to church in those days, and liked it.

The Castle of the Forest Sauvage is still standing, and you can see its lovely ruined walls with ivy on them, standing broached to the sun and wind. Some lizards live there now, and the starving sparrows keep warm on winter nights in the ivy, and a barn owl drives it methodically, hovering outside the little frightened congregations and beating the ivy with its wings, to make them fly out. Most of the curtain wall is down, though you can trace the foundations of the twelve round towers which guarded it. They are round, and stuck out from the wall into the moat, so that the archers could fire in all directions and command every part of the wall. Inside the towers there are circular stairs. These go round and round a central column, and this column is pierced with holes for shooting arrows. Even if the enemy had got inside the curtain wall and fought its way into the bottom of the towers, the defenders could retreat up the bends of the stairs and shoot at those who followed them up, inside, through the slits.

The stone part of the drawbridge with its barbican and the bartizans of the gatehouse are in good repair. These have many ingenious arrangements. Even if you got over the wooden bridge, which was pulled up so that you couldn't, there was a portcullis weighed with an enormous log which would squash you flat and pin you down as well. There was a large hidden trapdoor in the floor of the barbican, which would let you into the moat after all. At the other end of the barbican there was another portcullis, so that you could be trapped between the two and annihilated from above, while the bartizans, or hanging turrets, had holes in their floors through which the defenders could drop things on your head. Finally, inside the gatehouse, there was a neat little hole in the middle of the vaulted ceiling, which had painted tracery and bosses. This hole led to the room above, where there was a big cauldron, for boiling lead and oil in.

So much for the outer defences. Once you were inside the curtain wall, you found yourself in a kind of wide alleyway, probably full of frightened sheep, with another complete castle in front of you. This was the inner shell-keep, with its eight enormous round towers which still stand. It is lovely to climb the highest of them and to lie there looking out towards the Marches, from which all these old dangers came, with nothing but the sun above you and the little tourists trotting about below, quite regardless of arrows and boiling oil. Think of how many centuries that unconquerable tower has withstood. It has changed hands by secession often, by siege once, by treachery twice, but never by assault. On this tower the look-out moved. From here he kept the guard over the blue woods towards Wales. His clean old bones lie beneath the floor of the chapel now, so you must keep it for him.

If you look down and are not frightened of heights (the society for the Preservation of This and That have put up some excellent railings to preserve you from tumbling over), you can see the whole anatomy of the inner court laid out beneath you like a map. You can see the chapel, now quite open to its god, and the windows of the great hall with the solar over it. You can see the shafts of the huge chimneys and how cunningly the side flues were contrived to enter them, and the little private closets now public, and the enormous kitchen. If you are a sensible person, you will spend days there, possibly weeks, working out for yourself by detection which were the stables, which the mews, where were the cow byres, the armoury, the lofts, the well, the smithy, the kennel, the soldiers' quarters, the priest's room, and my lord's and lady's chambers. Then it will all grow about you again. The little people – they were much smaller than we are, and it would be a job for most of us to get inside the few bits of their armour and old gloves that remain – will hurry about in the sunshine, the sheep will baa as they always did, and perhaps from Wales there will come the fffff-putt of the triple-feathered arrow which looks as if it had never moved.

This place was of course, a complete paradise for a boy to be in. The Wart ran about it like a rabbit in its own complicated labyrinth. He knew everything, everywhere, all the special smells, good climbs, soft lairs, secret hiding-places, jumps, slides, nooks, larders and blisses. For every season he had the best place like a cat, and he yelled and ran and fought and upset people and snoozed and daydreamed and pretended he was a Knight, without ever stopping. Just now he was in the kennel.

People in those days had rather different ideas about the training of dogs to what we have today. They did it more by love than strictness. Imagine a modern M. F. H. going to bed with his hounds, and yet Flavius Arrianus says that it is "Best of all if they can sleep with a person because it makes them more human and because they rejoice in the company of human beings: also if they have had a restless night or been internally upset, you will know of it and will not use them to hunt next day." In Sir Ector's kennel there was a special boy, called the Dog Boy, who lived with the hounds day and night. He was a sort of head hound, and it was his business to take them out every day for walks, to pull thorns out of their feet, keep cankers out of their ears, bind the smaller bones that got dislocated, dose them for worms, isolate and nurse them in distemper, arbitrate in their quarrels and sleep curled up among them at night. If one more learned quotation may be excused, this is how the Duke of York who was killed at Agincourt described such a boy in his *Master of Game*: "Also I will teach the child to lead out the hounds to scombre twice in the day in the morning and in the evening, so that the sun be up, especially in winter. Then should he let them run and play long in a meadow in the sun, and then comb every hound after the other, and wipe them with a great wisp of straw, and this he shall do every morning. And then he shall lead them into some fair place where tender grass grows as corn and other things, that therewith they may feed themselves as if it is medicine for them." Thus, since the boy's "heart and his business be with the hounds," the hounds themselves become "Goodly and kindly and clean, glad and joyful and playful, and goodly to all manner of folks save to the wild beasts to whom they should be fierce, eager and spiteful."

Sir Ector's dog-boy was none other than the one who had had his nose bitten off by the terrible Wat. Not having a nose like a human, and being, moreover, subjected to stone-throwing by the other village children, he had become more comfortable with animals. He talked to them, not in baby-talk like a maiden lady, but correctly in their own growls and barks. They all loved him very much, and revered him for taking thorns out of their toes, and came to him with their little troubles at once. He always understood immediately what was wrong, and generally he could put it right. It was nice for the dogs to have their god with them, in visible form.

The Wart was fond of the Dog Boy, and thought him very clever to be able to do all these things with animals – for he could make them do almost anything just by moving his hands – while the Dog Boy loved the Wart in much the same way as his dogs loved him, and thought the Wart was almost holy because he could read and write. They spent much of their time together, rolling about with the dogs in the kennel.

The kennel was on the ground floor, near the mews, with a loft above it, so that it should be cool in summer and warm in winter. The hounds were alaunts, gaze-hounds, lymers and braches. They were called Clumsy, Trowneer, Phoebe, Colle, Gerland, Talbot, Luath, Luffra, Apollon, Orthros, Bran, Gelert, Bounce, Boy, Lion, Bungey, Toby and Diamond. The Wart's own special one was called Cavall, and he happened to be licking Cavall's nose – not the other way about – when Merlyn came in and found him.

"That will come to be regarded as an insanitary habit," said

Merlyn, "though I can't see it myself. After all, God made the creature's nose just as well as he made your tongue.

"If not better," added the philosopher pensively.

The Wart did not know what Merlyn was talking about, but he liked him to talk. He did not like the grown-ups who talked down to him like a baby, but the ones who just went on talking in their usual way, leaving him to leap along in their wake, jumping at meanings, guessing, clutching at known words, and chuckling at complicated jokes as they suddenly dawned. He had the glee of the porpoise then, pouring and leaping through strange seas.

"Shall we go out?" asked Merlyn. "I think it is about time we began our lessons."

The Wart's heart sank at this. His tutor had been there a month, and it was now August, but they had done no lessons so far. Now he suddenly remembered that this was what Merlyn was for, and he thought with dread of Summulae Logicales and the filthy astrolabe. He knew that it had to be borne, however, and got up obediently enough, after giving Cavall a last reluctant pat. He thought that it might not be so bad with Merlyn, who might be able to make even the old Organon interesting, particularly if he would do some magic.

They went out into the courtyard, into a sun so burning that the heat of haymaking seemed to have been nothing. It was baking. The thunder-clouds which usually go with hot weather were there, high columns of cumulus with glaring edges, but there was not going to be any thunder. It was too hot even for that. "If only," thought the Wart, "I did not have to go into a stuffy classroom, but could take off my clothes and swim in the moat."

They crossed the courtyard, having almost to take deep breaths before they darted across it, as if they were going quickly through an oven. The shade of the gatehouse was cool, but the barbican, with its close walls, was hottest of all. In one last dash across the desert they had achieved the draw-bridge – could Merlyn have guessed what he was thinking about? – and were staring down into the moat.

It was the season of water-lilies. If Sir Ector had not kept one section free of them for the boys' bathing, all the water would have been covered. As it was, about twenty yards on each side of the bridge were cut each year, and you could dive in from the bridge itself. The moat was quite deep. It was used as a stew, so that the inhabitants of the castle could have fish on Fridays, and for this reason the architects had been careful not to let the drains and sewers run into it. It was stocked with fish every year.

"I wish I was a fish," said the Wart.

"What sort of fish?"

It was almost too hot to think about this, but the Wart stared down into the cool amber depths where a school of small perch were aimlessly hanging about.

"I think I should like to be a perch," he said. "They are braver than the silly roach, and not quite so slaughterous as the pike."

Merlyn took off his hat, raised his staff of lignum vitae politely in the air, and said slowly, "Snylrem stnemilpmoc ot enutpen dna lliw eh yldnik tpecca siht yob sa a hsif?"

Immediately there was a loud blowing of sea-shells, conches and so forth, and a stout, jolly-looking gentleman appeared seated on a well-blown-up cloud above the battlements. He had an anchor tattooed on his tummy and a handsome mermaid with Mabel written under her on his chest. He ejected a quid of tobacco, nodded affably to Merlyn and pointed his trident at the Wart. The Wart found he had no clothes on. He found that he had tumbled off the draw-bridge, landing with a smack on his side in the water. He found that the moat and the bridge had grown hundreds of times bigger. He knew that he was turning into a fish.

"Oh, Merlyn," cried the Wart. "Please come too."

"Just for this once," said the large and solemn tench beside his ear, "I will come. But in future you will have to go by yourself. Education is experience, and the essence of experience is self-reliance."

The Wart found it difficult to be a fish. It was no good trying to swim like a human being, for it made him go corkscrew and much too slowly. He did not know how to swim like a fish.

"Not like that," said the tench in ponderous tones. "Put your chin on your left shoulder and do jack-knives. Never mind about the fins to begin with."

The Wart's legs had fused together into his backbone and his feet and toes had become a tail fin. His arms had become two more fins – also of a delicate pinkish colour – and he had sprouted some more somewhere about his tummy. His head faced over his shoulder, so that when he bent in the middle his toes were moving towards his ear instead of towards his forehead. He was a beautiful olive-green colour with rather scratchy plate-armour all over him, and dark bands down his sides. He was not sure which were his sides and which were his back and front, but what now appeared to be his tummy had an attractive whitish colour, while his back was armed with a splendid great fin that could be erected for war and had spikes in it. He did jack-knives as the tench directed and found that he was swimming vertically downwards into the mud.

"Use your feet to turn to left or right with," said the tench, "and spread those fins on your tummy to keep level. You are living in two planes now, not one."

The Wart found that he could keep more or less level by altering the inclination of his arm fins and the ones on his stomach. He swam feebly off, enjoying himself very much.

"Come back," said the tench solemnly. "You must learn to swim before you can dart."

The Wart turned to his tutor in a series of zig-zags and remarked, "I don't seem to keep quite straight."

"The trouble with you is that you don't swim from the shoulder. You swim as if you were a boy just bending at the hips. Try doing your jack-knives right from the neck downwards, and move your body exactly the same amount to the right as you are going to move it to the left. Put your back into it."

Wart gave two terrific kicks and vanished altogether in a clump of mare's tail several yards away.

"That's better," said the tench, now quite out of sight in the murky olive water, and the Wart backed himself out of his tangle with infinite trouble, by wriggling his arm fins. He undulated back towards the voice in one terrific shove, to show off.

"Good," said the tench, as they collided end to end, "but discretion is the better part of valour.

"Try if you can do this one," said the tench.

Without apparent exertion of any kind he swam off backwards under a water-lily. Without apparent exertion; but the Wart, who was an enterprising learner, had been watching the slightest movement of his fins. He moved his own fins anti-clockwise, gave the very tip of his own tail a cunning flick, and was lying alongside the tench.

"Splendid," said Merlyn. "Let's go for a little swim."

The Wart was on an even keel now, and reasonably able to move about. He had leisure to observe the extraordinary universe into which the tattooed gentleman's trident had plunged him. It was very different from the universe to which he had hitherto been accustomed. For one thing, the heaven or sky above him was now a perfect circle poised a few inches above his head. The horizon had closed in to this. In order to imagine yourself into the Wart's position, you will have to picture a round horizon, a few inches above your head, instead of the flat horizon which you have usually seen. Under this horizon of air you will have to imagine another horizon under water, spherical and practically upside down – for the surface of the water acted partly as a mirror to what was below it. It is difficult to imagine. What makes it a great deal more difficult to imagine is that everything which human beings would consider to be above the water level was fringed with all the colours of the spectrum. For instance, if you had happened to be fishing for the Wart, he would have seen you, at the rim of the tea saucer which was the upper air to him, not as one person waving a fishing-rod, but as seven people, whose outlines were red, orange, yellow, green, blue, indigo and violet, all waving the same rod whose colours were as varied. In fact, you would have been a rainbow man to him, a beacon of flashing and radiating colours, which ran into one another and had rays all about. You would have been burnt upon the water like Cleopatra in the poem by Herédia. The reference may possibly be to Shakespeare.

The next most lovely thing was that the Wart had no weight. He was not earth-bound any more and did not have to plod along on a flat surface, pressed down by gravity and the weight of the atmosphere. He could do what men have always wanted to do, that is, fly. There is practically no difference between flying in the water and flying in the air. The best of it was that he did not have to fly in a machine, by pulling levers and sitting still, but could do it with his own body. It was like the dreams people have.

Just as they were going to swim off their tour of inspection, a timid young roach appeared from between two waving bottle brushes of mare's tail and hung about, looking quite pale with agitation. It looked at them with big apprehensive eyes and evidently wanted something, but could not make up its mind.

"Approach," said Merlyn gravely.

At this the roach rushed up like a hen, burst into tears and began stammering its message.

"If you p-p-p-please, Doctor," stammered the poor creature, gabbling so that they could scarcely understand what it said, "we have such a d-dretful case of s-s-s-something or other in our family, and we w-w-w-wondered if you could s-s-s-spare the time? It's our d-d-d-dear Mamma, who w-w-w-will swim a-a-a-all the time upside d-d-d-down, and she d-d-d-does look so horrible and s-s-s-speaks so strange, that we r-r-r-really thought she ought to have a d-d-d-doctor, if it w-w-w-wouldn't be too much? C-C-C-Clara says to say so sir, if you s-s-s-see w-w-w-what I m-m-m-mean?"

Here the little roach began fizzing so much, what with its stammer and its tearful disposition, that it became perfectly inarticulate and could only stare at Merlyn with big mournful eyes.

"Never mind, my little man," said Merlyn. "There, there, lead me to your poor Mamma, and we shall see what we can do."

They all three swam off into the murk under the draw-bridge upon their errand of mercy.

"Very Russian, these roach," whispered Merlyn to the Wart, behind his fin. "It's probably only a case of nervous hysteria, a matter for the psychologist rather than the physician."

The roach's Mamma was lying on her back as he had described. She was squinting horribly, had folded her fins upon her chest, and every now and then she blew a bubble. All her children were gathered round her in a circle, and every time she blew a bubble they all nudged each other and gasped. She had a seraphic smile upon her face.

"Well, well, well," said Merlyn, putting on his best bedside manner, "and how is Mrs Roach today?"

He patted all the young roaches on the head and advanced with stately motions towards his patient. It should perhaps be mentioned that Merlyn was a ponderous, deep-beamed fish of about five pounds, red-leather coloured, with small scales, adipose in his fins, rather slimy, and having a bright marigold eye – a respectable figure.

Mrs Roach held out a languid fin, sighed emphatically and said, "Ah, Doctor, so you've come at last?"

"Hum," said Merlyn, in his deepest tones.

Then he told everybody to close their eyes – the Wart peeped – and began to swim round the invalid in a slow and stately dance. As he danced he sang. His song was this:

> Therapeutic,
> Elephantic,
> Diagnosis,
>   Boom!
> Pancreatic,
> Microstatic,
> Anti-toxic,
>   Doom!
> With normal catabolism,

> Gabbleism and babbleism,
> Snip, Snap, Snorum
> Cut out his abdonorum.
> Dyspepsia,
> Anaemia,
> Toxaemia,
> One, two, three,
> And out goes He,
> With a fol-de-rol-derido for the Five Guinea Fee.

At the end of his song he was swimming round his patient so close that he actually touched her, stroking his brown smooth-scaled flanks against her more rattly pale ones. Perhaps he was healing her with slime – for all fishes are said to go to the Tench for medicine – or perhaps it was by touch or massage or hypnotism. In any case, Mrs Roach suddenly stopped squinting, turned the right way up, and said, "Oh, Doctor, dear Doctor, I feel I could eat a little lob-worm now."

"No lob-worm," said Merlyn, "not for two days. I shall give you a prescription for a strong broth of algae every two hours, Mrs Roach. We must build up your strength you know. After all, Rome wasn't built in a day."

Then he patted all the little roaches once more, told them to grow up into brave little fish, and swam off with an air of great importance into the gloom. As he swam, he puffed his mouth in and out.

"What did you mean by that about Rome?" asked the Wart, when they were out of earshot.

"Heaven knows," said the tench.

They swam along, Merlyn occasionally advising him to put his back into it when he forgot, and all the strange under-water world began to dawn about them, deliciously cool after the heat of the upper air. The great forests of the weed were delicately traced, and in them there hung motionless many schools of sticklebacks learning to do their physical exercises in strict unison. On the word One they all lay still: at Two they faced about: at Three they all shot together into a cone, whose apex was a bit of something to eat. Water snails slowly ambled about on the stems of the lilies or under their leaves, while fresh-water mussels lay on the bottom doing nothing in particular. Their flesh was salmon pink, like a very good strawberry cream ice. The small congregations of perch – it was a strange thing, but all the bigger fish seemed to have hidden themselves – had delicate circulations, so that they blushed or grew pale as easily as a lady in a Victorian novel. Only their blush was a deep olive colour, and it was the blush of rage. Whenever Merlyn and his companion swam past them, they raised their spiky dorsal fins in menace, and only lowered them when they saw that Merlyn was a tench. The black bars on their sides made them look as if they had been grilled; and these also could become darker or lighter. Once the two travellers passed under a swan. The white creature floated above like a zeppelin, all indistinct except what was under the water. The latter part was quite clear and showed that the swan was floating slightly on one side with one leg cocked up over its back.

"Look," said the Wart, "it's the poor swan with the deformed leg. It can only paddle with one leg, and the other side of it is all hunched."

"Nonsense," said the swan snappily, putting its head into the water and giving them a frown with its black nares. "Swans like to rest in this position, and you can keep your fishy sympathy to yourself, so there." It continued to glare at them from up above, like a white snake suddenly let down through the ceiling, until they were out of sight.

"You swim along," said the tench in gloomy tones, "as if there was nothing to be afraid of in the world. Don't you see that this place is exactly like the forest you had to come through to find me?"

"Is it?"

"Look over there."

The Wart looked, and at first saw nothing. Then he saw a little translucent shape hanging motionless near the surface. It was just outside the shadow of a water-lily and was evidently enjoying the sun. It was a baby pike, absolutely rigid and probably asleep, and it looked like a pipe stem or a sea horse stretched out flat. It would be a brigand when it grew up.

"I am taking you to see one of those," said the tench, "the Emperor of all these purlieus. As a doctor I have immunity, and I daresay he will respect you as my companion as well. But you had better keep your tail bent in case he is feeling tyrannical."

"Is he the King of the Moat?"

"He is the King of the Moat. Old Jack they call him, and

some Black Peter, but for the most part they don't mention him by name at all. They just call him Mr M. You will see what it is to be a king."

The Wart began to hang behind his conductor a little, and perhaps it was as well that he did, for they were almost on top of their destination before he noticed it. When he did see the old despot he started back in horror, for Mr M. was four feet long, his weight incalculable. The great body, shadowy and almost invisible among the stems, ended in a face which had been ravaged by all the passions of an absolute monarch, by cruelty, sorrow, age, pride, selfishness, loneliness and thought too strong for individual brains. There he hung or hoved, his vast ironic mouth permanently drawn downwards in a kind of melancholy, his lean clean-shaven chops giving him an American expression, like that of Uncle Sam. He was remorseless, disillusioned, logical, predatory, fierce, pitiless: but his great jewel of an eye was that of a stricken deer, large, fearful, sensitive and full of griefs. He made no movement whatever, but looked upon them with this bitter eye.

The Wart thought to himself that he did not care for Mr M.

"Lord," said Merlyn, not paying any attention to his nervousness. "I have brought a young professor who would learn to profess."

"To profess what?" inquired the King of the Moat slowly, hardly opening his jaws and speaking through his nose.

"Power," said the tench.

"Let him speak for himself."

"Please," said the Wart, "I don't know what I ought to ask."

"There is nothing," said the monarch, "except the power that you profess to seek: power to grind and power to digest, power to seek and power to find, power to await and power to claim, all power and pitilessness springing from the nape of the neck."

"Thank you," said the Wart.

"Love is a trick played on us by the forces of evolution," continued the monster monotonously. "Pleasure is the bait laid down by the same. There is only power. Power is of the individual mind, but the mind's power alone is not enough. The power of strength decides everything in the end, and only Might is right.

"Now I think it is time that you should go away, young master, for I find this conversation excessively exhausting. I think you ought to go away really almost at once, in case my great disillusioned mouth should suddenly determine to introduce you to my great gills, which have teeth in them also. Yes, I really think you ought to go away this moment. Indeed, I think you ought to put your very back into it. And so, a long farewell to all my greatness."

The Wart had found himself quite hypnotized by all these long words, and hardly noticed that the thin-lipped tight mouth was coming closer and closer to him all the time. It came imperceptibly, as the cold suave words distracted his attention, and suddenly it was looming within an inch of his nose. On the last sentence it opened, horrible and vast, the thin skin stretching ravenously from bone to bone and tooth to tooth. Inside there seemed to be nothing but teeth, sharp teeth like thorns in rows and ridges everywhere, like the nails in labourers' boots, and it was only at the very last second that he was able to regain his own will, to pull himself together, recollect his instructions and to escape. All those teeth clashed behind him at the tip of his tail, as he gave the heartiest jack-knife he had ever given.

In a second he was on dry land once more, standing beside Merlyn on the piping drawbridge, panting in all his clothes.

Chapter Six

One Thursday afternoon the boys were doing their archery as usual. There were two straw targets fifty yards apart, and when they had shot their arrows at the one, they had only to go to it, collect them, and fire back at the other after facing about. It was still the loveliest summer weather, and there had been chickens for dinner, so that Merlyn had gone off to the edge of the shooting-ground and sat down under a tree. What with the warmth and the chickens and the cream he had poured over his pudding and the continual repassing of the boys and the tock of the arrows in the targets – which was as sleepy to listen to as the noise of a lawn-mower – and the dance of the egg-shaped sunspots between the leaves of his tree, the aged magician was soon fast asleep.

Archery was a serious occupation in those days. It had not yet been relegated to Red Indians and small boys, so that when you were shooting badly you got into a bad temper, just as the wealthy pheasant shooters do today. Kay was shooting badly. He was trying too hard and plucking on his loose, instead of leaving it to the bow.

"Oh, come on," said Kay. "I'm sick of these beastly targets. Let's have a shot at the popinjay."

They left the targets and had several shots at the popinjay – which was a large, bright-coloured artificial bird stuck on the top of a stick, like a parrot – and Kay missed these also. First he had a feeling of "Well, I *will* hit the filthy thing, even if I have to go without my tea until I do it." Then he merely became bored.

The Wart said, "Let's play Rovers then. We can come back in half an hour and wake Merlyn up."

What they called Rovers consisted of going for a walk with their bows and shooting one arrow each at any agreed mark which they came across. Sometimes it would be a mole hill, sometimes a clump of rushes, sometimes a big thistle almost at their feet. They varied the distance at which they chose these objects, sometimes picking a target as much as 120 yards away – which was about as far as these boys' bows could carry – and sometimes having to aim actually below a close thistle because the arrow always leaps up a foot or two as it leaves the bow. They counted five for a hit, and one if the arrow was within a bow's length, and added up their scores at the end.

On this Thursday they chose their targets wisely, and, besides, the grass of the big field had been lately cut. So they never had to search for their arrows for long, which nearly always happens, as in golf, if you shoot ill-advisedly near the hedges or in rough places. The result was that they strayed further than usual and found themselves near the edge of the savage forest where Cully had been lost.

"I vote," said Kay, "that we go to those buries in the chase, and see if we can get a rabbit. It would be more fun than shooting at these hummocks."

They did this. They chose two trees about a hundred yards apart, and each boy stood under one of them, waiting for the conies to come out again. They stood very still, with their bows already raised and arrows fitted, so that they would make the least possible movement to disturb the creatures when they did appear. It was not difficult for either of them to stand thus, for the very first test which they had had to pass in archery was standing with the bow at arm's length for half an hour. They had six arrows each and would be able to fire and mark them all, before they needed to frighten the rabbits back by walking about to collect. An arrow does not make enough noise to upset more than the particular rabbit that it is shot at.

At the fifth shot Kay was lucky. He allowed just the right amount for wind and distance, and his point took a young coney square in the head. It had been standing up on end to look at him, wondering what he was.

"Oh, well shot!" cried the Wart, as they ran to pick it up. It was the first rabbit they had ever hit, and luckily they had killed it dead.

When they had carefully gutted it with the little hunting knife which Merlyn had given – in order to keep it fresh –

and passed one of its hind legs through the other at the hock, for convenience in carrying, the two boys prepared to go home with their prize. But before they unstrung their bows they used to observe a ceremony. Every Thursday afternoon, after the last serious arrow had been fired, they were allowed to fit one more nock to their strings and to discharge the arrow straight up in the air. It was partly a gesture of farewell, partly of triumph, and it was beautiful. They did it now as a salute to their first prey.

The Wart watched his arrow go up. The sun was already westing towards evening, and the trees where they were had plunged them into a partial shade. So, as the arrow topped the trees and climbed into sunlight, it began to burn against the evening like the sun itself. Up and up it went, not weaving as it would have done with a snatching loose, but soaring, swimming, aspiring towards heaven, steady, golden and superb. Just as it had spent its force, just as its ambition had been dimmed by destiny and it was preparing to faint, to turn over, to pour back into the bosom of its mother earth, a terrible portent happened. A gore-crow came flapping wearily before the approaching night. It came, it did not waver, it took the arrow. It flew away, heavy and hoisting, with the arrow in its beak.

Kay was frightened by this, but the Wart was furious. He had loved his arrow's movement, its burning ambition in the sunlight, and besides it was his best arrow. It was the only one which was perfectly balanced, sharp, tight-feathered, clean-nocked, and neither warped nor scraped.

"It was a witch," said Kay.

"I don't care if it was ten witches," said the Wart. "I am going to get it back."

"But it went towards the Forest."

"I shall go after it."

"You can go alone, then," said Kay. "I'm not going into the Forest Sauvage, just for a putrid arrow."

"I shall go alone."

"Oh, well," said Kay. "I suppose I shall have to come too, if you're so set on it. And I bet we shall get nobbled by Wat."

"Let him nobble," said the Wart, "I want my arrow."

They went in the Forest at the place where they had last seen the bird of carrion.

In less than five minutes they were in a clearing with a well and a cottage just like Merlyn's.

"Goodness," said Kay, "I never knew there were any cottages so close. I say, let's go back."

"I just want to look at this place," said the Wart. "It's probably a wizard's."

The cottage had a brass plate screwed on the garden gate. It said:

MADAME MIM, B.A. (Dom–Daniel)

PIANOFORTE

NEEDLEWORK

NECROMANCY

No Hawkers,
Circulars or Income Tax
Beware of the Dragon

The cottage had lace curtains. These stirred ever so slightly, for behind them there was a lady peeping. The gore-crow was standing on the chimney.

"Come on," said Kay. "Oh, do come on. I tell you, she'll never give it back."

At this point the door of the cottage opened suddenly and the witch was revealed standing in the passage. She was a strikingly beautiful woman of about thirty, with coal-black hair so rich that it had the blue-black of the maggot-pies in it, sky bright eyes and a general soft air of butter-wouldn't-melt-in-my-mouth. She was sly.

"How do you do, my dears," said Madame Mim. "And what can I do for you today?"

The boys took off their leather caps, and Wart said, "Please, there is a crow sitting on your chimney and I think it has stolen one of my arrows."

"Precisely," said Madame Mim. "I have the arrow within."

"Could I have it back, please?"

"Inevitably," said Madame Mim. "The young gentleman shall have his arrow on the very instant, in four ticks and ere the bat squeaks thrice."

"Thank you very much," said the Wart.

"Step forward," said Madame Mim. "Honour the threshold. Accept the humble hospitality in the spirit in which it is given."

"I really do not think we can stay," said the Wart politely. "I really think we must go. We shall be expected back at home."

"Sweet expectation," replied Madame Mim in devout tones.

"Yet you would have thought," she added, "that the young gentleman could have found time to honour a poor cottager, out of politeness. Few can believe how we ignoble tenants of the lower classes value a visit from the landlord's sons."

"We would like to come in," said the Wart, "very much. But you see we shall be late already."

The lady now began to give a sort of simpering whine. "The fare is lowly," she said. "no doubt it is not what you would be accustomed to eating, and so naturally such highly-born ones would not care to partake."

Kay's strongly-developed feeling for good form gave way at this. He was an aristocratic boy always, and condescended to his inferiors so that they could admire him. Even at the risk of visiting a witch, he was not going to have it said that he had refused to eat a tenant's food because it was too humble.

"Come on, Wart," he said. "We needn't be back before vespers."

Madame Mim swept them a low curtsey as they crossed the threshold. Then she took them each by the scruff of the neck, lifted them right off the ground with her strong gypsy arms, and shot out of the back door with them almost before they had got in at the front. The Wart caught a hurried glimpse of her parlour and kitchen. The lace curtains, the aspidistra, the lithograph called the Virgin's Choise, the printed text of the Lord's Prayer written backwards and hung upside down, the sea-shell, the needle-case in the shape of a heart with A Present from Camelot written on it, the broomsticks, the cauldrons, and the bottles of dandelion wine. Then they were kicking and struggling in the back yard.

"We thought that the growing sportsmen would care to examine our rabbits," said Madame Mim.

There was indeed a row of large rabbit hutches in front of them, but they were empty of rabbits. In one hutch there was a poor ragged old eagle owl, evidently quite miserable and neglected: in another a small boy unknown to them, a wittol who could only roll his eyes and burble when the witch came near. In a third there was a moulting black cock. A fourth had a mangy goat in it, also black, and two more stood empty.

"Grizzle Greediguts," cried the witch.

"Here, Mother," answered the carrion crow.

With a flop and a squawk it was sitting beside them, its hairy black beak cocked on one side. It was the witch's familiar.

"Open the doors," commanded Madame Mim, "and Greediguts shall have eyes for supper, round and blue."

The gore-crow hastened to obey, with every sign of satisfaction, and pulled back the heavy doors in its strong beak, with three times three. Then the two boys were thrust inside, one into each hutch, and Madame Mim regarded them with unmixed pleasure. The doors had magic locks on them and the witch had made them to open by whispering in their keyholes.

"As nice a brace of young gentlemen," said the witch, "as ever stewed or roasted. Fattened on real butcher's meat, I daresay, with milk and all. Now we'll have the big one jugged for Sunday, if I can get a bit of wine to go in the pot, and the little one we'll have on the moon's morn, by jing and by jee, for how can I keep my sharp fork out of him a minute longer it fair gives me the croup."

"Let me out," said Kay hoarsely, "you old witch, or Sir Ector will come for you."

At this Madame Mim could no longer contain her joy. "Hark to the little varmint," she cried, snapping her fingers and doing a bouncing jig before the cages. "Hark to the sweet, audacious, tender little veal. He answers back and threatens us with Sir Ector, on the very brink of the pot. That's how I faint to tooth them, I do declare, and that's how I will tooth them ere the week be out, by Scarmiglione, Belial, Peor, Ciriato Sannuto and Dr D."

With this she began bustling about in the back yard, the herb garden and the scullery, cleaning pots, gathering plants for the stuffing, sharpening knives and cleavers, boiling water, skipping for joy, licking her greedy lips, saying spells, braiding her night-black hair, and singing as she worked.

First she sang the old witch's song:

> *Black spirits and white, red spirits and grey,*
> *Mingle, mingle, mingle, you that mingle may.*
>> *Here's the blood of a bat,*
>> *Put in that, oh, put in that.*
>> *Here's libbard's bane.*
>> *Put in again.*
> *Mingle, mingle, mingle, you that mingle may.*

Then she sang her work song.

Two spoons of sherry
Three oz. of yeast,
Half a pound of unicorn,
And God bless the feast.
Shake them in the collander,
Bang them to a chop,
Simmer slightly, snip up nicely,
Jump, skip, hop.
Knit one, knot one, purl two together,
Pip one and pop one and pluck the secret
feather.

Baste in a mod. oven.
God bless our coven.
Tra-la-la!
Three toads in a jar.
Te-he-he!
Put in the frog's knee.
Peep out of the lace curtain.
There goes the Toplady girl, she's up to
no good that's certain.
Oh, what a lovely baby!
How nice it would go with gravy.
Pinch the salt.

Here she pinched it very nastily

Turn the malt

Here she began twiddling round widdershins, in a vulgar way.

With a hey-nonny-nonny and I don't mean maybe.

At the end of this song, Madame Mim took a sentimental turn and delivered herself of several hymns, of a blasphemous nature, and of a tender love lyric which she sang sotto-voce with trills. It was:

> *My love is like a red, red nose*
> *His tail is soft and tawny,*
> *And everywhere my lovely goes*
> *I call him Nick or Horny.*

She vanished into the parlour, to lay the table.

Poor Kay was weeping in the corner of the end hutch, lying on his face and paying no attention to anything. Before Madame Mim had finally thrown him in, she had pinched him all over to see if he was fat. She had also slapped him, to see, as the butchers put it, if he was hollow. On top of this, he did not in the least want to be eaten for Sunday dinner and he was miserably furious with the Wart for leading him into such a terrible doom on account of a mere arrow. He had forgotten that it was he who had insisted on entering the fatal cottage.

The Wart sat on his haunches, because the cage was too small for standing up, and examined his prison. The bars were of iron and the gate was iron too. He shook all the bars, one after the other, but they were as firm as rock. There was an iron bowl for water – with no water in it – and some old straw in a corner for lying down. It was verminous.

"Our mistress," said the mangy old goat suddenly from the next pen, "is not very careful of her pets."

He spoke in a low voice, so that nobody could hear, but the carrion crow which had been left on the chimney to spy on them noticed that they were talking and moved nearer.

"Whisper," said the goat, "if you want to talk."

"Are you one of her familiars?" asked the Wart suspiciously.

The poor creature did not take offence at this, and tried not to look hurt.

"No," he said. "I'm not a familiar. I'm only a mangy old black goat, rather tattered as you see, and kept for sacrifice."

"Will she eat you too?" asked the Wart, rather tremblingly.

"Not she. I shall be too rank for her sweet tooth, you may be sure. No, she will use my blood for making patterns with on Walpurgis Night.

"It's quite a long way off, you know," continued the goat without self-pity. "For myself I don't mind very much, for I am old. But look at that poor owl there, that she keeps merely for a sense of possession and generally forgets to feed. That makes my blood boil, that does. It wants to fly, to stretch its wings. At night it just runs round and round and round like a big rat, it gets so restless. Look, it has broken all its soft feathers. For me, it doesn't matter, for I'm naturally of a sedentary disposition now that youth has flown, but I call that owl a rare shame. Something ought to be done about it."

The Wart knew that he was probably going to be killed

that night, the first to be released out of all that band, but yet he could not help feeling touched at the greatheartedness of this goat. Itself under sentence of death, it could afford to feel strongly about the owl. He wished he were as brave as this.

"If only I could get out," said the Wart. "I know a magician who would soon settle her hash, and rescue us all."

The goat thought about this for some time, nodding its gentle old head with the great cairngorm eyes. Then it said, "As a matter of fact I know how to get you out, only I did not like to mention it before. Put your ear nearer the bars. I know how to get you out, but not your poor friend there who is crying. I didn't like to subject you to a temptation like that. You see when she whispers to the lock I have heard what she says, but only at the locks on either side of mine. When she gets a cage away she is too soft to be heard. I know the words to release both you and me, and the black cock here too, but not your young friend yonder."

"Why ever haven't you let yourself out before?" asked the Wart, his heart beginning to bound.

"I can't speak them in human speech, you see," said the goat sadly, "and this poor mad boy here, the wittol, he can't speak them either."

"On, tell me then."

"You will be safe then, and so would I and the cock be too, if you stayed long enough to let us out. But would you be brave enough to stay, or would you run at once? And what about your friend and the wittol and the old owl."

"I should run for Merlyn at once," said the Wart. "Oh, at

once, and he would come back and kill this old witch in two twos, and then we should all be out."

The goat looked at him deeply, his tired old eyes seeming to ask their way kindly into the bottom of his heart.

"I shall tell you only the words for your own lock," said the goat at last. "The cock and I will stay here with your friend, as hostages for your return."

"Oh, goat," whispered the Wart. "You could have made me say the words to get you out first and then gone your way. Or you could have got the three of us out, starting with yourself to make sure, and left Kay to be eaten. But you are staying with Kay. Oh, goat, I will never forget you, and if I do not get back in time I shall not be able to bear my life."

"We shall have to wait till dark. It will only be a few minutes now."

As the goat spoke, they could see Madame Mim lighting the oil lamp in the parlour. It had a pink glass shade with patterns on it. The crow, which could not see in the dark, came quietly closer, so that at least he ought to be able to hear.

"Goat," said the Wart, in whose heart something strange and terrible had been going on in the dangerous twilight, "put your head closer still. Please, goat, I am not trying to be better than you are, but I have a plan. I think it is I who had better stay as hostage and you who had better go. You are black and will not be seen in the night. You have four legs and can run much faster than I. Let you go with a message for Merlyn. I will whisper you out, and I will stay."

He was hardly able to say the last sentence, for he knew

that Madame Mim might come for him at any moment now, and if she came before Merlyn it would be his death warrant. But he did say it, pushing the words out as if he were breathing against water, for he knew that if he himself were gone when Madame came for him, she would certainly eat Kay at once.

"Master," said the goat without further words, and it put one leg out and laid its double-knobbed forehead on the ground in the salute which is given to royalty. Then it kissed his hand as a friend.

"Quick," said the Wart, "give me one of your hoofs through the bars and I will scratch a message on it with one of my arrows."

It was difficult to know what message to write on such a small space with such a clumsy implement. In the end he just wrote Kay. He did not use his own name because he thought Kay more important, and that they would come quicker for him.

"Do you know the way?" he asked.

"My grandam used to live at the castle."

"What are the words?"

"Mine," said the goat, "are rather upsetting."

"What are they?"

"Well," said the goat. "you must say: Let Good Digestion Wait on Appetite."

"Oh, goat," said the Wart in a broken voice. "How horrible! But run quickly, goat, and come back safely, goat, and oh, goat, give me one more kiss for company before you go." The goat refused to kiss him. It gave him the Emperor's salute, of both feet, and bounded away into the darkness as soon as he had said the words.

Unfortunately although he had whispered too carefully for the crow to hear their speech, the release words had had to be said rather loudly to reach the next-door keyhole, and the door had creaked.

"Mother, mother!" screamed the crow. "The rabbits are escaping."

Instantly Madame Mim was framed in the lighted doorway of the kitchen.

"What is it, my Grizzle?" she cried. "What ails us, my halcyon tit?"

"The rabbits are escaping," shrieked the crow again.

The witch ran out, but too late to catch the goat or even to see him, and began examining the locks at once by the light of her fingers. She held these up in the air and a blue flame burnt at the tip of each.

"One little boy safe," counted Madame Mim, "and sobbing for his dinner. Two little boys safe, and neither getting thinner. One mangy goat gone, and who cares a fiddle? For the owl and the cock are left, and the wittol in the middle.

"Still," added Madame Mim, "it's a caution how he got out, a proper caution, that it is."

"He was whispering to the little boy," sneaked the crow, "whispering for the last half-hour together."

"Indeed?" said the witch, "whispering to the little dinner, hey? And much good may it do him. What about a sage stuffing, boy, hey? And what were you doing, my Greediguts, to let them carry on like that? No dinner for you, my little painted bird of paradise, so you may just flap off to any old tree and roost."

"Oh, Mother," whined the crow. "I was only adoing of my duty."

"Flap off," cried Madame Mim. "Flap off, and go broody if you like."

The poor crow hung its head and crept off to the other end of the roof, sneering to itself.

"Now my juicy toothful," said the witch, turning to the Wart and opening his door with the proper whisper of Enough-Is-As-Good-As-A-Feast, "we think the cauldron simmers and the oven is mod. How will my tender sucking pig enjoy a little popping lard instead of the clandestine whisper?"

The Wart ran about in his cage as much as he could, and gave as much trouble as possible in being caught, in order to save even a little time for the coming of Merlyn.

"Let go of me, you beast," he cried. "Let go of me, you foul hag, or I'll bite your fingers."

"How the creature scratches," said Madame Mim. "Bless us, how he wriggles and kicks, just for being a pagan's dinner."

"Don't you dare kill me," cried the Wart, now hanging by one leg. "Don't you dare lay a finger on me, or you'll be sorry for it."

"The lamb," said Madame Mim. "The partridge with a plump breast, how he does squeak.

"And then there's the cruel old custom," continued the witch, carrying him into the lamplight of the kitchen where a new sheet was laid on the floor, "of plucking the poor chicken before it is dead. The feathers come out cleaner so. Nobody could be so cruel as to do it nowadays, by Nothing or by Never, but of course a little boy doesn't feel any pain. Their clothes come off nicer if you take them off alive, and who would dream of roasting a little boy in his clothes, to spoil the feast?"

"Murdress," cried the Wart. "You will rue this ere the night is out."

"Cubling," said the Witch. "It's a shame to kill him, that it is. Look how his little downy hair stares in the lamplight, and how his poor eyes pop out of his head. Greediguts will be sorry to miss those eyes, so she will. Sometimes one could almost be a vegetarian, when one has to do a deed like this."

The witch laid the Wart over her lap, with his head between her knees, and carefully began to take his clothes off with a practised hand. He kicked and squirmed as much as he could, reckoning that every hindrance would put off the time when he would be actually knocked on the head, and thus increase the time in which the black goat could bring Merlyn to his rescue. During this time the witch sang her plucking song, of:

> *Pull the feather with the skin,*
> *Not against the grain — o.*
> *Pluck the soft one out from in,*

The great with might and main – o.
Even if he wriggles,
Never heed his squiggles,
For mercifully little boys are quite immune to pain – o.

She varied this song with the other kitchen song of the happy cook:

Soft skin for crackling,
Oh, my lovely duckling,
The skewers go here,
And the strings go there
And such is my scrumptious suckling.

"You will be sorry for this," cried the Wart, "Even if you live to be a thousand."

"He has spoken enough," said Madame Mim. "It is time that we knocked him on the napper.

"Hold him by the legs, and
When up goes his head,
Clip him with the palm-edge, and
Then he is dead."

The dreadful witch now lifted the Wart into the air and prepared to have her will of him; but at that very moment there was a fizzle of summer lightning without any crash and in the nick of time Merlyn was standing on the threshold.

"Ha!" said Merlyn. "Now we shall see what a double-first at Dom-Daniel avails against the private education of my master Bleise."

Madame Mim put the Wart down without looking at him, rose from her chair, and drew herself to her full magnificent height. Her glorious hair began to crackle, and sparks shot out of her flashing eyes. She and Merlyn stood facing each other for fully sixty seconds, without a word spoken, and then Madame Mim swept a royal curtsey and Merlyn bowed a frigid bow. He stood aside to let her go first out of the doorway and then followed her into the garden.

It ought perhaps to be explained, before we go any further, that in those far-off days, when there was actually a college for Witches and Warlocks under the sea at Dom-Daniel and when all wizards were either black or white, there was a good deal of ill-feeling between the different creeds. Quarrels between white and black were settled ceremonially, by means of duels. A wizard's duel was run like this. The two principals would stand opposite each other in some large space free from obstructions, and await the signal to begin. When the signal was given they were at liberty to turn themselves into things. It was rather like the game that can be played by two people with their fists. They say One, Two, Three, and at Three they either stick out two fingers for scissors, or the flat palm for paper, or the clenched fist for stone. If your hand becomes paper when your opponent's becomes scissors, then he cuts you and wins: but if yours had turned into stone, his scissors are blunted, and the win is yours. The object of the wizard in the duel was, to turn himself into some kind of animal, vegetable or mineral which would destroy the particular animal, vegetable or mineral which had been selected by his opponent. Sometimes it went on for hours.

Merlyn had Archimedes for his second, Madame Mim had the gore-crow for hers, while Hecate, who always had to be present at these affairs in order to keep them regular, sat on the top of a step-ladder in the middle to umpire. She was a cold, shining, muscular lady, the colour of moonlight. Merlyn and Madame Mim rolled up their sleeves, gave their surcoats to Hecate to hold and the latter put on a celluloid eye-shade to watch the battle.

At the first gong Madame Mim immediately turned herself into a dragon. It was the accepted opening move and Merlyn ought to have replied by being a thunderstorm or something like that. Instead he caused a great deal of preliminary confusion by becoming a field mouse, which was quite invisible in the grass, and nibbled Madame Mim's tail, as she stared about in all directions, for about five minutes before she noticed him. But when she did notice the nibbling, she was a furious cat in two flicks.

Wart held his breath to see what the mouse would become next – he thought perhaps a tiger which could kill the cat – but Merlyn merely became another cat. He stood opposite her and made faces. This most irregular procedure put Madame Mim quite out of her stride, and it took her more than a minute to regain her bearings and become a dog. Even as she became it, Merlyn was another dog standing opposite her, of the same sort.

"Oh, well played, sir!" cried the Wart, beginning to see the plan.

Madame Mim was furious. She felt herself out of her depth against these unusual stone-walling tactics and experienced an internal struggle not to lose her temper. She knew that if she did lose it she would lose her judgement, and the battle as well. She did some quick thinking. If whenever she turned herself into a menacing animal, Merlyn was merely going to turn into the same kind, the thing would become either a mere dog-fight or stalemate. She had better alter her own tactics and give Merlyn a surprise.

At this moment the gong went for the end of the first round. The combatants retired into their respective corners and their seconds cooled them by flapping their wings, while Archimedes gave Merlyn a little massage by nibbling with his beak.

"Second round," commanded Hecate. "Seconds out of the ring... Time!"

Clang went the gong, and the two desperate wizards stood face to face.

Madame Mim had gone on plotting during her rest. She had decided to try a new tack by leaving the offensive to Merlyn, beginning by assuming a defensive shape herself. She turned into a spreading oak.

Merlyn stood baffled under the oak for a few seconds. Then he most cheekily — and, as it turned out, rashly — became a powdery little blue-tit, which flew up and sat perkily on Madame Mim's branches. You could see the oak boiling with indignation for a moment; but then its rage became icy cold, and the poor little blue-tit was sitting, not on an oak, but on a snake. The snake's mouth was open, and the bird was actually perching on its jaws. The jaws clashed together, but only in the nick of time, the bird whizzed off as a gnat into the safe air. Madame Mim had got it on the run, however, and the speed of the contest now became bewildering. The quicker the attacker could assume a form, the less time the fugitive had to think of a form which would elude it, and now the changes were as quick as thought. The gnat was scarcely in the air when the snake had turned into a toad whose curious tongue, rooted at the front instead of the back of the jaw, was already unrolling in the flick which would snap it in. The gnat, flustered by the sore pursuit, was bounced into an offensive role, and the hard-pressed Merlyn now stood before the toad in the shape of a mollern which could attack it. But Madame Mim was in her element. The game was going according to the normal rules now, and in less than an eye's blink the toad had turned into a peregrine falcon which was diving at two hundred and fifty miles an hour upon the heron's back. Poor Merlyn, beginning to lose his nerve, turned wildly into an elephant – this move usually won a little breathing space – but Madame Mim, relentless, changed from the falcon into an aullay on the instant. An aullay was as much bigger than an elephant as an elephant is larger than a sheep. It was a sort of horse with an elephant's trunk. Madame Mim raised this trunk into the air, gave a shriek like a railway engine, and rushed upon her panting foe. In a flick Merlyn had disappeared.

"One," said Hecate. "Two. Three. Four. Five. Six. Seven. Eight. Nine – "

But before the fatal Ten which would have counted him out, Merlyn reappeared in a bed of nettles, mopping his brow. He had been standing among them as a nettle.

The aullay saw no reason to change its shape. It rushed upon the man before it with another piercing scream. Merlyn vanished again just as the thrashing trunk descended, and all stood still a moment, looking about them, wondering where he would step out next.

"One," began Hecate again, but even as she proceeded with her counting, strange things began to happen. The aullay got hiccoughs, turned red, swelled visibly, began whooping, came out in spots, staggered three times, rolled its eyes, fell rumbling to the ground. It groaned, kicked and said Farewell. The Wart cheered, Archimedes hooted till he cried, the gore-crow fell down dead, and Hecate, on the top of her ladder, clapped so much that she nearly tumbled off. It was a master stroke.

The ingenious magician had turned himself successively into the microbes, not yet discovered, of hiccoughs, scarlet fever, mumps, whooping cough, measles and heat spots and from a complication of all these complaints the infamous Madame Mim had immediately expired.

CHAPTER SEVEN

TILTING AND HORSEMANSHIP had two afternoons a week because they were easily the most important branches of a gentleman's education in those days. Merlyn grumbled a good deal about athletics, saying that nowadays people seemed to think that you were an educated man if you could knock another man off a horse and that the craze for games was the ruination of true scholarship – nobody got scholarships like they used to do when he was a boy, and all the public schools had been forced to lower their standards – but Sir Ector, who was an old tilting blue, said that the battle of Cressy had been won upon the playing fields of Camelot. This made Merlyn so furious that he gave Sir Ector rheumatism two nights running before he relented.

Tilting was a great art and needed an enormous amount of practice. When two knights jousted they held their lances in their right hands, but they directed their horses at one another so that each man had his opponent on his near side. The base of the lance, in fact, was held on the opposite side of the body to the side at which the enemy was charging. This seems rather inside out to anybody who is in the habit, say, of opening gates with a hunting-crop, but it had its reasons. For one thing, it meant that the shield was on the left arm, so that the opponents charged shield to shield, fully covered. It also meant that the man could be unhorsed with the side or edge of the lance, in a kind of horizontal swipe, if you did not feel sure of hitting him with your point. This was the humblest or least skilful blow in jousting.

A good jouster, like Launcelot or Tristram, always used the blow of the point, because, although it was liable to miss in unskilful hands, it made contact sooner. If one knight charged with his lance held rigidly sideways, with a view to sweeping his opponent out of the saddle, the other knight with his lance held directly forward would knock him down a lance length before the sweep came into effect.

Then there was how to hold your lance for the point stroke. It was no good crouching in the saddle and clutching it in a rigid grip preparatory to the great shock, for if you held it inflexibly like this its point bucked up and down to every movement of your thundering mount and you were practically certain to miss your aim. On the contrary, you had to sit quite loosely in the saddle with the lance easy and balanced against the horse's motion. It was not until the actual moment of striking that you clamped your knees into the horse's sides, threw your weight forward in your seat, clutched the lance with the whole hand instead of with your finger and thumb, and hugged your right elbow to your side to support its butt.

There was the size of spear. Obviously a man with a spear one hundred yards long would strike down an opponent with a normal spear of ten or twelve feet before the latter came anywhere near him. But it would have been impossible to make a spear one hundred yards long, and, if made, impossible to carry. The jouster had to find out the greatest length which he could manage with the greatest speed, and stick to that. Sir Launcelot, who came some time after this story, had several sizes of spear and would call for his Great Spear or his Lesser Spear as occasion demanded.

There were the places on which the enemy should be hit. In the armoury of the Castle of the Forest Sauvage there was a big picture of a knight in armour with circles round his vulnerable points. These varied with the style of armour, so that you had to study your opponent before the charge and select a point. The good armourers – the best lived at Warrington, and still live there – were careful to make all the forward or entering sides of their suits convex, so that the spear point glanced off them. Curiously enough, the shields were more inclined to be concave. It was better that a spear point should stay on your shield, rather than glance off upwards or downwards, and perhaps hit a more vulnerable point of your body armour. The best place of all for hitting people was on the very crest of the tilting helm, that is, if the person in question were vain enough to have a large metal crest in whose folds and ornaments the point would find a ready lodging. Many were vain enough to have these armorial crests, with bears and dragons or even ships or castles on them, but Sir Launcelot always contented himself with a bare helmet, or a bunch of feathers which would not hold spears, or, on one occasion, a soft lady's sleeve.

It would take too long to go into all the interesting details of proper tilting which the boys had to learn, for in those days one had to be a master of one's craft from the bottom upwards. You had to know what wood was best for spears, and why, and even how to turn them so that they would not splinter or warp. There were a thousand disputed questions about arms and armour, all of which had to be understood.

Just outside Sir Ector's castle there was a jousting field for tournaments, although there had been no tournaments in it since Kay was born. It was a green meadow, kept short, with a broad grassy bank raised around it on which pavilions could be erected. There was an old wooden grandstand at one side, lifted on stilts for the ladies. At present it was only used as a practice-ground for tilting, so a quintain had been erected at one end and a ring at the other. The quintain was a very horrible wooden saracen on a pole. He was painted with a bright blue face and red beard and glaring eyes. He had a shield in his left hand and a flat wooden sword in his right. If you hit him in the middle of the forehead all was well, but if your lance struck him on the shield or on any part to left or right of the middle line, then he spun round with great rapidity, and usually caught you a wallop with his sword as you galloped by, ducking. His paint was somewhat scratched and the wood picked up over his right eye. The ring was just an ordinary iron ring tied to a kind of gallows by a thread. If you managed to put your point through the ring, the thread broke, and you could canter off proudly with the ring round your spear.

The day was cooler than it had been for some time, for the autumn was almost within sight, and the two boys were in the tilting yard with the master armourer and Merlyn. The master armourer, or sergeant-at-arms, was a stiff, pale, bouncy gentleman with waxed moustaches. He always marched about with his chest stuck out like a pouter pigeon, and called out "On the word One – " on every possible occasion. He took great pains to keep his tummy in, and often tripped over his feet because he could not see them over his chest. He was always making his muscles ripple, which annoyed Merlyn.

Wart lay beside Merlyn in the shade of the grandstand and scratched himself for harvest bugs. The saw-like sickles had only lately been put away, and the wheat stood in stooks of eight among the tall stubble of those times. The Wart still itched. He was also sore about the shoulders and had a burning red ear, from making bosh shots at the quintain – for, of course, practice tilting was done without armour. Wart was pleased that it was Kay's turn to go through it now and lay drowsily in the shade, snoozing, scratching, twitching like a dog and partly attending to the fun.

Merlyn, sitting with his back to all this athleticism, was

practising a spell which he had forgotten. It was a spell to make the sergeant's moustaches uncurl, but at present it only uncurled one of them and the sergeant had not noticed it. He absent-mindedly curled it up again every time that Merlyn did the spell, and Merlyn said, "Drat it!" and began again. Once he had made the sergeant's ears flap by mistake, and the latter gave a startled look at the sky.

"How's goat?" asked Merlyn lazily, getting tired of these activities.

They had set free all Madame Mim's poor captives on the night of the great duel, but the goat had insisted on coming home with them. They had found him lurking on the edge of the battle ground, having galloped all the way back to see the fun and help the Wart as best he could if Madame Mim should have proved the victor.

"He has made friend with Cavall," said Wart, "and decided to sleep in the kennels. It was funny at first, because Clumsy and Apollon thought it was cheek and tried to run him out. He just stood in a corner so that they could not nip his hocks, and gave them such a bunt each with his knobbly forehead that now, whenever he gives them one of his looks, they get up from whatever they are doing and go somewhere else. The Dog-Boy says that Clumsy believes that he is the devil."

From far off at the other side of the tilting ground the sergeant's voice came floating on the still air.

"Nah, Nah, Master Kay, that ain't it at all. *Has* you were. *Has* you were. The spear should be 'eld between the thumb and forefinger of the right 'and, with the shield in line with the seam of the trahser leg…"

The Wart rubbed his sore ear and sighed.

"What are you grieving about now?" asked Merlyn.

"I wasn't grieving. I was just thinking."

"What were you thinking?"

"Oh, it wasn't anything. I was thinking about Kay learning to be a knight."

"And you may well grieve," exclaimed Merlyn hotly. "A lot of brainless unicorns swaggering about and calling themselves educated just because they can push each other off a horse with a bit of stick! It makes me tired. Why, I believe Sir Ector would have been gladder to get a by-our-lady tilting blue for your tutor, that swings himself along on his knuckles like an anthropoid ape, rather than a magician of known probity and international reputation with first-class honours from every European university. The trouble with the English Aristocracy is that they are games-mad, that's what it is, games-mad."

He broke off indignantly and deliberately made the sergeant's ears flap twice, in unison.

"I wasn't thinking quite about that," said the Wart. "As a matter of fact, I was thinking how nice it would be to be a knight, like Kay."

"Well, you'll be one soon enough, won't you?" asked Merlyn impatiently.

The Wart did not answer.

"Won't you?"

Merlyn turned round and looked closely at the Wart through his spectacles.

"What's the matter now?" said Merlyn in his nastiest voice. His inspection had showed him that the Wart was trying not to cry, and that if he spoke in a kind voice the Wart would break down and do it.

"I shall not be a knight," replied the Wart coldly. Merlyn's trick had worked and he no longer wanted to weep: he wanted to kick Merlyn. "I shall not be a knight because I am not a proper son of Sir Ector's. They will knight Kay, and I shall be his squire."

Merlyn's back was turned again, but his eyes were twinkling behind his curious spectacles. "That's too bad," said Merlyn, without any commiseration.

The Wart burst out with all his thoughts aloud. "Oh," he cried, "but I should have liked to be born with a proper father and mother, so that I could be a knight errant."

"What would you have done?"

"I should have had a splendid suit of armour and dozens of spears and a black horse standing eighteen hands, and I should have called myself The Black Knight. And I should have hoved at a well or a ford or something and made all true knights that came that way to joust with me for the honour of their ladies, and I should have spared them all after I had given them a great fall, and I should live out of doors all the year round in a pavilion, and never do anything but joust and go on quests and bear away the prize at tournaments, and I shan't ever tell anybody my name."

"Your wife won't enjoy the life very much," said Merlyn reflectively.

"Oh, I'm not going to have a wife. I think they're stupid.

"I shall have to have a lady-love, though," added the Wart uncomfortably, "so that I can wear her favour in my helm, and do deeds in her honour."

A humble bee came zooming between them, under the grandstand and out into the sunlight.

"Would you like to see some real knights errant?" asked Merlyn slowly. "Now, for the sake of your education?"

"Oh, I would," cried the Wart. "We've never even had a tournament since I was here."

"I suppose it could be managed."

"Oh, please do. You could take me to some like you did to the fish."

"I suppose it's educational in a way."

"It's very educational," said the Wart. "I can't think of anything more educational than to see some real knights fighting. Oh, won't you please do it?"

"Do you prefer any particular knights?"

"King Pellinore," said the Wart immediately. He had a weakness for this gentleman since their strange encounter in the Forest Sauvage.

Merlyn said, "That will do very well. Put your hands to your sides and relax your muscles. *Cabricias arci thuram, catalamus, singulariter, nominativo, haec musa.* Shut your eyes and keep them shut. *Bonus, Bona, Bonum.* Here we go. *Deus Sanctus, est-ne oratio Latinas? Etiam, oui, quare? Pourquoi? Quia substantivo et adjectivum concordat generi, numerum et casus.* Here we are."

While this incantation was going on, Wart experienced

some queer sensations. First he could hear the sergeant calling out to Kay, "Nah then, nah then, keep the 'eels dahn and swing the body from the 'ips." Then the words got smaller and smaller, as if he were looking at his feet through the wrong end of a telescope, and began to swirl round into a cone, as if they were at the pointed bottom end of a whirlpool which was sucking him into the air. There was nothing but a loud rotating roaring and hissing noise which rose to such a tornado that he felt he could not stand it any more. Finally there was utter silence and Merlyn saying, "Here we are." All this happened in about the time that it would take a sixpenny rocket to start off with its fiery swish, bend down from its climax and disperse itself in thunder and coloured stars. He opened his eyes just at the moment when you would have heard the invisible stick hitting the ground.

They were lying under a beech tree in the Forest Sauvage.

"Here we are," said Merlyn. "Get up and dust your clothes.

"And there, I think," continued the magician, in a tone of great satisfaction because his spells had worked for once without a hitch, "is your friend, King Pellinore, pricking towards us o'er the plain."

"Hallo, hallo," cried King Pellinore, popping his visor up and down. "it's the young boy with the feather bed, isn't it. Ay say, what?"

"Yes, it is," said the Wart. "And I am very glad to see you. Did you manage to catch the Beast?"

"No," said King Pellinore. "Didn't catch the Beast. Oh, do come here, you brachet, and leave that bush alone. Tcha! Tcha!

Naughty, naughty! She runs riot, you know, what. Very keen on rabbits. Ay tell you there's nothing in it, you beastly dog. Tcha! Tcha! Leave it, leave it! Oh, do come to heel, like Ay tell you.

"She never does come to heel," added King Pellinore.

At this the dog put a cock pheasant out of the bush, which rocketed off with a tremendous clatter, and the dog became so excited that it ran round its master three or four times at the end of its rope, panting hoarsely as if it had asthma. King Pellinore's horse stood quite patiently while the rope was being wound round its legs, and Merlyn and the Wart had to catch the brachet and unwind it before the conversation could proceed.

"Ay say," said King Pellinore. "Thank you very much, Ay must say. Won't you introduce me to your friend, what?"

"This is my tutor Merlyn, a great magician."

"How de do," said the King. "Always like to meet magicians. In fact Ay always like to meet anybody, you know. It sort of passes the time away, what, on a quest."

"Hail," said Merlyn, in his most mysterious manner.

"Hail," replied the King, anxious to make a good impression.

They shook hands.

"Did you say Hail?" inquired the King, looking about him nervously. "Ay thought it was going to be fine, meself."

"He meant How-do-you-do," explained the Wart.

"Ah, yes, How-de-do?"

They shook hands again.

"Good afternoon," said King Pellinore. "What do you think the weather looks like now?"

"I think it looks like an anticyclone," said Merlyn.

"Ah, yes," said the King. "An anticyclone. Well, Ay suppose Ay ought to be getting along."

At this the King trembled very much, opened and shut his visor several times, coughed, wove his reins into a knot, exclaimed, "Ay beg your pardon?" and showed signs of cantering away.

"He is a white magician," said the Wart. "You needn't be afraid of him. He is my best friend, your majesty, and in any case he generally gets his spells muddled up."

"Ah, yes," said King Pellinore. "A white magician, what? How small the world is, is it not? How-de-do?"

"Hail," said Merlyn.

"Hail," said King Pellinore.

They shook hands for the third time.

"I shouldn't go away," said Merlyn, "if I were you. Sir Grummore Grummursum is on the way here to challenge you to a joust."

"No, you don't say? Sir What-you-may-call-it coming here to challenge me to a joust?"

"Assuredly."

"Good handicap man?"

"I should think it would be a pretty even match."

"Well, Ay must say," exclaimed the King, "it never hails but it pours."

"Hail," said Merlyn.

"Hail," said King Pellinore.

"Hail," said the Wart involuntarily.

"Now Ay really won't shake hands with anybody else," announced the monarch. "We shall simply assume that we have all met before."

"Is Sir Grummore really coming," inquired the Wart, hastily changing the subject, "to challenge King Pellinore to battle?"

"Look yonder," said Merlyn, and both of them looked in the direction of the outstretched finger.

Sir Grummore Grummursum was cantering up the clearing in full panoply of war. Instead of his ordinary helmet with a visor he was wearing the proper tilting-helm, which looked like a large coal-scuttle, and as he cantered he clanged.

He was singing his old school song:

"We'll tilt together
Steady from crupper to poll,
And nothin' in life shall sever
Our love for the dear old coll.
Follow-up, follow-up, follow-up,
    follow-up, follow-up,
Till the shield ring again and again
With the clanks of the clanky true men."

"Goodness," exclaimed King Pellinore. "It's about two months since Ay had a proper tilt, and last winter they put me up to eighteen. That was when they had the new handicaps, you know."

Sir Grummore had arrived while he was speaking, and had recognized the Wart.

"Mornin'," said Sir Grummore. "You're Sir Ector's boy, ain't you? And who's that chap in the comic hat?"

"That's my tutor," said the Wart hurriedly, "Merlyn, the magician."

Sir Grummore looked at Merlyn – magicians were considered rather middle-class by the true jousting set in those days – and said distantly, "Ah, a magician. How-de-do?"

"And this is King Pellinore," said the Wart. "Sir Grummore Grummursum – King Pellinore."

"How-de-do?" said Sir Grummore.

"Hail," said King Pellinore. "No, Ay mean it won't hail, will it?"

"Nice day," said Sir Grummore.

"Yes it is nice, what, isn't it?"

"Been questin' today?"

"Oh, yes, thank you. Always am questing, you know. After the Questing Beast."

"Interestin' job that, very."

"Yes, it is interesting. Would you like to see some fewmets?"

"By jove, yes. Like to see some fewmets."

"Ay have some better ones at home, but these are quite good, really."

"Bless my soul. So these are her fewmets."

"Yes, these are her fewmets."

"Interestin' fewmets."

"Yes, they are interesting, aren't they? Only you get tired of them," added King Pellinore.

"Well, well. It's a fine day, isn't it?"

"Yes, it is rather fine."

"Suppose we'd better have a joust, eh, what?"

"Yes, Ay suppose we had better," said King Pellinore, "really."

"What shall we have it for?"

"Oh, the usual thing, Ay suppose. Would one of you kindly help me on with my helm?"

They all three had to help him on eventually, for, what with the unscrewing of screws and the easing of nuts and bolts which the King had clumsily set on the wrong thread when getting up in a hurry that morning, it was quite a feat of engineering to get him out of his helmet and into his helm. The helm was an enormous thing like an oil drum, padded inside with two thicknesses of leather and three inches of straw.

As soon as they were ready the two knights stationed themselves at each end of the clearing and then advanced to meet in the middle.

"Fair knight," said King Pellinore. "Ay pray thee tell me thy name."

"That me regards," replied Sir Grummore, using the proper formula.

"That is uncourteously said," said King Pellinore, "what? For no knight ne dreadeth for to speak his name openly, but for some reason of shame."

"Be that as it may, I choose that thou shalt not know my

name as at this time, for no askin'.""

"Then you must stay and joust with me, false knight."

"Haven't you got that wrong, Pellinore?" inquired Sir Grummore. "I believe it ought to be 'thou shalt'."

"Oh, Ay'm sorry, Sir Grummore. Yes, so it should, of course. Then thou shalt stay and joust with me, false knight."

Without further words the two gentlemen retreated to the opposite ends of the clearing, fewtred their spears, and prepared to hurtle together in the preliminary charge.

"I think we had better climb up this tree," said Merlyn. "You never know what will happen in a joust like this."

They climbed up the big beech, which had low easy branches sticking out in all directions, and the Wart stationed himself towards the end of a smooth bough about fifteen feet up, where he could get a good view. Nothing is so uncomfortable to sit in as a big beech.

In order to be able to picture the terrible battle which now took place, there is one thing which ought to be known: a knight in his full armour in those days was generally carrying as much or more than his own weight in metal. He weighed no less than twenty-two stone, and sometimes as much as twenty-five. This meant that his horse had to be a slow and enormous weight-carrier, like the farm-horse of today, and that his own movements were so hampered by his burden of iron and padding that they were toned down into slow motion like the cinema.

"They're off!" cried the Wart, holding his breath with excitement.

Slowly and majestically, the ponderous horses lumbered into a walk. The spears, which had been pointing in the air, bowed down to a horizontal line and pointed at each other. King Pellinore and Sir Grummore could be seen to be thumping their horses' sides with their heels for all they were worth and in a few minutes the splendid animals had shambled into an earth-shaking imitation of a trot. Clank, rumble, thumpity-thump, and now the two knights were flapping their elbows and legs in unison, showing a good deal of daylight at their seats. There was a change in tempo, and Sir Grummore's horse could be definitely seen to be cantering. In another minute King Pellinore's was doing so too. It was a terrible spectacle.

"Oh, dear!" exclaimed the Wart, feeling slightly ashamed that his own blood-thirstiness had been responsible for making those two knights joust before him. "Do you think they will kill each other?"

"Dangerous sport," said Merlyn, shaking his head.

"Now!" cried the Wart.

With a blood-curdling thumping of iron hoofs the mighty equestrians came together. Their spears wavered for a moment within a few inches of each other's helms – each had chosen the difficult point-stroke – and then they were galloping off in opposite directions. Sir Grummore drove his spear deep into the beech tree where they were sitting and stopped dead. King Pellinore, who had been run away with, vanished altogether behind his back.

"Is it safe to look?" inquired the Wart, who had shut his

eyes tight at the critical moment.

"Quite safe," said Merlyn, "it will take them some time to get back."

"Whoa, whoa, Ay say!" cried King Pellinore in muffled and distant tones, far away among some gorse bushes.

"Hi, Pellinore, Hi!" shouted Sir Grummore. "Come back, my dear fellah, I'm over here."

There was a long pause, while the complicated stations of the two knights readjusted themselves, and then King Pellinore was at the opposite end from that at which he had started, while Sir Grummore faced him from his original position.

"Traitor knight!" cried Sir Grummore.

"Yield, recreant, what?" cried King Pellinore.

They fewtred their spears again, and thundered into the charge.

"Oh," said the Wart. "I hope they don't hurt themselves."

But the two mounts were patiently blundering together, and the two knights had simultaneously decided upon the sweeping stroke. Each held his spear straight out at right angles towards the left, and before the Wart could say anything further there was a terrific yet melodious thump. Clang! said the armour, like a motor omnibus in collision with a smithy, and the jousters were sitting side by side on the green sward, while their horses cantered off in opposite directions.

"A splendid fall," said Merlyn.

The two horses pulled themselves up, their duty done, and began resignedly to eat the sward. King Pellinore and Sir

Grummore sat looking straight before them, each with the other's spear clasped hopefully under his arm.

"Well!" said the Wart. "What a bump! They both seem to be all right, so far."

Sir Grummore and King Pellinore laboriously got up.

"Defend thee," cried King Pellinore.

"God save thee," cried Sir Grummore.

With this they drew their swords and rushed together with such ferocity that each, after dealing the other a dint on the helm sat down suddenly backwards.

"Bah!" cried King Pellinore.

"Booh!" cried Sir Grummore, also sitting down.

"Mercy," exclaimed the Wart. "What a combat!"

The knights had now lost their tempers and the battle was joined in earnest. It did not matter much, however, for they were so encased in metal that they could do each other little damage. It took them so long to get up, and the dealing of a blow when you weighed the eighth part of a ton was such a cumbrous business, that every stage of the contest could be marked and pondered.

In the first stage King Pellinore and Sir Grummore stood opposite each other for about half an hour, and walloped each other on the helm. There was only opportunity for one blow at a time, and so they more or less took it in turns, King Pellinore striking while Sir Grummore was recovering, and vice versa. At first, if either of them dropped his sword or got it stuck in the ground, the other put in two or three extra blows while he was patiently fumbling for it or trying to tug it out. Later, they fell into the rhythm of the thing more perfectly, like the toy mechanical people who saw wood on Christmas trees. Eventually the exercise and the monotony restored their good humour and they began to get bored.

The second stage was introduced as a change, by common consent. Sir Grummore stumped off to one end of the clearing, while King Pellinore plodded off to the other. Then they turned round and swayed backwards and forwards once or twice, in order to get their weight on their toes. When they leant forward they had to run forward, in order to keep up with their weight, and if they leant too far backwards they fell down. So even walking was a bit complicated. When they had got their weight properly distributed in front of them, so that they were just off their balance, each broke into a trot to keep up with himself. They hurtled together as it had been two boars.

They met in the middle, breast to breast, with a noise of shipwreck and great bells tolling, and both, bouncing off, fell breathless on their backs. They lay thus for a few minutes, panting. Then they slowly began to heave themselves to their feet, and it was obvious that they had lost their tempers once again.

King Pellinore had not only lost his temper but seemed to have been a bit astonished by the impact. He got up facing the wrong way, and could not find Sir Grummore. There was some excuse for this, since he had only a tiny slit to peep through, and that was three inches away from his eye owing to the padding of straw, but he looked a bit muddled as well.

Perhaps he had broken his spectacles. Sir Grummore was quick to seize his advantage.

"Take that!" cried Sir Grummore, giving the unfortunate monarch a two-handed swipe on the nob as he was slowly turning his head from side to side, peering in the opposite direction.

King Pellinore turned round morosely, but his opponent had been too quick for him. He had ambled round so that he was still behind the King, and now gave him another terrific blow in the same place.

"Where are you?" asked King Pellinore.

"Here," cried Sir Grummore, giving him another.

The poor king turned himself round as nimbly as possible, but Sir Grummore had given him the slip again.

"Tally-ho back!" shouted Sir Grummore, with another wallop.

"Ay think you're a cad," said the King.

"Wallop!" replied Sir Grummore, doing it.

What with the preliminary crash, the repeated blows on the back of the head, and the puzzling invisible nature of his opponent, King Pellinore could now be seen to be visibly troubled in his brains. He swayed backwards and forwards under the hail of blows which were administered, and feebly wagged his arms.

"Poor King," said the Wart. "I wish he wouldn't hit him so."

As if in answer to his wish, Sir Grummore paused in his labours.

"Do you want Pax?" asked Sir Grummore.

King Pellinore made no answer.

Sir Grummore favoured him with another whack and said, "If you don't say Pax, I shall cut your head off."

"I won't," said the King.

Whang! went the sword on the top of his head.

Whang! it went again.

Whang! for the third time.

"Pax," said King Pellinore, mumbling rather.

Then, just as Sir Grummore was relaxing with the fruits of victory, he swung round upon him, shouted "Non!" at the top of his voice, and gave him a good push in the middle of the chest.

Sir Grummore fell over backwards.

"Well!" exclaimed the Wart. "What a cheat! I wouldn't have thought it of him."

King Pellinore hurriedly sat down on his victim's chest, thus increasing the weight upon him to a quarter of a ton and making it quite impossible for him to move, and began to undo Sir Grummore's helm.

"You said Pax!"

"Ay said Pax Non under my breath."

"It's a swizzle."

"It isn't, so sucks to you."

"You cad."

"No, Ay'm not."

"Yes, you are."

"No, Ay'm not."

"Yes, you are."

"Ay said Pax Non."

"You said Pax!"

"No, Ay didn't."

"Yes, you did."

"No, Ay didn't."

"Yes, you did."

By this time Sir Grummore's helm was unlaced and they could see his bare head glaring at King Pellinore, quite purple in the face.

"Yield thee, recreant," said the King.

"Shan't," said Sir Grummore.

"You've got to yield, or Ay shall cut off your head."

"Cut if off them."

"Oh, come on," said the King. "You know you have to yield when your helm is off."

"Feign I," said Sir Grummore.

"Well, Ay shall just cut your head off."

"I don't care."

The King waved his sword menacingly in the air.

"Go on," said Sir Grummore. "I dare you to."

The King lowered his sword and said, "Oh, Ay say, do yield, please."

"You yield," said Sir Grummore.

"But I can't yield, you know. Ay am on top of you after all, am not Ay, what?"

"Well, I've feigned yieldin'."

"Oh, come on, Grummore. Ay do think you are a cad not to yield. You know very well Ay can't cut your head off."

"I wouldn't yield to a cheat who started fightin' after he'd said Pax."

"Ay'm not a cheat."

"You are a cheat."

"No, Ay'm not."

"Yes, you are."

"No, Ay'm not."

"Yes, you are."

"Very well," said King Pellinore. "You can bally well get up and put on your helm and we'll have a fight. Ay won't be called a cheat for anybody."

"Cheat," said Sir Grummore.

They stood up and fumbled together with the helm, hissing, "No, Ay'm not," and "Yes, you are," until it was safely on. Then they retreated to opposite ends of the clearing, got their weight upon their toes, and came rumbling and thundering together like two runaway trams.

Unfortunately they were now so cross that they had both ceased to be vigilant, and in the fury of the moment they missed each other altogether. The momentum of their armour was too great for them to stop till they had passed each other handsomely, and then they manoeuvred about in such a manner that neither happened to come within the other's range of vision. It was a bit funny watching them, because King Pellinore, having already been caught from behind once, was continually spinning round to look behind him, and Sir Grummore, having used the stratagem himself, was doing the same thing. Thus they wandered for some five minutes, standing still, listening, clanking, crouching, creeping, peering, walking on tiptoe, and occasionally making a chance swipe behind their backs. Once they were standing within a few feet of each other, back to back, only to stalk off in opposite directions with infinite precaution, and once King Pellinore did hit Sir Grummore with one of his back strokes, but they both immediately spun round so often that they became giddy and mislaid each other afresh.

After five minutes, Sir Grummore said, "All right, Pellinore. It's no use hidin'. I can see where you are."

"Ay'm not hiding," exclaimed King Pellinore indignantly. "Where am Ay?"

They discovered each other and went up close together, face to face.

"Cad," said Sir Grummore.

"Yah," said King Pellinore.

They turned round and marched off to their corners, seething with indignation.

"Swindler," shouted Sir Grummore.

"Beastly bully," shouted King Pellinore.

With this they summoned all their energies together for one decisive encounter, leant forward, lowering their heads like two billy-goats, and positively sprinted together for the final blow. Alas, their aim was poor. They missed each other by about five yards, passed at full steam doing at least eight knots, like ships that pass in the night but speak not to each other in passing, and hurtled onwards to their doom. Both knights began waving their arms like windmills, anti-clockwise, in the vain effort to slow up. Both continued with undiminished speed. Then Sir Grummore rammed his head against the beech in which the Wart was sitting, and King Pellinore collided with a chestnut at the other side of the clearing. The trees shook, the forest rang. Blackbirds and squirrels cursed and wood-pigeons flew out of their leafy perches half a mile away. The two knights stood to attention while you could count three. Then, with a last unanimous melodious clang, they both fell prostrate on the fatal sward.

"Stunned," said Merlyn, "I should think."

"Oh, dear," said the Wart. "Oughtn't we to get down and help them?"

"We could pour water on their heads," said Merlyn reflectively, "if there were any water. But I don't suppose they'd thank you for making their armour rusty. They'll be all right. Besides, it's time that we were home."

"But they might be dead!"

"They're not dead, I know. In a minute or two they'll come round and go off home to dinner."

"Poor King Pellinore hasn't got a home."

"Then Sir Grummore will invite him to stay the night. They'll be the best of friends when they come to. They always are."

"Do you think so?"

"My dear boy, I know so. Shut your eyes and we'll be off."

The Wart gave in to Merlyn's superior knowledge. "Do you think," he asked with his eyes shut, "that Sir Grummore has a feather bed?"

"Probably."

"Good," said the Wart. "That will be nice for King Pellinore, even if he was stunned."

The Latin words were spoken and the secret passes made. The funnel of whistling noise and space received them. In two twos they were laying under the grandstand, and the sergeant's voice was calling from the opposite side of the tilting ground. "Nah then, Master Art, nah, then. You've been a snoozing there long enough. Come aht into the sunlight 'ere with Master Kay, one-two, one-two, and see some real tilting."

CHAPTER EIGHT

IT WAS A cold wet evening, such as may happen even towards
the end of August, and the Wart did not know how to bear
himself indoors. He spent some time in the kennels, talking to
goat and Cavall, then wandered off to help them turn the spit
in the kitchen. But there it was too hot. He was not forced to
stay indoors because of the rain, by his female supervisors, as
happens all too frequently to the decadent children of the
present generation, but the mere wetness and dreariness in the
open discouraged him from going out. He hated everybody.

"Confound the boy," said Sir Ector. "For goodness' sake
stop mopin' by the window there, and go and find your tutor.
When I was a boy we always used to study on wet days, yes,
and eddicate our minds."

"Wart's stupid," said Kay.

"Ah, run along, my duck," said their old Nurse. "I ha'n't

got time to attend to thy mopseys now, what with all this sorbent washing."

"Now then, my young master," said Hob. "Let thee run off to thy quarters, and stop confusing they fowls."

"Nah, nah," cried the sergeant. "You op orf art of 'ere. I got enough to do polishing of this ber-lady harmour."

Even the Dog Boy barked at him when he went back to the kennels.

Wart draggled off to the tower-room, where Merlyn was busy knitting himself a woollen night-cap for the winter.

"I cast off two together at every other line," said Merlyn, "but for some reason it seems to end too sharply. Like an onion, you know. It's the turning of the heel that does you, every time."

"I think I ought to have some more eddication," said the Wart. "I can't think of anything to do."

"You think that education is something that ought to be done when all else fails?" inquired Merlyn nastily, for he was in a bad mood too.

"Well," said the Wart, "some sorts of education."

"Mine?" asked the magician with flashing eyes.

"Oh, Merlyn," exclaimed the Wart without answering, "please give me something to do, because I feel so miserable. Nobody wants me for anything today, and I just don't know how to be sensible. It rains so."

"You should learn to knit."

"Couldn't I go out and be something, a fish or anything like that?"

"You've been a fish," said Merlyn. "Nobody with any go

needs to do their education twice."

"Well, could I be a bird?"

"If you knew anything at all," said Merlyn, "which you don't, you would know that a bird doesn't like to fly in the rain because it wets its feathers and makes them stick together. They get bedraggled."

"I could be a hawk in Hob's mews," said the Wart stoutly. "Then I should be indoors and shouldn't get wet."

"That's pretty ambitious," said Merlyn, "to want to be a hawk."

"You know you will turn me into a hawk when you want to," shouted the Wart. "But you like to plague me because it's wet. I won't have it."

"Hoity-toity," said Merlyn.

"Please," said the Wart, "dear Merlyn, turn me into a hawk. If you don't do that I shall do something. I don't know what."

Merlyn put down his knitting and looked at his pupil over the top of his spectacles. "My boy," he said, "you shall be everything in the world, animal, vegetable or mineral for all I care, before I've done with you, but you really will have to trust to my superior foresight — or is it backsight? The time is not ripe for you to be a hawk — for one thing Hob is still in the mews feeding them — and you may just as well sit down for the moment and learn to be a human being."

"Very well," said the Wart, "if that's a go." And he sat down.

After several minutes he said, "Is one allowed to speak as a human being, or does the thing about being seen and not heard have to apply?"

"Everybody can speak."

"That's good, because I wanted to mention that you have been knitting your beard into that night-cap for three rows now."

"Well, I'll be fiddled."

"I should think the best thing would be to cut off the end of your beard. Shall I fetch some scissors?"

"Why didn't you tell me before?"

"I wanted to see what would happen."

"You run a grave risk, my boy," said Merlyn coldly, "of being turned into a piece of bread, and toasted."

With this he slowly began to unpick his beard, muttering to himself meanwhile and taking the greatest precautions not to drop a stitch.

"Will it be as difficult to fly," asked the Wart when he thought his tutor had calmed down, "as it was to swim?"

"You won't need to fly. I don't mean to turn you into a loose hawk, but only to set you in the mews for the night, so that you can talk to the others. That's the way to learn, by listening to the experts."

"Will they talk?"

"They talk every night, deep into the darkness. They say about how they were taken, and what they can remember of their homes: about their lineage and the great deeds of their ancestors, about their training and what they have learnt and will learn. It is military talk really, like you might have in the mess of a crack cavalry regiment: tactics, small arms, maintenance, betting, famous hunts, wine, women and song.

"Another subject they have," continued Merlyn, "is food. It's a depressing thought, but of course they are mainly trained by hunger. They're a hungry lot, poor chaps, thinking of the best restaurants where they used to go, and how they had champagne and caviar and gipsy music. Of course, they all come of noble blood."

"What a shame that they should be kept prisoners and hungry."

"Well, they don't really understand that they are prisoners, any more than the cavalry officers do. They look on themselves as being dedicated to their profession, like an order of knighthood or something like that. You see, the membership of the mews is after all restricted to the raptors, and that does help a lot. They know that none of the lower classes can get in. Their screen perches don't carry blackbirds or such trash as that. And then, as to the hungry part, they are far from starving or that kind of hunger. They are in training, you know, and like everybody in strict training, they think about food."

"How soon can I begin?"

"You can begin now, if you want to, for my insight tells me that Hob has this minute finished for the night. But first of all you must choose what kind of hawk you would prefer to be."

"I should like to be a merlin," said the Wart politely.

This answer pleased the magician. "A very good choice," he said, "and if you please we will proceed at once."

The Wart got up from his stool and stood in front of his tutor. Merlyn put down his knitting.

"First you go small," said Merlyn, pressing him on the top of the head until he was a bit smaller than a pigeon. "Then you stand on the ball of your toes, bend at the knees, hold your elbows to your sides, lift your hands to the level of your shoulders, and press your first and second fingers together, as also your third and fourth. Look, it is like this."

With these words the aged magician stood upon tiptoe and did as he had explained.

The Wart copied him carefully and wondered what would happen next. What did happen was that Merlyn, who had been saying the final spells under his breath, suddenly turned himself into a condor, leaving the Wart standing on tiptoe unchanged. He stood there as if he were drying himself in the sun, with a wing-spread of about eleven feet, a bright orange head and a magenta carbuncle. He looked very surprised and rather funny.

"Come back," said the Wart. "You've changed the wrong one."

"It's this by-our-lady spring cleaning," exclaimed Merlyn, turning back into himself. "Once you let a woman into your study for half an hour, you don't know where to lay your hands on the right spell, not if it was ever so. Stand up and we'll try again."

This time the now tiny Wart felt his toes shooting out and scratching on the floor. He felt his heels rise and stick out behind, and his knees draw into his stomach. His thighs got quite short. A web of skin grew from his wrists to his shoulders, while his primary feathers burst out into little soft quills from the end of his fingers and quickly grew. His secondaries sprouted out along his forearms, and a charming little false primary sprang from the end of each thumb.

The dozen feathers of his tail, with the double deck-feathers in the middle, grew out in the twinkling of an eye, and all the covert feathers of his back and breast and shoulders slipped out of the skin to hide the roots of the more important plumes. Wart looked quickly at Merlyn, ducked his head between his legs and had a look through there, rattled his feathers into place, and began to scratch his chin with the sharp talon of one toe.

"Good," said Merlyn. "Now hop up on my hand – ah, be careful and don't gripe – and listen to what I have to tell you. I shall take you into the mews now that Hob has locked up for the night, and I shall put you loose and unhooded beside Balin and Balan. Now pay attention. Don't go close to anybody without speaking first. You must remember that most of them are hooded and might be startled into doing something rash. You can trust Balin and Balan, also the kestrel and the sparhawk. Don't go within reach of the falcon unless she invites you to. On no account must you stand beside Cully's special enclosure, for he is unhooded and will go for you through the mesh if he gets half a chance. He is not quite right in his brains, poor chap, and if he once grips you, you will never leave that grip again. Remember that you are visiting a kind of spartan military mess. These fellows are regulars. As the junior subaltern your only business is to keep your mouth shut, speak when you're spoken to and not interrupt."

"I bet I'm more than a subaltern," said the Wart, "if I am a merlin."

"Well, as a matter of fact you are. You will find that both the kestrel and the spar-hawk are polite to you, but for all sake's sake don't interrupt the senior merlins or the falcon. She's the honorary colonel of the regiment you know. And as for Cully, well, he's a colonel too, even if he is infantry, so you must mind your p's and q's."

"I will be careful," said the Wart, who was beginning to feel rather scared.

"Good. I shall come for you in the morning before Hob is up."

All the hawks were silent as Merlyn carried their new companion into the mews, and silent for some time afterwards when they had been left in the dark. The rain had given place to a full August moonlight, so clear that you could see a woolly bear caterpillar fifteen yards away out of doors, as it climbed up and up the knobbly sandstone of the great keep, and it took the Wart only a few moments for his eyes to become accustomed to the diffused brightness inside the mews. The darkness became watered with light, with silver radiance, and then it was an eerie sight which dawned upon his vision. Each hawk or falcon stood in the silver upon one leg, the other tucked up inside the apron of its panel, and each was a motionless statue of a knight in armour. They stood gravely in their plumed helmets, spurred and armed. The canvas or sacking screens of their perches moved heavily in a breath of wind, like banners in a chapel, and the rapt nobility of the air kept their knight's vigil in knightly patience. In those days they used to hood everything they could, even the goshawk and the merlin, which are no longer hooded according to the modern practice.

Wart drew his breath at the sight of all these stately figures, standing so still that they might have been cut of stone. He was overwhelmed by their magnificence, and felt no need of Merlyn's warning that he was to be humble and behave himself.

Presently there was a gentle ringing of a bell. The great peregrine falcon had bestirred herself and now said, in a high nasal voice which came from her aristocratic nose, "Gentlemen, you may converse."

There was dead silence.

Only, in the far corner of the room, which had been netted off for Cully – loose there, unhooded and deep in moult – they could hear a faint muttering from the choleric infantry colonel. "Damned niggers," he was mumbling. "Damned administration. Damned politicians. Is this a damned dagger that I see before me, the handle towards my hand? Damned spot. Now Cully hast thou but one brief hour to live, and then thou must be damned perpetually."

"Colonel," said the peregrine coldly, "not before the young officers."

"I beg your pardon, Mam," said the poor colonel at once. "It's something that gets into my head, you know. Some deep damnation."

There was silence again, formal, terrible and calm.

"Who is the new officer?" inquired the first fierce and beautiful voice.

Nobody answered.

"Speak for yourself, sir," commanded the peregrine, looking straight before her as if she were talking in her sleep.

They could not see him through their hoods.

"Please," began the Wart, "I am a merlin…"

And he stopped, scared in the stillness.

Balan, who was one of the real merlins standing beside him, leant over and whispered quite kindly in his ear, "Don't be afraid. Call her Madam."

"I am a merlin, Madam, an it please you."

"A merlin. That is good. And what branch of the Merlins do you stoop from?"

The Wart did not know in the least what branch he stooped from but he dared not be found out now in his lie.

"Madam," said the Wart, "I am one of the Merlins of the Forest Sauvage."

There was silence at this again, the silver silence which he had begun to dread.

"There are the Yorkshire Merlins," said the honorary colonel in her slow voice at last, "and the Welsh Merlins, and the McMerlins of the North. Then there are the Salisbury ones and several from the neighbourhood of Exmoor. I don't think I have ever heard of any family in the Forest Sauvage."

"It would be a cadet branch, Madam," said Balan, "I dare say."

"Bless him," thought the Wart. "I shall catch him a special

sparrow tomorrow and give it to him behind Hob's back."

"That will be the solution, Captain Balan, no doubt."

The silence fell again.

At last the peregrine rang her bell. She said, "We will proceed with the catechism, prior to swearing him in."

The Wart heard the spar-hawk to his left giving several nervous coughs at this, but the peregrine paid no attention.

"Merlin of the Forest Sauvage," said the peregrine. "What is a Beast of the Foot?"

"A Beast of the Foot," replied the Wart, blessing his stars that Sir Ector had chosen to give him a First Rate Eddication, "is a horse, or a hound, or a hawk."

"Why are these called beasts of the foot?"

"Because these beasts depend upon the powers of their feet, so that, by law, any damage to the feet of hawk, hound or horse, is reckoned as damage to its life. A lamed horse is a murdered horse."

"Good," said the peregrine. "What are your most important members?"

"My wings," said the Wart after a moment, guessing because he did not know.

At this there was a simultaneous tintinnabulation of all the bells, as each graven image lowered its raised foot in distress. They stood up on both feet now, disturbed.

"Your what?" cried the peregrine sharply.

"He said his damned wings," said Colonel Cully from his private enclosure. "And damned be he who first cries Hold, enough!"

"But even a thrush has wings!" cried the humble kestrel, speaking for the first time in his sharp-beaked alarm.

"Think!" whispered Balan, under his breath.

The Wart thought feverishly.

A thrush had wings, tail, eyes, legs – apparently everything. "My talons!"

"It will do," said the peregrine kindly, after one of her dreadful pauses. "The answer ought to be Feet just as it is to all the other questions, but Talons will do."

All the hawks, and of course we are using the term loosely, for some were hawks and some were falcons, raised their belled feet again and sat at ease.

"What is the first law of the foot?"

("Think," said friendly little Balan, behind his false primary.)

The Wart thought, and thought right.

"Never let go," he said.

"Last question," said the peregrine. "How would you, as a Merlin, kill a pigeon bigger than yourself?"

Wart was lucky in this one, for he had heard Hob giving a description of how Balan did it one afternoon, and he answered warily, "I should strangle her with my foot."

"Good!" said the peregrine.

"Bravo!" cried all the others, raising their feathers.

"Ninety per cent," said the spar-hawk after a quick sum. "That is, if you give him a half for the talons."

"The devil damn me black!"

"Colonel, please!"

Little Balan whispered to the Wart, "Colonel Cully is not quite right in his wits. It is his liver, we believe, but the kestrel says it is the constant strain of living up to her ladyship's standard. He says that her ladyship spoke to him from her full rank once, cavalry to infantry, you know, and that he just closed his eyes and got the vertigo. He has never been the same since."

"Captain Balan," said the peregrine, "it is rude to whisper. We will proceed to swear the new officer in. Now, padre, if you please."

The poor spar-hawk, who had been getting more and more nervous for some time, blushed deeply and began faltering out a complicated oath about varvels, jesses and hoods. "With this varvel," the Wart heard, "I thee endow… love, honour and obey… till jess us do part."

But before the padre had got to the end of it, he broke down altogether and sobbed out, "Oh, please your ladyship. I beg your pardon, but I've forgotten to keep any tirings."

("Tirings are bones and things," explained Balan, "and of course you have to swear on bones.")

"Forgotten to keep any tirings? But it is your duty to keep tirings."

"I – I know."

"What have you done with them?"

The spar-hawk's voice broke at the enormity of his confession. "I – I ate 'em," wept the unfortunate priest.

Nobody said anything. The dereliction of duty was too terrible for mere words. All stood on two feet and turned their blind heads towards the culprit. Not a word of reproach was spoken. Only, during an utter silence of five minutes, they could hear the incontinent priest snivelling and hiccoughing to himself.

"Well," said the peregrine at last, "the initiation will be put off till tomorrow."

"If you will excuse me, Madam," said Balin, "perhaps we could manage the ordeal part of it tonight? I believe the candidate is loose, for I did not hear him being tied up."

At the mention of ordeal the Wart trembled within himself and privately determined that Balin should have not one feather of Balan's sparrow next day.

"Thank you, Captain Balin. I was reflecting upon that subject myself."

Balin shut up.

"Are you loose, candidate?"

"Oh, Madam, yes, I am, if you please: but I don't think I want an ordeal."

"The ordeal is customary."

"Let me see," continued the honorary colonel reflectively. "What was the last ordeal we had? Can you remember, Captain Balan?"

"My ordeal, Mam," said the friendly merlin, "was to hang by my jesses during the third watch."

"If he's loose he can't do that."

"You could strike him yourself, Mam," said the kestrel. "Judiciously, you know."

"Send him over to stand by Colonel Cully while we ring

thrice," said the other merlin.

"Oh, no!" cried the crazy colonel in an agony out of his remoter darkness. "Oh, no, your ladyship. I beg of you not to do that. I am such a damned villain, your ladyship, that I don't answer for the consequences. Spare the poor boy, your ladyship, and lead us not into temptation."

"Colonel, control yourself. That ordeal will do very well."

"Oh, Madam, I was warned not to stand by Colonel Cully."

"Warned? And by whom?"

The poor Wart realized now that he must choose between confessing himself a human, and learning no more of their secrets, or going through with his ordeal in order to earn his education. He did not want to be a coward.

"I will stand by the Colonel, Madam," he said, immediately noticing that his voice sounded insulting.

The peregrine falcon paid no attention to the tone.

"It is well," she said. "But first we must have the hymn. Now, padre, if you haven't eaten your hymns as well as your tirings, will you be so kind as to lead us in Ancient but not Modern No. 23? The Ordeal Hymn."

"And you, Mr Kee," she added to the kestrel, "you had better keep quiet, for you are always too high."

The hawks stood still in the moonlight, while the sparhawk counted "One, Two, Three." Then all those curved or toothed beaks opened in their hoods to a brazen unison, and this is what they fiercely chanted:

Life is blood, shed and offered.
  The eagle's eye can face this dree.
To beasts of chase the lie is proffered
  Timor Mortis Conturbat Me.

The beast of foot sings Holdfast only,
  For flesh is bruckle and foot is slee.
Strength to the strong and the lordly and lonely.
  Timor Mortis Exultat Me.

Shame to the slothful and woe to the weak one,
  Death to the dreadful who turn to flee.
Blood to the tearing, the talon'd, the beaked one.
  Timor Mortis is me.

"Very nice," said the peregrine. "Captain Balin, I think you were a little off on the top C. And now, candidate, you will go over and stand next to Colonel Cully's enclosure, while we ring our bells thrice. On the third ring you may move as quickly as you like."

"Very good, Madam," said the Wart, quite fearless with resentment. He flipped his wings and was sitting on the extreme end of the screen perch, next to Cully's enclosure of string netting.

"Boy, boy!" cried the Colonel in an unearthly voice, "don't come near me, don't come near. Ah, tempt not the foul fiend to his damnation."

"I don't fear you, sir," said the Wart. "Don't vex yourself, for no harm will come to either of us."

"No harm, quotha! Ah, go, before it is too late. I feel eternal longings in me."

"Never fear, sir. They have only to ring three times."

At this all the knights lowered their raised legs and gave them a solemn shake. The first sweet persuasive tinkling filled the room.

"Madam, Madam!" cried the Colonel in torture. "Have pity, have pity on a damned man of blood. Ring out the old, ring in the new. I can't hold off much longer."

"Be brave, sir," said the Wart softly.

"Be brave, sir! Why, but two nights since, one met the duke 'bout midnight in a lane behind Saint Mark's Church, with the leg of a man upon his shoulder: and he howled fearfully."

"It's nothing," said the Wart.

"Nothing! Said he was a wolf, only the difference was a wolf's skin was hairy on the outside, his on the inside. Rip up my flesh and try. Ah, for quietus, with a bare bodkin!"

The bells rang for the second time.

The Wart's heart was thumping heavily and pleading for the third release, but now the Colonel was sidling towards him along the perch. Stamp, stamp, he went, striking the wood he trod on with a convulsive grip at every pace. His poor, mad, brooding eyes glared in the moonlight, shone against the persecuted darkness of his scowling brow. There was nothing cruel about him, no ignoble passion. He was terrified of the Wart, not triumphing, and he must slay.

"If it were done when 'tis done," whispered the Colonel,

"then 'twere well it were done quickly. Who would have thought the young man had so much blood in him?"

"Colonel!" said the Wart, but held himself there.

"Boy!" cried the Colonel. "Speak, stop me, mercy!"

"There is a cat behind you," said the Wart calmly, "or a pine-marten. Look."

The Colonel turned, swift as a wasp's sting, and menaced into the gloom. There was nothing. He swung his wild eyes again upon the Wart, guessing at the trick. Then, in the cold voice of an adder, "The bell invites me," he hissed for the last time. "Hear it not, Merlin, for it is a knell that summons thee to heaven or to hell."

The third bells were indeed ringing as he spoke, and honour was allowed to move. The ordeal was over and the Wart might fly. But as he moved, but as he flew, quicker than any movement or flight in the world, the terrible sickles had shot out from the Colonel's plated legs – not flashed out, for they moved too quick for sight – and with a thump, with a clutch, with an apprehension, like being arrested by a big policeman, the great scimitars had fixed themselves in his retreating thumb.

They fixed themselves, and fixed irrevocably. Gripe, gripe, the enormous thigh muscles tautened in two convulsions. Then the Wart was four yards further down the screen, and Colonel Cully was standing on one foot with a few meshes of string netting and the Wart's false primary, with its covert-feathers, vice-fisted in the other. Two or three minor feathers drifted softly in a moonbeam towards the floor.

"Well stood!" cried Balan, delighted.

"A very gentlemanly exhibition," said the peregrine, not minding that Captain Balan had spoken before her.

"Amen, Amen!" said the spar-hawk.

"Brave heart!" cried the kestrel.

"Might we give him the Triumph Song?" asked Balan, now relenting.

"Certainly," said the peregrine.

And they all sang together, led by Colonel Cully at the top of his voice, all belling triumphantly in the terrible moonlight.

> "The mountain birds are sweeter
>   But the valley birds are fatter,
> And so we deemed it meeter
>   To carry off the latter.
> We met a cowering coney
>   And struck him through the vitals.
> The coney was like honey
>   And squealed our requitals.
> Some struck the lark in feathers
>   Whose puffing clouds were shed off.
> Some plucked the partridge's nethers,
>   While others pulled his head off.
> But Wart the King of Merlins
>   Struck foot most far before us.
> His birds and beasts
> Supply our feasts.
>   And his feasts our roarious chorus."

"Mark my words," cried the beautiful Balan, forgetful of all etiquette. "We shall have a regular king in that young candidate. Now then, boys, chorus altogether for the last time:

> "But Wart the King of Merlins
>> Struck foot most far before us.
> His birds and beasts
> Supply our feasts

"And his – " ("Damn fine show," cried Colonel Cully, with most lamentable infantry manners, at the top of his crazy voice, quite out of tune) "our Roarious Chorus!"

CHAPTER NINE

"WELL!" SAID THE Wart, as he woke up in his own bed next morning. "What a horrible, grand crew!"

Kay sat up in bed and began scolding like a squirrel. "Where were you all last night?" he cried. "I believe you climbed out. I shall tell my father and get you tanned. You know we aren't allowed out after curfew. What have you been doing? I looked for you everywhere. I know you climbed out."

The boys had a way of sliding down a rainwater pipe into the moat, which they could swim on secret occasions when it was necessary to be out at night — to wait for a badger for instance, or to catch tench, which can only be taken just before dawn.

"Oh, shut up," said the Wart. "I'm sleepy."

Kay said, "Wake up, wake up, you beast. Where have you been?"

"I shan't tell you."

He was sure that Kay would not believe the story, but only call him a liar and get angrier than ever.

"If you don't tell me I shall kill you."

"You won't, then."

"I will."

The Wart turned over on his other side.

"Beast," said Kay. He took a fold of the Wart's arm between the nails of first finger and thumb and pinched for all he was worth. Wart kicked like a salmon which had been suddenly hooked, and hit Kay wildly in the eye. In a trice they were out of bed, pale and indignant, and looking rather like skinned rabbits – for in those days nobody wore clothes in bed – and whirling their arms like windmills in the effort to do each other mischief.

Kay was older and bigger than the Wart, so that he was bound to win in the end, but he was more nervous and imaginative. He could imagine the effect of each blow that was aimed at him, and this weakened his defence. Wart was only an infuriated hurricane.

"Leave me alone," shouted the Wart again and again. "Leave me alone, can't you?" And all the while he did not leave Kay alone, but with head down and swinging arms made it impossible for Kay to do as he was bid. They punched entirely at each other's faces, as boys will.

Kay had a longer reach and a heavier fist. He straightened his arm out, more in self-defence than in anything else, and the Wart smacked his own eye upon the end of it. The sky became a noisy and shocking black, streaked outwards with a blaze of meteors. The Wart began to sob and pant. He managed to get in a blow upon his opponent's nose, and this began to bleed. Kay lowered his defence, turned his back upon the Wart, and said in a cold, snuffing, reproachful voice, "Now it's bleeding." The battle was over.

Kay lay upon his back on the stone floor, bubbling blood out of his nose, and the Wart, with a black eye, fetched the enormous key out of the door to put down Kay's back. Neither of them spoke.

Presently Kay turned over on his face and began to sob. He said, "Merlyn does everything for you, but he never does anything for me."

At this the Wart felt he had been a beast. He dressed himself in silence and hurried off to find Merlyn.

On the way he was caught by his nurse.

"Ah, you little helot," exclaimed she, shaking him by the arm. "You've been a-battling again with that there Master Kay. Look at your poor eye, I do declare. It's enough to baffle the college of sturgeons."

"It's all right," said the Wart.

"No, that it isn't, my poppet," cried his nurse, getting crosser and showing signs of slapping him. "Come now, how did you do it, before I have you whipped?"

"I knocked it on the bedpost," said the Wart sullenly.

The old nurse immediately folded him to her broad bosom, patted him on the back, and said, "There, there, my dowsabel. It's the same story Sir Ector told me when I caught him with a blue eye, gone forty year. Nothing like a good family for sticking to a good lie. There, my innocent, you come along of me to the kitchen and we'll slap a nice bit of steak across him in no time. But you hadn't ought to fight with people bigger than yourself."

"It's all right," said the Wart again, disgusted by this fuss, but fate was bent on punishing him and the old lady was inexorable. It took him half an hour to escape, and then only at the price of carrying with him a juicy piece of raw beef which he was supposed to hold over his eye. "Nothing like a mealy rump for drawing out the humours," his nurse had said, and the cook had answered, "Us hant seen a sweeter bit of raw since Easter, no, nor a bloodier."

"I will keep the foul thing for Balan," thought the Wart, resuming his search for his tutor.

He had found him without trouble in the tower-room which he had chosen when he arrived. All philosophers prefer to live in towers, as may be seen by visiting the room which Erasmus chose in his college at Cambridge, but Merlyn's tower was even more beautiful than his. It was the highest room in the castle, directly below the look-out of the great tower, and from its window you could gaze across the open field – with its rights of warren – across the park, and the chase, until your eye finally wandered out over the distant blue tree-tops of the Forest Sauvage. This sea of leafy timber rolled away and away in knobs like the surface of porridge, until it was finally lost in remote mountains which nobody had ever visited, and the cloud-capped towers and gorgeous palaces of heaven.

Merlyn's comments upon the black eye were of a philosophic nature.

"The discolouration," he said, "is caused by haemorrhage into the tissues (ecchymosis) and passes from dark purple through green to yellow before it disappears."

There seemed to be no sensible reply to this.

"I suppose you had it," continued Merlyn, "fighting with Kay?"

'Yes. How did you know?"

"Ah, well, there it is."

"I came to ask you about Kay."

"Speak. Demand, I'll answer."

"Well, Kay thinks it unfair that you are always turning me into things and not him. I haven't told him about it but I think he guesses. I think it's unfair too."

"It is unfair."

"So will you turn us both next time that we are turned?"

Merlyn had finished his breakfast, and was puffing at the meerschaum pipe which made his pupil believe that he breathed fire. Now he took a very deep puff, looked at the Wart, opened his mouth to speak, changed his mind, blew out the smoke and drew in another lungful.

"Sometimes," he said, "life does seem to be unfair. Do you know the story of Elijah and the Rabbi Jachanan?"

"No," said the Wart. He sat down resignedly upon the most comfortable part of the floor, perceiving that he was in for something like the parable of the looking-glass.

"This Rabbi," said Merlyn, "went on a journey with the

prophet Elijah. They walked all day, and at nightfall they came to a humble cottage of a poor man, whose only treasure was a cow. The poor man ran out of his cottage, and his wife ran too, to welcome the strangers for the night and to offer them all the simple hospitality which they were able to give in straitened circumstances. Elijah and the Rabbi were entertained with plenty of cow's milk, sustained by home-made bread and butter, and they were put to sleep in the best bed while their kindly hosts lay down before the kitchen fire. But in the morning the poor man's cow was dead."

"Go on."

"They walked all the next day, and came that evening to the house of a very wealthy merchant, whose hospitality they craved. The merchant was cold and proud and rich, and all that he would do for the prophet and his companion was to lodge them in a cowshed and feed them on bread and water. In the morning, however, Elijah thanked him very much, and sent for a mason to repair one of his walls, which happened to be falling down, as a return for his kindness.

"The Rabbi Jachanan, unable to keep silence any longer, begged the holy man to explain the meaning of his dealings with human beings.

"'In regard to the poor man who received us so hospitably,' replied the prophet, 'it was decreed that his wife was to die that night, but in reward for his kindness God took the cow instead of the wife. I repaired the wall of the rich miser because a chest of gold was concealed near the place, and if the miser had repaired the wall himself he would have discovered the treasure. Say not therefore to the Lord: What doest thou? but say in thy heart: Must not the Lord of all the earth do right?' "

"It's a nice sort of story," said the Wart, because it seemed to be over.

"I am sorry," said Merlyn, "that you should be the only one to get my extra tuition, but then, you see, I was only sent for that."

"I don't see that it would do any harm for Kay to come too."

"Nor do I. But the Rabbi Jachanan didn't see why the miser should have had his wall repaired."

"I understand that," said the Wart doubtfully, "but I still think it's a shame that the cow died. Couldn't I have Kay with me just once?"

Merlyn said gently, "Perhaps what is good for you might be bad for him. Besides, remember he has never asked to be turned into anything."

"He wants to be turned, for all that. I like Kay, you know, and I think people don't understand him. He has to be proud because he is frightened."

"You still don't follow what I mean. Suppose he had gone as a merlin last night, and failed in the ordeal, and lost his nerve?"

"How do you know about that ordeal?"

"Ah, well, there it is again."

"Very well," said the Wart obstinately. "But suppose he hadn't failed in the ordeal, and hadn't lost his nerve. I don't see why you should have to suppose that he would have."

"Oh, flout the boy!" cried Merlyn passionately. "You don't seem to see anything this morning. What is it that you want me to do?"

"Turn me and Kay into snakes or something."

Merlyn took off his spectacles, dashed them on the floor and jumped upon them with both feet.

"Castor and Pollux blow me to Bermuda!" he exclaimed, and immediately vanished with a frightful roar.

The Wart was still staring at his tutor's chair in some perplexity, a few moments later, when Merlyn reappeared. He had lost his hat and his hair and beard were all tangled up, as if by a hurricane. He sat down again, straightening his gown with trembling fingers.

"Why did you do that?" asked the Wart.

"I didn't do it on purpose."

"Do you mean to say that Castor and Pollux did blow you to Bermuda?"

"Let this be a lesson to you," replied Merlyn, "not to swear. I think we had better change the subject."

"We were talking about Kay."

"Yes and what I was going to say before my – ahem! – my visit to the still vexed Bermoothes, was this. I can't change Kay into things. The power was not deputed to me when I was sent. Why this was so, neither you nor I am able to say, but such remains the fact. I have tried to hint at some of the reasons for the fact, but you won't take them, so you must just accept the fact in its naked reality. Now please stop talking until I have got my breath back, and my hat."

The Wart sat quietly while Merlyn closed his eyes and began to mutter to himself. Presently a curious black cylindrical hat appeared on his head.

Merlyn examined it with a look of disgust, said bitterly, "And they call this service!" and handed it back to the air. He closed his eyes and produced with growing indignation, in rapid succession, this

and this

and this.

Finally he stood up in a passion and exclaimed, "Come here!"

The Wart and Archimedes looked at each other, wondering which was meant – Archimedes had been sitting all the while on the window-sill and looking at the view, for, of course, he never left his master – but Merlyn did not pay them any attention.

"Now," said Merlyn furiously, apparently to nobody, "do you think you are being funny?

"Very well then, why do you do it?

"That's no excuse. Naturally I meant the one I was wearing.

"But wearing now, of course, you fool. I don't want a hat I was wearing in 1800. Have you no sense of time at all?"

Merlyn took off his sailor hat and held it out to the air for inspection.

"This is an anachronism," he said severely. "That's what it is, a beastly anachronism."

Archimedes seemed to be accustomed to these scenes, for he now said in a reasonable voice: "Why don't you ask for the hat by name, Master? Say, 'I want my magician's hat,' not, 'I want the hat I was wearing.' Perhaps the poor chap finds it as difficult to live backwards in time as you do."

"I want my magician's hat," said Merlyn sulkily.

Instantly the long pointed cap was standing on his head.

The tension in the air relaxed; Wart sat down again on the floor, and Archimedes resumed his toilet, pulling his pinions and tail feathers through his beak to smooth the barbs together. Each barb had hundreds of little hooks or barbules on it, by means of which the barbs of the feather were held together. He was stroking them into place.

Merlyn said, "I beg your pardon. I am not having a very good day today, and there it is."

"About Kay," said the Wart. "Even if you can't change him into things, couldn't you give us both an adventure without changing?"

Merlyn made a visible effort to control his temper again, and to consider this question dispassionately. He was sick of the subject altogether.

"I can't do any magic for Kay," he said slowly, "except my own magic that I have anyway. Backsight and insight and that. Do you mean anything I could do with that?"

"What does your backsight do?"

"It tells me what you would say is going to happen, and the insight sometimes says what is or was happening in other places."

"Is there anything happening just now, anything that Kay and I could go to see?"

Merlyn immediately struck himself on the brow and exclaimed excitedly, "Now I see it all. Yes, of course, there is, and you are going to see it. Yes, you must take Kay and hurry up about it. You must go immediately after Mass. Have breakfast first and go immediately after Mass. Yes, that's it. Go straight to Hob's strip of barley in the open field and follow that line until you come to something. That will be splendid, yes, and I shall have a nap this afternoon instead of that filthy Summulae Logicales. Or have I had the nap?"

"You haven't had it," said Archimedes. "That's still in the future yet, Master."

"Splendid, splendid. And mind, Wart, don't forget to take Kay with you so that I can have my nap."

"What shall we see?" asked the Wart.

"Ah, don't plague me about a little thing like that. You run along now, there's a good boy, and mind you don't forget to take Kay with you. Why ever didn't you mention it before? Don't forget to follow beyond the strip of barley. Well, well, well. This is the first half-holiday I've had since I started this confounded tutorship. First I think I shall have a little nap before luncheon, and then I think I shall have a little nap before tea. Then I shall have to think of something I can do before dinner. What shall I do before dinner, Archimedes?"

"Have a little nap, I expect," said the owl coldly, turning his back upon his master, because he, as well as the Wart, enjoyed to see life.

CHAPTER TEN

WART KNEW THAT if he told the elder boy about his conversation with Merlyn, Kay would very probably refuse to be condescended to, and not come. So he said nothing. It was strange, but their battle had made them friends again, and each could look the other in the eye, with a kind of confused affection. They went together unanimously though shyly, without the need for explanations, and found themselves standing at the end of Hob's barley strip after Mass, without the Wart having to use any ingenuity. When they were there it was easy.

"Come on," said the Wart. "Merlyn told me to tell you that there was something along here that was specially for you."

"What sort of thing?" asked Kay.

"An adventure."

"How do we get to it?"

"We ought to follow along the line which this strip makes, and I suppose that would take us into the forest. We should have to keep the sun just there on our left, but allow for its moving."

"All right," said Kay. "What is the adventure?"

"I don't know."

They went along the strip, and followed its imaginary line over the park and over the chase, keeping their eyes skinned all the time for some miraculous happening. They wondered whether half a dozen young pheasants they started had anything curious about them, and Kay was ready to swear that one of them was white. If it had been white, and if a black eagle had suddenly swooped down upon it from the sky, they would have known quite well that wonders were afoot, and that all they had to do was to follow the pheasant – or the eagle – until they reached the maiden in the enchanted castle. However, the pheasant was not white and no eagle appeared.

At the end of the forest Kay said, "I suppose we shall have to go into this?"

"Merlyn said to follow the line."

"Well," said Kay. "I'm not afraid. If the adventure was specially for me, it's bound to be a jolly good one."

They went in, and were surprised to find that the going was not bad at all. It was about the same as a big wood might be nowadays, whereas the common forest of those times was much more like a jungle on the Amazon. There were no pheasant-shooting proprietors then, to see that the undergrowth was thinned, and not one thousandth part of the number of the present-day timber merchants who prune away judiciously at the few remaining woods. The most of the Forest Sauvage was almost impenetrable, an enormous barrier of eternal trees, the dead ones fallen against the live and held to them by ivy, the living struggling up in competition with each other towards the sun which gave them life, the floor boggy through lack of drainage, or tindery from old wood so that you might suddenly tumble through a decayed tree trunk into an ant's nest, or laced with brambles and bindweed and honeysuckle and convolvulus and teazles and the stuff which country people call sweethearts, until you would be torn to pieces in three yards.

This part was good. Hob's line pointed down what seemed to be a succession of glades, shady and murmuring places in which the wild thyme was droning with bees. The insect season was past its peak, for it was really the time for wasps on fruit, but there were many fritillaries still, with tortoiseshells and red admirals on the flowering mint. Wart pulled a leaf of this, and munched it like chewing-gum as they walked.

"It's queer," he said, "but there have been people here. Look, there is one hoof-mark, and it was shod."

"You don't see much," said Kay, "for there is a man."

Sure enough, there was a man at the end of the next glade, sitting with a wood-axe by the side of a tree which he had felled. He was a queer-looking, tiny man, with a hunchback and a face like mahogany, and he was dressed in numerous pieces of old leather which he had secured about his brawny legs and arms with pieces of cord. He was eating a hunch of bread and cheese with a knife which years of sharpening had worn into a mere streak, leaning his back against one of the highest trees that they had ever seen. The white flakes of wood lay all about him. The dressed stump of the felled tree looked very new. His eyes were bright like a fox's.

"I expect he will be the adventure," whispered Wart.

"Pooh," said Kay. "You have knights-in-armour, or dragons or things like that in a adventure, not dirty old men cutting wood."

"Well, I'm going to ask him what happens along here, anyway."

They went up to the small munching woodman, who did not seem to have seen them, and asked him where the glades were leading to. They asked two or three times before they discovered that the poor fellow was either deaf or mad, or both. He neither answered nor moved.

"Oh, come on," said Kay. "He's probably loopy like Wat, and doesn't know what he is at. Let's go and leave the old fool."

They went on for nearly a mile, and still the going was good. There were no paths exactly, and the glades were not continuous. Anybody who came there by chance would have thought that there was just the one glade which he was in, a couple of hundred yards long, unless he went to the end of it and discovered another one, screened by a few trees. Now and then they found a cut stump with the marks of the axe on it, but mostly these had been carefully covered over with brambles or altogether grubbed up. The Wart considered that the glades must have been made.

Kay caught the Wart by the arm, at the edge of the clearing, and pointed silently towards its further end. There was a grass bank there, swelling up gently towards a gigantic sycamore, upwards of ninety feet high, which stood upon its top. On the bank there was an equally gigantic man lying at his ease, with a dog beside him. This man was as notable as the sycamore, for he stood or lay seven feet without his shoes, and he was dressed in nothing but a kind of kilt made of Lincoln green worsted. He had a leather bracer on his left forearm. His enormous brown chest supported the dog's head – it had pricked its ears and was watching the boys, but made no other movement – which the muscles gently lifted as they rose and fell. The man appeared to be fast asleep. There was a seven-foot bow beside him, with some arrows more than a cloth-yard long. He, like the woodman, was the colour of mahogany, and the curled hairs on his chest made a golden haze where the sun caught them.

"He's it," whispered Kay excitedly.

They went up to the man cautiously, for fear of the dog; but the dog only followed them with its eyes, keeping its chin pressed firmly to the chest of its beloved master, and giving them the least suspicion of a wag from its tail. It moved its tail without lifting it, two inches in the grass. The man opened his eyes – obviously he had not been asleep at all – smiled at the boys, and jerked his thumb in the direction which pointed further up the glade. Then he stopped smiling and shut his eyes.

"Excuse me," said Kay, "what happens up there?"

The man made no answer and kept his eyes closed, but he lifted his hand again and pointed onwards with his thumb.

"He means us to go on," said Kay.

"It certainly is an adventure," said the Wart. "I wonder if that dumb woodman could have climbed up the big tree he was leaning against and sent a message to this tree that we were coming? He certainly seems to have been expecting us."

At this the naked giant opened one eye and looked at Wart in some surprise. Then he opened both eyes, laughed all over his big twinkling face, sat up, patted the dog, picked up his bow, and rose to his feet.

"Very well, then, young measters," he said, still laughing. "Us will come along with 'ee after all. Young heads still meake the sharpest, they do say."

Kay looked at him in blank surprise. "Who are you?" he asked.

"Naylor," said the giant, "John Naylor in the wide world it were, till us come to be a man of the 'ood. Then t'were John Little for some time, in the 'ood like, but mostly folks put it backward now, and calls us Little John."

"Oh!" cried the Wart in delight. "I've heard of you, often, when they tell stories in the evening, of you and Robin Hood."

"Not Hood," said Little John reprovingly. "That bain't the way to name 'un, measter, not in the 'ood."

"But it's Robin Hood in the stories," said Kay.

"Ah, them book-learning chaps. They don't know all.

How'm ever, 'tis time us be stepping along."

They fell in on either side of the enormous happy man, and had to run one step in three to keep up with him, for, although he talked very slowly, he walked on his bare feet very fast. The dog trotted at heel.

"Please," asked the Wart, "where are you taking us?"

"Why, to Robin 'ood, seemingly. Ant you sharp enough to guess that also, Measter Art?"

The giant gave him a sly peep out of the corner of his eye at this, for he knew quite well that he had set the boys two problems at once — first, what was Robin's real name, and second, how did he come to know the Wart's.

The Wart fixed on the second question first.

"How did you know my name?"

"Ah," said Little John. "Us knowed."

"Does Robin 'ood know we are coming?"

"Nay, my duck, a young scholar like thee should speak his name scholarly."

"Well, what is his name?" cried the Wart, between exasperation, and being out of breath from running to keep up. "You said 'ood."

"So it is 'ood, my duck. Robin 'ood, like the 'oods you'm running through. And a grand fine name it is."

"Robin Wood!"

"Aye, Robin 'ood. What else should un be, seeing as he loves 'em? They'm free pleaces, the 'oods, and fine pleaces. Let thee sleep in 'em, come summer, come winter, without brick nor thatch; and hunt in 'em with the good earth in the springtime; and number of 'em as they brings forward their comely bright leaves, according to order, or loses of 'em by the same order backards: let thee stand in 'em that thou be'st not seen, and move in 'em that thou be'st not heard, and warm thee with 'em i' the golden light of their timbers as thou fall'st on sleep – ah, they'm proper fine pleaces, the 'oods, for a free man of hands and heart."

Kay said, "But I thought all Robin Wood's men wore hose and jerkins of Lincoln green?"

"That us do," replied Little John. "In the winter like, when us needs 'em, or with leather leggings at 'ood 'ork: but here by summer 'tis more seasonable thus for the pickets, who have nought to do save watch."

"Were you a sentry then?"

"Aye, and so were wold Much, as you spoke to by the felled tree."

"And I think," exclaimed Kay triumphantly, "that this next big tree which we are coming to will be the stronghold of Robin Wood!"

They were indeed approaching the monarch of the forest. It was a lime tree as great as that which used to grow at Moor Park in Herefordshire, no less that one hundred feet in height and seventeen feet in girth, a yard above the ground. Its smooth beech-like trunk was embellished with a sort of beard of little twigs at the bottom, and, where each of the great branches had sprung from the trunk, the bark had split and was now discoloured with rain water or sap. The bees zoomed among its bright and sticky leaves, higher and higher towards heaven, and a rope ladder disappeared among the foliage. Nobody could have climbed that tree without a ladder, even with irons.

"You think well, Measter Kay," said Little John. "And there be Measter Robin, a-dallying atween her roots."

The boys who had been more interested in the lookout man perched in a crow's nest at the very top of that swaying and whispering glory of the earth, lowered their eyes at once and clapped them upon Robin Wood.

He was not, as they had expected, a romantic man – or not at first. Nearly as tall as Little John – these two, of course, were the only people in the world who have ever shot an arrow the distance of a mile, with the English long-bow – or at any rate more than six feet high, he was a sinewy fellow whose body did not carry an ounce of fat. He was not half-naked, like John, but clad discreetly in faded green with a silvery bugle at his side. He was clean shaven, sunburnt, nervous, gnarled like the roots of the trees which he loved; but gnarled and mature with weather and with poetry rather than with age, for he was about thirty years old. (Eventually he lived to be eighty-seven, and attributed his long life to smelling the turpentine in the pines.) At the moment he was lying flat on his back and looking upwards, but not into the sky.

It had been beautiful to see little leather-clad Much sitting complacently at his dinner, more beautiful to see the great limbs of Little John sprawling in company with his dog. But now there was something which was most beautiful of all, for Robin Wood lay happily with his head in Marian's lap. She sat between the roots of the lime tree, clad in a one-piece smock of green girded in with a quiver of arrows, and her feet and arms were bare. She had let down the brown shining waterfall of her hair, which was usually kept braided in pigtails for convenience in hunting and cookery, and with the falling waves of this she framed his up-looking head. She was singing a duet with him softly, and tickling the end of his nose with the finest hairs. Nobody nowadays could write the song which they were singing:

> "Under the greenwood tree," sang Maid Marian,
> "Who loves to lie with me,
> And tune his merry note
> Unto the sweet bird's throat."

"Come hither, come hither, come hither," sang Robin.

> "Here shall he see
> No enemy
> But winter and rough weather."

They laughed happily and began again, singing lines alternately:

> "Who doth ambition shun
> And loves to lie i' the sun,
> Seeking the food he eats
> And pleased with what he gets,"

Then, both together:

> "Come hither, come hither, come hither:
> Here shall he see
> No enemy
> But winter and rough weather."

The song ended in laughter, and Robin, who had been twisting his brown fingers in and out of the silk-fine threads which fell about his face, gave them a shrewd tug and scrambled to his feet.

"Now, John," he said, seeing them at once.

"Now, measter," said Little John.

"So you've brought the young squires?"

"They brought me," said Little John.

"Welcome whatever way," said Robin. "I never heard ill spoken of Sir Ector, nor reason why his sounders should be pursued. How are you, Kay and Wart, and who set you so luckily into the forest at my glades, on this day of all days?"

"Robin," interrupted Maid Marian at this point reproachfully. "You can't mean to take them with you on a venture like this. They are far too young."

"Why not, my sweetheart? The people are their people, and they would wish to be there."

"But they are children."

"And none the worst of that. If they are worth their salt they can move quicker than we can, and hide better, and I'll warrant me, they can shoot well enough with the bow. There is no need that they should come to close quarters at the end, maid, any more than thou."

"I think it's inhuman," said Maid Marian, and began to do up her hair.

"Can you shoot?" asked Robin.

"Trust me," said the Wart.

"I can try," said Kay, more reserved, as they laughed at the Wart's comical assurance.

"Come, Marian," said Robin, "let us have one of thy bows."

Maid Marian handed him a bow and half a dozen arrows twenty-eight inches long.

"Shoot the popinjay," said Robin, handing them to the Wart.

Wart now looked and saw the popinjay set up full five score paces away. He guessed that he had been a fool and said cheerfully, "I'm sorry, Robin Wood, but I'm afraid it is much too far away for me."

"Never mind," said the outlaw. "Have a shot at it anyway. I can tell all I want to know by the way you shoot."

The Wart fitted his arrow as quickly and neatly as he was able, set his feet wide in the same line as he wished his arrow to go, squared his shoulder, drew the bow to his chin, sighted on the mark, raised his point through an angle of about twenty degrees, aimed two yards to the right because he always pulled to the left in his loose, and sped his arrow. It missed, but not so badly.

"Now, Kay," said Robin.

Kay went through the same motions and also made a pretty good shot. Each of them had held the bow the right way up, had quickly found the cock feather and set it outwards, each had taken hold of the string to draw the bow – most boys who have not been taught are inclined to catch hold of the nock of the arrow when they draw, between their finger and thumb, but, of course, a proper archer pulls back the string with his first two or three fingers and lets the arrow follow it – neither of them had allowed the point to fall away towards the left as they drew, nor struck their left forearms with the bow-string, two common faults with people who don't know, and each had loosed evenly without a pluck.

"Good," said Robin. "No lute-players here."

"Ah," said Little John, "it warn't bad for boys, but suppose you show 'em, measter 'ood."

"Is it a match, John?" asked Robin smiling: these two men were the oldest of rivals with a bow in England, and could never forbear to take one another on in competition.

"Go on," said Marian. "You two are like children."

"Us han't never fled afore a challenge, Measter 'ood," said Little John slowly, his eyes twinkling, "as thee knows to thy cost."

"Get on, man," said Robin. "You know I could beat you with one hand behind my back."

Little John deliberately put the toe of his great bow against the inside of his instep, pulled the grip outward with his mighty right fist, and slipped the string into place with his left hand. It was a movement like an absent-minded caress, but probably nobody else except Robin could have strung his bow.

"'Tis for a buffet, measter?" he inquired, grinning at Robin with sly challenge.

"A buffet," said the captain of the outlaws. "Go on and I'll let you off with a light stroke."

Little John lumbered himself into position and remarked philosophically, "Folks say the last laugh rings merriest."

With this, in a limber flash which had nothing to do with his bear-like movements and slow speech, the fugitive who had once been called Naylor had raised, drawn, loosed and lowered his bow, apparently without aiming it, and the arrow was saying Phutt! in the heart of the popinjay, before cleaving straight through it and burying its point in the ground.

"A shaky loose," said Robin, from two yards behind him, and, as Little John turned round to smile at his captain, but before he could turn back again towards the popinjay, the captain's arrow also was cutting through the bird of straw.

Wart noticed that where he and Kay had been compelled to aim their woman's bow twenty degrees above the mark, Robin and Little John were still loosing well below it, although it was a hundred yards away. The boys had been given Maid Marian's bow to shoot with because they could not have drawn any other. Its draw was a horizontal pull of only twenty-five or thirty pounds, while Robin and his lieutenant were opening arcs with a force of anything up or above a hundred. If you have ever attempted to lift a hundredweight upwards from the ground, with all your stature to help you, you will be able to appreciate the steady force which the two greatest English archers were able to exert, not upwards but horizontally.

"Robin," said Maid Marian sharply, "you are being a baby. You will just go on and on until each of you has had a dozen shots, and then one or the other of you will miss and the conqueror will claim the right to give him a smack. How can you be so childish?"

"I want to beat John here," said Robin Wood, plausibly, "because otherwise he will become insubordinate."

"Insubordinate fiddlesticks. Leave your silly competition and send these boys away to their father."

"That I won't do," said Robin, "unless they wish to go. It is their quarrel as much as it is mine."

"What is the quarrel?" asked Kay.

Robin threw down his bow and sat cross-legged on the ground, drawing Maid Marian to sit beside him. His face had suddenly gone grim.

"It's the Anthropophagi," he said.

The boys looked so blank that he took a breath and began to explain.

"Perhaps you have never heard of the Anthropophagi? I don't blame you. There were none of these bad creatures in our old England until a few years ago, when my lord of Lilford liberated a pair at Oundle. Now they swarm and increase daily: to the menace of true woodmen of the old breed. They live like outlaws in the woods, just as we do, but the arrows they use are poisoned. They are cannibals too. Nobody can stand against them, for our arrows are not mortal unless they strike a mortal blow, while theirs kill horribly, even with a scratch."

"What sort of arrows are they?"

"They paint them black and yellow, like wasps. They are cunning archers, especially the Nisites from Sirbithim, and their murders grow more pestilent every week. It is not that they waylay fat abbots, or occasionally string up an oppressive money-lender or an unjust nobleman protected by the laws of his class. They are bad, wild creatures. They give nothing to the poor. Only, living in the worst quarters of the forest, they creep out like wolves or adders and assassinate any person that they see. They kill us for the pot."

"There were wold Matthew," said Little John bitterly, "struck as he were making huddles. Peter they killed sleeping. Walter fell as he stooped to draw water, and Colin at my side barked like a dog afore he fell on his face."

"They had a shot at me once," said the Wart.

"They make no distinction of man, woman or child."

"Are you at war with these people?" asked Kay.

"I am sworn to exterminate them," said Robin.

A silence fell upon the four speakers under the tree. Robin sat with an arrow in his hand and cut moodily at the turf with its point.

"For four months now," said he, "my scouts have sought their stronghold. By day and by night, in all weathers, they have rested where the track took them, eaten little, slept less. They have come back to me weary with their reports, and fallen on sleep when they had scarce done speaking. Many have not come back. Last week we traced them to their nest.

"It must be a surprise attack. They are wasps and must be destroyed like wasps. If we marched upon them in daylight or offered them fair battle they would fly. Their troops would melt away before us in the undergrowth, only to hang about our wings on the march home and to shoot invisibly, using their deadly arrows.

"It must be an attack from which not one escapes. We shall make it in the darkness this evening, because then they will hold a feast. What this feast is concerns you, Kay and Wart, more than it concerns me."

"Have they caught one of our people?"

"They have caught the Dog Boy. This morning, when he took the hounds out for their roll in the grass, Cavall chased a rabbit into the edge of the forest. The Dog Boy called him, but he did not come. He went after him, and could see nothing. He turned round at a slight noise and found himself surrounded by Sciopodes, one of whom was holding Cavall by the muzzle so that he could not bark. This news came to me from my northward trees, at about the same time that Much and Little John told me of your approach from the east."

"We must rescue them."

"Are they alive?"

"They will keep them alive until the feast begins, for the sake of freshness. They have kept one other alive also, for tonight is to be one of their nights of sacrifice."

"Who is the other?"

"It is an old man called Wat, a harmless old person who used to live wild in the forest, supporting himself on grass and roots and acorns. He has no nose."

"That is our man too," said the Wart. "He lived in our village before he lost his wits. Why, it was he who bit off the Dog Boy's nose. Fancy his living on acorns! We all thought he was a terrible old man who bit off children's noses, a sort of ogre of the forest."

"Well," said Robin, "he is a tamed ogre now, poor fellow."

"What of it, then, Measter Kay?" asked Little John after a long pause. "Will 'ee leave thy men to be eaten?"

"Or," said Robin, "do you come with us?"

There was no need to reply.

CHAPTER ELEVEN

THEY PASSED THE morning pleasantly, getting accustomed to two of Maid Marian's bows. Robin had insisted on this, saying that no man could shoot with another's bow any more than he could cut with another scythe. For their midday meal they had cold venison pattie, with mead, as also did everybody else. The outlaws drifted in for the meal like a conjuring trick. At one moment there would be nobody on the edge of the clearing, at the next half a dozen right inside it: green or sunburnt men who had silently materialized out of the bracken or the trees. In the end there were about a hundred of them, eating merrily and laughing. The food was dished out from a leafy bower, where Marian and her attendants cooked.

The outlaws usually posted a sentry to take the tree messages, and slept during the afternoon, partly because so much of their hunting had to be done in the times when most workmen sleep, and partly because generally the wild beasts take a nap in the afternoon and so should their hunters. This afternoon, however, Robin called them to council.

"Now, men," he said, when they had assembled. "You know about these Anthropophagi, and how we have lost Matthew, Peter, Walter, Colin and many others. God rest their souls. You know how Guido found their Nest last week. Tonight the Anthropophagi are holding one of their feasts of sacrifice and it behoves us to slay them at it."

All the men made a deep murmur at this.

"I have much to tell you, men," continued Robin "and the success of our plan certainly, the safety of all our lives possibly, depends upon your listening. You know the Anthropophagi, and how many varieties they have. The Scythians, who wrap themselves in their ears, can hear a twig break half a mile away. The Pitanese, who live by smell, can detect a man upwind for three miles. The Nisites, with three or four eyes, can distinguish the faintest movement anywhere. All these men, or beasts if you prefer to call them so, are wild, ferocious and desperate. They are armed with poison arrows. Many of them, particularly the Sciopodes, are much swifter of foot than we can ever be. Our chances are small.

"Men, our hope is to take them by surprise. If we can surround them in the darkness, while their attention is all concentrated upon the fires of their sacrifice, we may be able to get within bow-shot without being heard or scented or seen. Then, while they stand in the firelight and we in gloom, the difference between poisoned arrows and English cloth-yards will be evened up.

"It is a dastardly way to fight. None of us likes it.

"But remember that these creatures are poisonous and cannibals. At that very moment they will be preparing to eat two servants of our neighbour Sir Ector. Remember also that on their own ground they are invincible, that our only hope of ourselves escaping from their slow decimation is by surprise. It will be difficult enough, considering their acute senses, even to surround them; this will need all our woodcraft. They must be slaughtered, every one, tonight. Not one wasp, or adder shall I call him, must escape our shafts.

"Now, men. There will be five troops. Their leaders will be Marian, John Little, Much the Miller's son, Will Scathelocke and myself. Friar Tuck will stay at the tree as look-out. These five troops will move individually for the first stage, each man for himself, until we are met at the great oak that was struck in the storm year. That oak is four miles away from the nest, and downwind of it, as the air lies at present. We must hope it will not change. After the great oak the men will separate into their bands, my own band and John Little's going four hundred yards to the left and right. It will be dark by then. The other three bands will spread into a semicircle and, after giving us a start of twenty rosaries, will advance upon the Nest upwind. Once more, and for the last time, I must warn every man that a Pitanese can smell three miles, the Scythians hear a twig at half a mile, and the Nisites see like hawks in every direction.

"My band and John Little's will be advancing on your wings, a few hundred yards in front. It will be the business of these two bands to close in upon the Anthropophagi from the other side. It will be these bands who will be heard or scented sooner or later, for it will be their necessity to go upwind of the Nest. We must hope that they will not be scented too soon.

"The other three bands will take up their stations on the downward side of the sacrificial fire, close enough for shooting point blank, but far enough to be invisible in the firelight. They will wait for news of my band and John's. If we manage to take up a good position on the other side undetected, I shall blow my horn. This will be the signal for all to fire. If we do not manage to take up a good position, but disturb the Anthropophagi, that disturbance may also be taken as an order to fire. We shall have to surround them then, each man for himself again, as best we may.

"These two boys will go with Marian's band. I think that is all. No, there is one thing. If you can distinguish them in the firelight I want you to spare the Pitanese and the Indians. They are perfectly harmless. You know what they look like.

"That is all, men. Remember the silence of the woods, and move like them. God bless us. Now then."

As soon as Robin Wood had finished his speech, which was listened to in perfect silence, an odd thing happened. He began it again at the beginning and spoke it from start to finish in exactly the same words. On finishing it for the second time, he said, "Now, captains," and all those hundred men split into groups of twenty which went to different parts of the clearing and stood round Marian, Little John, Much, Scarlett and Robin. From each of these little groups a humming noise rose to the sky.

"What on earth are they doing?" asked Kay.

"Listen," said the Wart.

They were repeating the speech, word for word. Probably none of them could read or write, but they had learnt to listen and to remember. This was the way in which Robin kept touch with his raiders by night, by knowing that each man knew by heart all that the leader himself knew, and why he was able to trust them, when necessary, to move each man by himself.

When all the men had repeated their instructions, and every one was word perfect in that long speech, there was an issue of war arrows, a dozen to each man. These arrows had bigger heads, ground to razor sharpness, and they were heavily feathered in a square cut. There was a bow inspection, and two or three men were issued with new strings. Then all fell silent.

"Now then," cried Robin cheerfully.

He waved his arms in a generous gesture, and the men, smiling, raised their bows in salute. Then there was a sigh, a rustle, a snap of one incautious twig, and the clearing of the giant lime tree was as empty as it had been before the days of man.

"Come with me," said Marian, touching the boys on the shoulder. Behind them the bees hummed in the leaves.

It was a long march and a tedious one. The artificial glades which converged upon the lime tree in the form of a cross were no longer of use after the first half-hour. After that they had to make their way through the virgin forest as best they might. It would not have been so bad if they had been able to kick and slash their way through it, but they were supposed to move in silence. Maid Marian showed them how to go sideways, one side after the other; how to stop at once when a bramble caught them, and take it patiently out; how to put their feet down sensitively and then roll their weight to that leg as soon as they were certain that no twig was under the foot; how to distinguish at a glance the places which gave most hope of an easy passage; and how a kind of rhythm in their movements would help them in spite of all these obstacles. Although there were a hundred invisible men on every side of them, moving towards the same goal, they heard no sounds but their own.

The boys had felt a little disgruntled at first, at being put into Marian's band. They would have preferred to have gone with Robin, and thought that being put under Marian was like being entrusted to a governess. They soon found out their mistake. She had objected to their coming, but, now that their coming was ordered, she accepted them as companions in war. Nor was it easy to be a companion of hers. In the first place it was impossible to keep up with her unless she waited for them – for she could move on all fours or even wriggle like a snake almost as quickly as they could walk – and in the second place she was an accomplished soldier, which they were not. One of the bits of advice which she gave them before talking had to be stopped was this: Aim high when you shoot in war, rather than low. A low arrow strikes only the ground, a high one may kill in the second rank.

"If I am ever made to get married," thought the Wart, who had doubts on this subject, "I will marry a girl like this: a kind of golden vixen."

As a matter of fact, though the boys did not know it, Marian could hoot like an owl by blowing into her fists, or whistle that shrill blast between tongue and teeth with the fingers in the corner of the mouth; could bring all the birds to her by imitating their calls, and understand much of their small language – such as when the tits exclaim that a hawk is coming; could hit the popinjay twice for three times of Robin's; and could turn cartwheels. But none of these accomplishments was necessary at the moment.

The twilight fell mistily – it was the very first of the autumn mists – and in the dimity the undispersed families of the tawny owl called to each other, the young with *keewick* and the old with the proper *Hooroo, Hooroo*. Proportionately as the brambles and obstacles became harder to see, so did they become easier to feel. It was odd, but in the deepening silence the Wart found himself able to move more silently, instead of the reverse. Being reduced to touch and sound, he found himself in better accord with these, and could go quietly and quick.

It was about compline, or, as we should call it, at nine o'clock at night – and they had covered at least seven miles of that toilsome forest – when Marian touched Kay on the shoulder and pointed into the blue darkness. They could see in the dark now, as well as human beings can see in it and much better than townspeople will ever manage to, and there in front of them, struck through seven miles of trackless forest by Marian's woodcraft, was the smitten oak. They decided with one accord, without even a whisper, to creep up to it so silently that even the members of their own army, who might already be waiting there, would not know of their arrival. They crept.

But a motionless man has always the advantage of a man in motion, and they had hardly reached the outskirts of the roots when friendly hands took hold of them, patted their backs with pats as light as thistle down, and guided them to seats. The roots were crowded. It was like being a member of a band of starlings, or of roosting rooks. In the night mystery a hundred men breathed on every side of Wart, like the surge of our own blood which we can hear when we are writing or reading in the late and lonely hours. They were in the dark and stilly womb of night.

Presently the Wart noticed that the grasshoppers were creaking their shrill note, so tiny as to be almost extra-audible, like the creak of the bat. They creaked one after another. They creaked, and when Marian had creaked thrice in order to account for Kay and Wart as well as for herself, one hundred times. All the outlaws were present, and it was time to go.

There was a rustle, as if the wind had moved in the last few leaves of that nine-hundred-year-old oak: then an owl hooted soft, a field mouse screamed, a rabbit thumped, a dog-fox barked his deep, single lion's cough, and an aerymouse twittered above their heads. The leaves rustled again more lengthily while you could count a hundred, and then Maid Marian, who had done the rabbit's thump, was surrounded by her band of twenty plus two. The Wart felt a man on either side of him take his hand, as they stood in a circle, and then he noticed that the stridulation of the grasshoppers had begun again. It was going round in a circle, towards him, and as the last grasshopper rubbed its legs together, the man on his right squeezed his hand. Wart stridulated. Instantly the man on his left did the same, and pressed his hand also. There were twenty-two grasshoppers before Maid Marian's band was ready for its last stalk of four miles through the silent forest.

The last stalk might have been a nightmare, but to the Wart it was heavenly. Suddenly he found himself filled with an exaltation of might, and felt that he was bodiless, silent, or transported. He felt that he could have walked upon a feeding rabbit and caught her up by the ears, furry and kicking, before she knew his presence. He felt that he could have run between the legs of the men on either side of him, or taken their bright daggers from their sheaths while they still moved on undreaming. The passion of nocturnal secrecy was a wine that triumphed in his blood. He really was small and young enough to move as secretly as the warriors. Their age and weight made them lumber, in spite of all their woodcraft, and his youth and lightness made him mobile, in spite of his lack of it.

It was an easy stalk, except for its added danger. The bushes thinned out and the sounding bracken grew rarely in the swampy earth, so that they could move three times as fast. They went in a dream, unguided by owl's hoot or bat's twitter, but only kept together by the necessary pace which the sleeping forest imposed upon them. Some of them were fearful, some revengeful for their lost comrades, some, as it were, disbodied in the horrible sleep-walk of their stealth.

There was a glimmer in front of them, a rosy sunrise in the

trees. There were noises and shadows that moved before it, something like a queer phantasmagoria of village celebrations which have been seen in these late years of grace for jubilee and coronations.

There was a clearing lit by firelight, and in it huts of mud. Their round walls were saffron in the glow, beehives of light and darkness, and three stakes or spits stood in the centre of the night. The wild men intended to roast poor Cavall as well as the Dog Boy and Wat, and the third stake was for him. Wart could see the firelight gleaming red from the coating of Maid Marian's eye, as she fitted the nock of her arrow to the string.

But the people in the Nest of Anthropophagi were more strange than all. They were busy about their tasks of roasting, plainly visible to their slayers in the outer gloom. Some with their heads growing beneath their shoulders ran about their errands of torture with set expressions, like people intent upon something they have lost upon the ground. Others, with the heads of dogs, howled with slow melodious accents before the fire. The Pygmaei Spythamei, whose eternal enemies are cranes, ran about with tiny logs for the roast, themselves only a few hands high. The Æthiopians, or Sciopodes, had only one foot, but this is so huge that they could use it as a sunshade to protect themselves when sleeping. These creatures hopped on their single feet with incredible agility, like hares, landing on their heels and taking off with their toes in industrious bounds which were directed towards conveying all the necessaries for the sacrifice. Some of the men had lower lips so large that they could cover their heads with them to keep off the rain, others had six fingers or eight toes, others again, the Nisites, were glaring in all directions from four eyes, bloodshot by the bonfire light, while the women among them had long beards but were quite bald. Perhaps the most curious of all these flame-fringed cannibals were the stork-men, creatures with beautiful human bodies, but the necks, heads and beaks of the heron family. They moved before the hellish tapestry poking their heads forwards and back, tick-tock like a metronome, as they balanced their beaks against the forward pace. In a far corner of the clearing, by a stream, distant from all this business, the Indians and Pitanese – or Astomes – were clustered; the former innocuous water mammals like manatees, who were covered with hair, had six hands, and lived only by browsing in the stream; the latter a timid race who had no mouths, but existed entirely upon what they smelt, and who could be slain by a stink.

All these, with the Scythians who were accustomed to wrap themselves up in their ears at night, moved in the strange light of the sacrificial flame.

The boys lay and listened with their troop for a time which seemed eternity. They fitted their arrows to their strings, so that they would be ready to loose off at the very first note of Robin's horn, but no sound came. Only the cruel uproar of the Nest came to them down the wind. They saw the poor Dog Boy and old Wat led out to their stakes, and Cavall also, howling dismally. He was terrified by the dog-headed men, whom he supposed to be demons. The Dog Boy seemed very angry and anxious to fight his captors in spite of his bonds, but old Wat did not know what was being done to him and walked between two Scythians with a happy smile. He, unlike Cavall, believed that he was in the hands of angels. The huge ears of the Scythians, moving like wings, made him think this.

The victims were tied to their stakes and the faggots piled about them. Then the Anthropophagi joined hands in a circle and began to prance round and round the sacrifice as if they were doing a Paul Jones. They shouted, squealed, hooted, honked or barked as they pranced, according to the several natures of their heads. The stork-men jerked their sharp beaks backwards and forwards quicker and quicker, looking very strange in their tallness as they skipped perhaps hand in hand with one of the pygmies. The Sciopodes went ker-thump ker-thump, bounding on their huge and single feet. It was a terrible spectacle.

The Wart was watching one of the Nisites who appeared to be the leader of the band – partly on account of his enormous size and four red eyes, partly because he carried the sacrificial bow which would be used to despatch the victims as soon as their faggots had been truly lit – when the Paul Jones stopped of its own accord. There had been no sound of movement which the outlaws could distinguish, but suddenly the dance was stilled. For a moment the Nisites shaded all their eyes and frowned into the darkness on the other side of the clearing, while the Scythians, unfolding their elephant ears, stood in black silhouettes and waved them sensitively in the same direction. Then the poor Pitanese or Astomes, huddles at the far end of the settlement and taking no parts in these barbaric orgies, set up a dreadful wail through their twitching noses, and stampeded. There were shrieks and a terrible din of animal voices. On top of the uproar, and riding on it proudly like the voice of an Arabian Bird, Robin Wood's fierce horn of silver began to blow.

"Tone, ton, tavon, tontavon, tantontavon, tontantontavon," went the horn, and again, "Moot, trout, troutoutout, troutoutoutout. Troot, troot. Tran, tran, tran, tran."

Robin was blowing his hunting music and now all the ambushed archers leaped up. They set forward their left foot in the same movement and let fly such a shower of arrows as it had been snow.

The Wart saw the leader of the Nisites stagger in his tracks, a cloth-yard shaft suddenly sprouting from between his shoulder blades. He saw his own arrow fly wide of a crane-man, and eagerly bent forward to snatch another from the ground. Each man of the waiting troops had stuck his twelve arrows point downwards in the ground before him, for convenience in loading. He saw the rank of his companion archers sway forward as if by a preconcerted signal, when each man stooped for a second shaft. He heard the bow-strings twang again, the purr of the feathers in the air. He saw the phalanx of arrows gleam like an eye-flick in the firelight. All his life up to then he had been shooting into straw targets which made a noise like Phutt! He had often longed to hear the noise that these gay, true, clean and deadly missiles of the air would make in solid flesh. He heard it.

The Anthropophagi were yelling, falling and running

about. Some had snatched up their poisonous bows and were firing wildly into the dark. Others, strangely transfixed, were tumbling with their ears pinned to their bodies or their lips to their chests. The pygmies scuttled for the huts. The Scythians made a trumpeting noise and charged the dark. They ran madly upon their assailants, but stumbled, coughed or barked, and fell on their faces or sat down backwards in a few yards. As they leapt out the arrows leapt to meet them. The Sciopodes, more swift in flight, bounded towards the sheltering darkness in skips of twenty or thirty feet. One of them coming straight at the Wart. He could see the pointed ears, the wild eyes slit like a cat's, and the one huge foot by whose action it bounded. It squealed as it came, and let fly one of its poisoned arrows at random. It saw the Wart and leapt into the air like a kangaroo.

The Wart was fitting an arrow to his bow. The cock feather would not go right. Everything was in slow motion once again.

He saw the huge body flying blackly through the glare, felt the foot take him in the chest. He felt himself turning somersaults on top of him. He saw Kay's face somewhere in the cartwheel of the universe, flushed with flame-lit excitement, and Maid Marian's on the other side with its mouth open, shouting something. He thought; before he slid into blackness, that it was shouting something nice.

CHAPTER TWELVE

THEY PICKED THE Wart out from under the Sciopod, and found his arrow sticking through its chest. It had died in its leap. Wart was unconscious, and the battle was over.

Then there was a time which made him feel sick, while Robin set his broken collarbone and made him a sling out of the green cloth of his hood, and after that all lay down indiscriminately to sleep, dog-tired, among the slain. The Wart lay propped against a tree. It was too late to get back to the castle that night, or even to get back to the outlaw's camp by the lime tree. All that could be done was to make up the fires, post sentries, and sleep where they were.

Wart did not sleep much. He leant against his tree, watching the red sentries pass to and fro in the firelight, hearing their quiet passwords and thinking about the excitements of the day. These went round and round in his head, sometimes losing their proper order and happening backwards or by bits. He saw the leaping Sciopod, heard Marian shouting "Good shot", listened to the humming of the bees muddled up with the stridulation of the grasshoppers, and shot and shot, hundreds and thousands of times, at popinjays which turned into Sciopodes. Kay and the liberated Dog Boy slept twitching beside him, looking alien and incomprehensible as people do when they are asleep, and Cavall, lying at his good shoulder, occasionally licked his hot cheeks. The dawn came slowly, so slowly and pausingly that it was quite impossible to determine when it really had dawned, as is its habit during the summer months.

"Well," said Robin, when they had all wakened and eaten the breakfast of bread and cold venison which they had brought with them, "you will have to love us and leave us, Kay. Otherwise I shall have Sir Ector fitting-out an expedition against me, to fetch you back. Thank you both for your help. Can I give you any little present as a reward for it?"

"It has been lovely," said Kay. "Absolutely lovely. Can I have the Scythian I shot?"

"He will be a bit heavy to carry. Why not just take his head?"

"That would do," said Kay, "if somebody wouldn't mind cutting it off. It was that Scythian there."

"What are you going to do about old Wat?" asked the Wart.

"It depends on his preferences. Perhaps he will like to run off by himself and eat acorns, as he used to do, or if he likes to join our band we shall be glad of him. He ran away from your village in the first place, so I don't suppose he will care to go back there. What do you think?"

"If you are going to give me a present," said the Wart slowly, "I should like to have him. Do you think that would be all right?"

"As a matter of fact," said Robin, "I don't. I don't think you can very well give people as presents: they might not like it. What did you intend to do with him?"

"Oh, I don't want to keep him or anything like that. You see, we have a tutor who is a pretty good magician and I thought he might be able to restore Wat to his wits."

"Good boy," said Robin. "Have him by all means. I'm sorry I made a mistake. At least, we'll ask him if he would like to go."

When somebody had gone off to fetch Wat, Robin said, "You had better talk to him yourself."

They brought the poor old man, smiling, confused, hideous and very dirty, and stood him up before Robin.

"Go on," said Robin.

The Wart did not know quite how to put it, but he said, "I say, Wat, would you like to come home with me, please, just for a little?"

"AhnaNanaWarraBaaBaa," said Wat, pulling his forelock, smiling, bowing and gently waving his arms in various directions.

"Come with me?"

"WanaNanaWanawana."

"Dinner?" asked the Wart in desperation. "Yum, yum?"

"Yum, yum!" cried the poor creature affirmatively, and his eyes glowed with pleasure at the prospect of being given something to eat.

"That way," said the Wart, pointing in the direction which he knew by the sun to be that of his guardian's castle. "Dinner. Come with. I take."

"Measter," said Wat, suddenly remembering just one word, the word which he had always been accustomed to offer to the great people who made him a present of food, his only livelihood. It was concluded.

"Well," said Robin. "It has been a good adventure and I'm sorry you're going. I hope I shall see you again one day."

"Come any time," said Marian, "if you are feeling bored. You have only to follow those glades. And you, Wart, be careful of that collarbone for a few days."

"I will send some men with you to the edge of the chase," said Robin. "After that you must go by yourselves. I expect the Dog Boy can carry the Scythian's head."

"Goodbye," said Kay.

"Goodbye," said Robin.

"Goodbye," said the Wart.

"Goodbye," said Marian smiling, "and always shoot like you did last night."

"Goodbye," cried all the outlaws, waving their bows.

And Kay and the Wart and the Dog Boy and Wat and Cavall and their escort set off on the long track home.

★ ★ ★

They had an immense reception. The return on the previous day of all the hounds, except Cavall and the Dog Boy, and in the evening the failure to return of Kay and the Wart, had set the household in an uproar. Their nurse had gone into hysterics, Hob had stayed out till midnight scouring the purlieus of the forest, the cooks had burnt the joint for dinner, and the sergeant-at-arms had polished all the armour twice and sharpened all the swords and axes to a razor blade in expectation of an immediate invasion. At last somebody had thought of consulting Merlyn, whom they had found in the middle of his third nap. The magician, for the sake of peace and quietness to go on with his nap in, had used his insight to tell Sir Ector exactly what the boys were doing, where they were, and when they might be expected to come back. He had prophesied their return to the minute.

So, when the small procession of returning warriors came within sight of the drawbridge, they were greeted by the entire household. Sir Ector was standing in the middle with a thick walking-stick with which he proposed to whack them for going out of bounds and causing so much trouble; the nurse had insisted on bringing out a banner which used to be put up when Sir Ector came home for the holidays, as a small boy, and this said WELCOME HOME; Hob had forgotten all about his beloved hawks and was standing on one side, shading his eagle eyes to get the first view; the cooks and all the kitchen staff were banging pots and pans and singing "Will Ye No Come Back Again?" out of tune; the kitchen cat was yowling; the hounds had escaped from the kennel because there was nobody to look after them, and were preparing to chase the kitchen cat; the sergeant-at-arms was blowing out his chest with pleasure, so far that he looked as if he might burst at any moment, and was commanding everybody in a very important voice to get ready to cheer when he said "One, Two!"

"One, Two!" cried the sergeant.

"Huzza!" cried everybody obediently, including Sir Ector.

"Look what I've got," shouted Kay. "I've shot a Scythian and the Wart has been wounded."

"Yow-yow-yow," barked all the hounds, and poured over the Dog Boy, licking his face, scratching his chest, sniffing him all over to see what he had been up to, and looking hopefully at the Scythian's head which the Dog Boy held high in the air so that they could not eat it.

"Bless my soul," exclaimed Sir Ector.

"Alas, the poor Phillip Sparrow," cried the nurse, dropping her banner, "pity his poor arm all to-brast in a green sling, God bless him."

"It's all right," said the Wart. "Ah, don't catch hold of me. It hurts."

"May I have it stuffed?" asked Kay.

"Well, I be dommed," said Hob. "Be'nt thick wold chappie our Wat, that erst run lunatical?"

"My dear, dear boys," said Sir Ector. "I *am* so glad to see you back."

"Wold chuckle-head," exclaimed the nurse triumphantly. "Where be thy girt cudgel now?"

Chapter Twelve

"Hem!" said Sir Ector. "How dare you go out of bounds and put us all to this anxiety?"

"It's a real Scythian," said Kay, who knew there was nothing to be afraid of. "I shot dozens of them. Wart shot a Sciopod and broke his collarbone. We rescued the Dog Boy and Wat."

"That comes of teaching the young Hidea 'ow to shoot," said the sergeant proudly.

Sir Ector kissed the boys and commanded the Scythian to be displayed before him.

"Well!" he exclaimed. "What a monster! We'll have him stuffed in the dinin'-hall. What did you say his measurements were?"

"Eighty-two inches from ear to ear. Robin said it might be a record."

"We shall have to write to the *Field*."

"It is rather a good one, isn't it?" remarked Kay with studied calm.

"I shall have it set up by Rowland Ward," Sir Ector went on in high delight, "with a little ivory card with KAY'S FIRST ANTHROPOPHAGUS on it in black letters, and the date."

"Arrah, leave thy childishness," exclaimed the nurse. "Now Master Art, my innocent, be off with thee to thy bed upon the instant. And thou, Sir Ector, let thee think shame to be playing wi' monsters' heads like a godwit when the poor child stays upon the point of death. Now, sergeant, leave puffing of thy chest. Stir, man, and take horse to Cardoyle for the chirurgeon."

She waved her apron at the sergeant, who collapsed his chest and retreated like a shoo'd chicken.

"It's all right," said the Wart. "I tell you. It is only a broken collarbone, and Robin set it for me last night. It doesn't hurt a bit."

"Leave the boy, nurse," commanded Sir Ector, taking sides with the men against the women, and anxious to re-establish his superiority after the matter of the cudgel. "Merlyn will see to him if he needs it, no doubt. Who is this Robin?"

"Robin Wood," cried both the boys together.

"Never heard of him."

"You call him Robin Hood," explained Kay in superior tones. "But it's Wood really, like the Wood that he's the spirit of."

"Well, well, well, so you've been foragin' with the rascal! Come in to breakfast, boys, and tell me all about him."

"We've had breakfast," said the Wart, "hours ago. May I please take Wat with me to see Merlyn?"

"Why, it's the old man who went wild and started rootin' in the forest. Where ever did you get hold of him?"

"The Anthropophagi had captured him with the Dog Boy and Cavall. They were going to eat them, roasted."

"But we shot them," Kay put in. "I shot a hundred."

"So now I want to see if Merlyn can restore him to his wits."

"Master Art," said the nurse sternly. She had been breathless up to now on account of Sir Ector's rebuke. "Master Art, thy room and thy bed is where thou art tending to, and that this instant. Wold fools may be wold fools, whether by yea or by nay, but I hant served the Family for fifty years without a-learning of my duty. A flibberty-gibberting about wi' a lot of want-wits, when thy own arm may be dropping to the floor at any moment!"

"Yes, thou wold turkey-cock," she added, turning fiercely upon Sir Ector. "And thou canst keep thy magician away from the poor mite's room till he's rested, that thou canst."

"A wantoning wi' monsters and lunaticals," continued the victor as she led her helpless captive from the stricken field. "I never heard the like."

"Please someone to tell Merlyn to look after Wat," cried the victim over his shoulder, in diminishing tones.

"Popaguys, indeed," they heard her concluding. "I'll give him Popaguys."

The Wart woke up in his cool bed, feeling better. The dear old fire-eater who looked after him had covered the windows with a curtain, so that the room was dark and comfortable, but he could tell by the one ray of sunlight which shot golden across the floor that it was late afternoon. He not only felt better. He felt very well indeed, so well that it was quite impossible to stay in bed. He moved quickly to throw back the sheet, but stopped with a hiss at the creak or scratch of his shoulder, which he had forgotten about in his sleep. Then he got out more carefully, by sliding down the bed and pushing himself upright with one hand, shoved his bare feet into a pair of slippers, and managed to wrap a dressing-gown round him more or less. He padded off through the stone passages up the worn circular stairs to find Merlyn.

When he reached the schoolroom, he found that Kay was continuing his First Rate Eddication. He was evidently doing dictation, for as Wart opened the door he heard Merlyn pronouncing in measured tones, "*Sciant presentes et futuri Quod*," and Kay saying, "Wait a bit. My pen has gone all squee-gee."

"You'll catch it," remarked Kay, when he saw him. "You're supposed to be in bed, dying of gangrene or something."

"Merlyn," said the Wart, "what have you done with Wat?"

"You should try to speak without assonances," said Merlyn. "For instance, 'The beer is never clear near here, dear' is unfortunate, even as an assonance. And then again, your sentence is ambiguous to say the least of it. 'What what?'; I might reply, taking it to be a conundrum, or if I were King Pellinore, 'What what, what?' Nobody can be too careful about their habits of speech."

Kay had evidently been doing his dictation well and the old gentleman was in good humour.

"You know what I mean," said the Wart. "What have you done with the old man with no nose?"

"He's cured him," said Kay.

"Well," said Merlyn, "you might call it that, and there again you might not. Of course, when one has lived in the world as long as I have, and backwards at that, one does learn to know a thing or two about pathology. The wonders of analytical psychology and plastic surgery are, I am afraid, to this generation but a closed book."

He leant back in high delight.

"What did you do to him?"

"Oh, I just psychoanalysed him, you know," said Merlyn grandly. "That, and of course I sewed on a new nose on both of them."

"What kind of nose?" asked the Wart.

"It's too funny," said Kay. "He wanted to have the Scythian's nose for one, but I wouldn't let him. So then he took the noses off two young pigs which we are going to have for supper, and used those. Personally I think they will both grunt."

"A ticklish operation," said Merlyn, "but a successful one."

"Well," said Wart doubtfully. "I hope it will be all right. What did they do then?"

"They went off to the kennels together. Old Wat is very sorry for what he did to the Dog Boy, but he says he can't remember having done it. He says that suddenly everything went black, when they were throwing stones once, and he can't remember anything since. The Dog Boy forgave him and said he didn't mind a bit. They are going to work together in the kennels in future, and not think of what's past any more. The Dog Boy says that the old man was very good to him while they were prisoners of the Anthropophagi, and that he knows he ought not to have thrown stones at him in the first place. He says he often thought about that when the other boys were throwing stones at *him*."

"Well," said the Wart. "I'm glad it's all turned out for the best. Do you think I could go and visit them?"

"For heaven's sake, don't do anything to annoy your nurse," exclaimed Merlyn, looking about him anxiously. "That old woman hit me with a broom when I came to see you this forenoon, and broke my spectacles. Couldn't you wait until tomorrow?"

On the morrow Wat and the Dog Boy were the firmest of friends. Their common experiences of being stoned by a mob and then sacrificed by cannibals served as a bond and a topic of reminiscence, as they lay among the dogs at night, for the rest of their lives; and, by the morning, they had both pulled off the noses which Merlyn had so kindly given them. They explained that they had got used to having no noses, now, and anyway they preferred to live with the dogs.

CHAPTER THIRTEEN

THE SUMMER WAS over at last, and nobody could deny any longer that the autumn was definitely there. It was that rather sad time of year when for the first time for many months the fine old sun still blazes away in a cloudless sky, but does not warm you, and the hoar-frosts and the mists and the winds begin to stir their faint limbs at morning and evening, with the gossamer, as the sap of winter vigour remembers itself in the cold corpses which brave summer slew. The leaves were still on the trees, and still green, but it was the leaden green of old leaves which have seen much since the gay colours and happiness of spring – that seems so lately and, like all happy things, so quickly to have passed. The sheep fairs had been held. The plums had tumbled off the trees in the first big winds, and here and there, in the lovely sunlight too soon enfeebled, a branch of beech or oak was turning yellow: the one to die quickly and mercifully, the other perhaps to hold grimly to the frozen tree and to hiss with its papery skeletons all through the east winds of winter, until the spring was there again.

The Wart's arm did not hurt any more, but he was not allowed to do his martial exercises under the sergeant-at-arms in the afternoons, for fear of spoiling it before it was properly mended. He went for walks instead, kept watch on a playful family of five hobbies, who shouted "Cui-Cui-Cui-Cui-Cui," and would be migrating any day now – they were late already – and he collected the enormous caterpillars of moths which had been through all their changes and now sought lumberingly for a convenient place in which to turn into the chrysalis. His best capture was the four-inch plum and apricot upholstery of a Goat Moth, which buried itself quite cheerfully among trails of silk in a box of loose earth which he kept beside his bed. It had taken three years to reach its present size and would lie perdue for another, before the big dun moth crept out of its old armour and pumped the blood into the veins of its expanding wings.

Merlyn caught a male grass snake on one of these walks. They met by chance, face to face, as each was turning the corner of a big bed of seeded nettles from opposite directions, and the magician pounced upon the reptile before it had time to flick its black tongue twice. He held it up, wriggling, hissing and smelling strongly of acetylene, while the Wart examined it in horror.

"Don't be afraid of it," said Merlyn: "It is only a piece of olive lightning with a ochre V behind its shining black head. It can't sting you and won't bite you. It has never done harm to anybody, and can only flee and stink.

"See," he said, and began stroking it from the head downwards: a touch which the poor creature tried to evade but soon accepted, in its ceaseless efforts to pour and pour away.

"Everybody kills them," said Merlyn indignantly. "Some by-our-lady fool once said that you could tell an adder because it had a V on its head, which stood for viper. It would take you five minutes to find the mark on an adder's head anyway, but these helpless beauties with their bright yellow black-bordered V get bashed to death in consequence. Here, catch hold of him."

The Wart took the serpent gingerly into his hands, taking care to hold it well away from the vent from which the white smell came. He had thought that snakes were slimy as well as dangerous, but this was not. It was dry as a piece of living rope, and had, like rope, a pleasing texture to the fingers, on account of its scales. Every ounce of it was muscle, every plate of its belly was a strong moving foot. He had held toads before, and they, the fat philosophical warty creatures, had been a little clammy on account of their loose flesh. This creature, on the other hand, was dry and delicately rough and liquid power. It was the same temperature as the ground on which it basked.

"You asked to be turned into a snake once," said Merlyn. "Do you still want that?"

"Yes, please."

"It isn't much of a life. I don't think you'll get anything very exciting to happen to you. This chap probably only eats about once a week or once a fortnight, and the rest of the time he dreams. Still, if I turned you into one, you might get him to talk. It won't be more than that."

"I should like it all the same."

"Well, it will be a rest after shooting Anthropophagi."

Merlyn loosed the grass-snake, which immediately flashed off into the nettles. Then he exchanged a few words in Greek with an invisible gentleman called Aesculapius, and turned to the Wart.

He said, "I shall stay here for an hour or two, and perhaps I shall sit down against that tree and have a nap. Then I want you to come out to me when I call you. Goodbye."

The Wart tried to say Goodbye, but found that he was dumb. He looked quickly at his hands, but they were not there. Aesculapius had accepted him so gently that he had not noticed it, and he was lying on the ground.

"Pour off, then," said Merlyn. "Go and search for him in the nettles."

Some people say that snakes are deaf, and others that they deafen themselves in order to escape being charmed by music. The thoughtful adder, for instance, is said by many learned persons to lay one ear upon the ground and to stick the point of his tail into the other so that he cannot hear your music. Wart found that as a matter of fact snakes were not deaf. He had an ear anyway, which was conscious of deep roaring sounds that were approximate to the noises which he had learnt as a boy. For instance if somebody bangs on the side of the bath or if the pipes begin to gurgle when your ears are under water, you hear sounds which are different to those which would be heard in a normal position. But you would soon get accustomed to these sounds, and connect the roaring and bumbling with water-pipes, if you kept your head under water for long. In fact, although you heard a different kind of noise, you would still be hearing the pipes which human beings hear in the upper air. So the Wart could hear what Merlyn said, though it sounded very thin and high, and he therefore hoped to be able to talk to the snake. He darted out his tongue, which he used as a sort of feeler such as the long stick with which an explorer might probe the bogs in front of him, and he slid off into the nettles in search of his companion.

The other snake was lying flat on its face in a state of great agitation. It had managed to push itself into the very roots of the coarse grass among the nettles, for there is always a kind of empty layer between the green grass and the actual mud. The top green layer is supported on pillars of bleached roots, and it was in this secret acre-huge chamber, which covers every grass field, floored with mud and roofed with green, that the poor snake had sought concealment. It was lamenting to itself in a very sweet, cold, simple voice and crying, "Alas, Alas!"

It is difficult to explain the way in which snakes talk, except by this. Everybody knows that there are rays of light, the infra-red and the ultra-violet and those beyond them, in which ants, for instance, can see, and men cannot. Just so there are waves of sound higher than the bat's squeak, which Mozart once heard delivered by Lucrezia Ajugari in 1770, and lower than the distant thunder which pheasants hear (or is it that they see the flash?) before man. It was in these profound melodious accents that the snake conversed.

"Who are you?" asked the snake, trembling, as Wart poured himself into the secret chamber beside it. "Did you see the human? It was an *H. Sapiens*, I believe. I only just got away."

It was in such a flutter that it did not wait for its question to be answered, but went on excitedly, "Oh, the horrid creature. Did you notice how it smelt? Well, I shan't go out again in a hurry, that I will say. Look what a mess I have got myself in. It was an *H. Sapiens barbatus*, as far as I could see. They are quite common round here. You take my advice and lie close for a day or two. I just went out for a moment with the idea of getting a frog or two before hibernating, and it pounced upon me like a hedgehog. I don't believe I was ever so frightened in my life. Do you think it would be best to hibernate at once?"

"I shouldn't worry," said the Wart. "That particular human is fond of snakes, as I happen to know."

"To eat?" stammered the serpent.

"No, no. He is friendly with them, and has some as pets. We – he, I mean – that is, he spends most of the botany hours looking for frogs to feed them on. It's wonderful how few frogs there are, once you begin looking for them – only toads. And of course snakes don't eat toads."

"I ate a toad once," said the other, who was beginning to

calm down. "It was a small one, you know, but it wasn't very nice. Still, I don't think I should like to be a pet of that creature's however many frogs it caught. Do you happen to know its sex?"

"It was a male," said the Wart.

"*H. Sapiens barbatus* ♂," repeated the snake, feeling safer now that he had got the subject classified. "And what is your name, my child?"

The Wart did not know what to answer, so he simply told the truth.

"It's a funny sort of name," said the snake doubtfully.

"What is yours?" asked the Wart.

"*T. Natrix.*"

"Does the T. stand for anything?"

"Well, not Tommy, " said the snake rather coolly, "if that's what you mean. It's *Tropidonotus* in my family always."

"I'm sorry."

"If you don't mind my saying so," remarked the snake, "it seems to me that your education has been neglected. First you have a mother who calls you Wart, just as if you were one of those vulgar Bufonidae, and then you can't distinguish a *T. Natrix* when you see him. Did you never have a mother?"

"As a matter of fact, I didn't."

"Oh, I am sorry," exclaimed the snake. "I hope I haven't hurt your feelings. Do you mean to say you never had anybody to teach you the Legends and Dreams and that?"

"Never."

"You poor newt. What do you do then when you hibernate?"

"I suppose I just go to sleep."

"And not dream?"

"No," said the Wart. "I don't think so. Not much."

It turned out that *T. Natrix* was an affectionate and tender-hearted creature, for it now shed a small, clear tear — through its nose — and exclaimed indignantly, "What a shame! Fancy the poor little reptile crawling into its lonely hole for all those months with not a mother to remember, and not a single Dream to keep it company. I suppose they haven't even taught you History?"

"I know some History," said the Wart doubtfully. "About Alexander the Great, and that."

"Some trashy modern stuff, no doubt," said the snake. "How in earth you get through the winter I don't know. Did anybody tell you about *Atlantosaurus immanis* and *Ceratosaurus nasicornis*?"

"I don't think so."

"Well, I don't know what to say."

"Couldn't you tell me about them yourself?"

"It certainly seems the kindest thing to do," replied the snake, "and by Aesculapius I will do it, too, if it takes me all the afternoon. Why, I should hardly be able to sleep the whole winter, thinking of you shivering in that hole with nothing to muse about."

"It would be very kind of you if you would."

"And I will," said the gentle reptile. "I will teach you the sort of thing that all snakes revolve in their small, slow, winter brains, what time the snow shuffles down outside, or for that matter in the summer too, as they snooze beside warm stones. Would you rather have History or Legends?"

"I think History," said the Wart.

"History," murmured the snake, drawing a film over its eyes because it could not close them. "History," it repeated softly. "Ah.

"I wonder," said the snake after a minute. Then it gave a gentle sigh and gave it up.

"You must forget about us," it said absently. "There is no History in me or you. We are individuals too small for our great sea to care for. That is why I don't have any special name, but only *T. Natrix* like all my forefathers before me. There is a little History in *T. Natrix*, but none in me."

It stopped, baffled by its own feelings, and then began again in its slow voice.

"There is one thing which all we snakes remember, child. Except for two people, we are the oldest in the world. Look at that ridiculous *H. Sapiens barbatus* which gave me such a fright just now. It was born when? Ten or twenty thousand years ago. What do the tens and twenties matter? The earth cooled. The sea covered it. It was a hundred million years ago that Life came to the Great Sea, and the fishes bred within it. They were the oldest people, the Fish. Their children climbed out of it and stood upon the bosky shores, and they were the Amphibia like our friends the newts. The third people, who sprang from them, were the Reptiles, of which we are one. Think of those old faces of the world upon which *T. Natrix* moved in the slime, and of the millions of years. Why, the birds which you see every day are our descendants: we are their parents, but can persist to live along with them."

"Do you mean that when you were born there were no birds or men?"

"No birds or men: no monkeys, or reindeer or elephants or any such animals: only the amphibia and the reptiles and the fishes and the Mesozoic world.

"That's history," added the snake thoughtfully. "One of those *H. Sapiens barbatus* ♂ might think of that next time he murders *T. Natrix* for being a viper.

"There is something strange about the Will of the Sea. It is bound up with the History of my family. Did you ever hear the story of *H. Sapiens armatus georgius sanctus*?"

"I don't think I did," said the Wart.

"Once very long ago, when even *T. Natrix* was a young and hopeful, there were two families called *Atlantosaurus immanis* and *Ceratosaurus nasicornis. Atlantosaurus* was a hundred and fifteen feet long. He had not many brains, although I did hear once that he had something like an extra brain at the other end of him, to take care of his tail, and he lived by browsing on the trees. He was timid, ruminant and harmless, except to the tree-frogs which he munched by mistake among the boughs. He lived very long and thought all the time, so that, although he did not think very well, he had generally thought a good deal by the end of it. So far as I can remember, he had solved the problem of being a giant, without breaking on account of his own weighty height of twenty feet, by having his bones hollow. The birds do that too, you know, for other reasons. However, perhaps I am muddling him up with another of the Dinosauria.

"*Ceratosaurus nasicornis* was quite small. He was only seventeen feet long. But he had teeth, great, crushing and tearing teeth, which fitted into each other so badly that he leapt always with his slaughterous mouth half open, in a grin of terror. He leaped like a kangaroo, a death-dealing kangaroo, and he generally leaped upon poor *Atlantosaurus immanis*. He had a horn upon his nose, like a rhinoceros, with which he could rip an opening in that big trundling old body, and his clashing teeth could meet in the flesh as in ripe fruit and tear it out in mouthfuls by the action of his muscular neck. What is more terrible, he leaped in packs.

"*Ceratosaurus nasicornis* was at war with *Atlantosaurus immanis*, in that strange war which the Spirit of the Waters wills, the war of competition and evolution which makes the trees fight upwards for the sun on the Amazon, and in the course of which, for the boon of life, many of my cousins have been content to sacrifice the benefits of limbs and teeth and eyesight.

"*Ceratosaurus* was savage and aggressive, *Atlantosaurus* timid and old. Their combat lasted for as many centuries as will be needed by *H. Sapiens* also, in which to destroy himself. At the end of that time it was the defender who triumphed. The ferocious kangaroo had dealt death on every side, had decimated his adversaries and fed upon their carcases, but carcases cannot continue their species and in the end the kangaroos had consumed the very flesh on which they lived. Too remorseless for the Spirit of the Waters, too bloodthirsty for the hierarchy of progressive victims, the last *Ceratosaurus* roamed the thick-leaved jungles in a vain search for the food which could satisfy his gnashing jaws: then died and slept with his fathers.

"The last *Atlantosaurus* thrust her forty-foot neck out of the jungle in which she had been hiding, and surveyed the emaciated corpse of her starved persecutor. She had preserved her life, as the sensible wood pigeon does, by specializing in escape. She had learnt to flee, to hide, to stand still, to control her scent, to conceal herself in waters. By humility she had survived her enemy, who had slain her own husband; and now she carried the children of the latter inside her, the last of the victorious race. They would be born in a few years.

"*H. Sapiens* had come meanwhile. He also had suffered from the terror of the kangaroo. In order to protect himself from its rapine, he had developed a sub-class called *H. Sapiens armatus*, a class which was concealed in metal scales and carried a lance by means of which it defended itself against the Dinosauria. This sub-class had perfected an order called *H. Sapiens armatus georgius sanctus*, which was sufficiently unobservant to classify all the Dinosaurs together as its enemies.

"*Atlantosaurus* thrust out her neck, and thought with triumph of her unborn children. She had never killed in her life, and these, the future, would perpetuate a vegetarian race. She heard the clank of *H. Sapiens armatus georgius sanctus*, and turned the comely reptile head towards him in her kindly curiosity."

"Go on," said the Wart.

"He killed her, of course," concluded the serpent with sudden brevity, turning its own head away. "She was a reptile of my race."

"I am sorry," said the Wart. "I don't know what to say."

"There is nothing, dear," said the patient serpent, "that you can say. Perhaps I had better tell you a Legend or Dream, to change the subject."

The Wart said, "I don't think I want to hear it, if it is sad."

"There is nothing sad," said the other, "except History. All these things are only something to muse upon while you are hibernating."

"It is a good thing to muse?"

"Well, it passes the time. Even *H. Sapiens* has museums, you know: and as far as that goes, he has put the chalky bones of *Atlantosaurus* in many of them, along with the scales of *georgius sanctus*."

"It you knew a fairly cheerful Legend," said the Wart, "I think I could bear to hear that."

"Ridiculous newt," said *T. Natrix* affectionately – for Newt seemed to be one of his pet words. "I suppose I shall have to tell you a Legend of my dangerous cousins, for whom I suffer."

"Is it cheerful?"

"Well, it just goes on to the end, you know, and then stops – as Legends do."

"Tell it," said the Wart.

"This Legend," said the snake in its sing-song voice, after a preparatory cough, "comes from Burma, a place of which you have probably never heard.

"Once upon a time there was only one poisonous serpent in the world, and this was the python. As you know, he is no longer venomous, and the story of how he lost his venom is an interesting one. In those days he was perfectly white. He happened to make the acquaintance of the wife of a human being whose name was Aunt Eu, and in course of time they fell in love with each other. Aunt Eu left her husband and went off to live with the python, whose name was *P. reticulatus*. She was in some ways an old-fashioned kind of person, the kind which delights in making carpet slippers for curates among the humans, and she soon set about weaving a most handsome and closely woven skin for her python. It was an ornamental affair, what with black lozenges and yellow dots, and here and there at regular intervals cubes and cross-stitches of amber, such as the humans use in rug-making or working samplers. *P. reticulatus* was pleased with it, and wears it always, so that now he is not white any more.

"At this time the python was interested in making experiments with his unique venom. Since he was the only poisonous snake, he naturally contained within himself all the poison which is nowadays spread out among the snakes. So concentrated was this terrible poison, therefore, that he could kill a man, however far away he was, simply by biting any footprint which the man had happened to leave on the ground. *P. reticulatus* was naturally proud of this accomplishment, but he could never get ocular proof of it. He could not be there to see the man die, and at the same time three or four miles away to bite his footprint. Yet he wanted very much to establish the truth of the experiment.

"One day he decided that he would have to rely on evidence. He persuaded a crow that was a friend of his to go off to a village of the Karens – this was the name of the men in that district – and to watch and see if the man did die while he was biting the footprint.

"Now the Karens had a curious habit of celebrating a death or funeral, not by tears and lamentations, but by laughing, singing, dancing, jumping and beating on drums. When the crow arrived to watch events from a tree, and after the man had died, the Karens began to perform their usual rites in front of the hut in which he lay stricken. So the crow, after looking on for some time, returned to the python, and reported that, so far from slaying by the venom of his bite, it had only the effect of causing extreme joy to human beings and of transporting them into the seventh heaven. The python was so furious that he climbed up to the very top of a tree and sicked up every ounce of his useless poison.

"Of course the python had to fall on something. Although the python had lost his power to sting, the tree itself became venomous – and its juice is used to this day by the Anthropophagi to poison their arrows – while several creatures which happened to be underneath it received a due share. The cobra, the water snake and the frog were among them.

"Now Aunt Eu naturally had a soft spot for her fellow mortals, and, when it was discovered that the poison was venomous after all, she upbraided *P. reticulatus* for spreading the power to slay among so many beings. *P. reticulatus*, who was grateful for his woven coat, felt remorse for what he had done, and hurried off to see how he could improve matters. He explained the nature of the poison to all the creatures which had received it, and asked them to promise that their use of it should not be tyrannical.

"The cobra agreed to the remarks of the python, and said, 'If there be transgression so as to dazzle my eyes, to make my tears fall seven times in one day, I will bite; but only then.' So said most of the kindlier creatures. But the water snake and the silly frog said that they did not see what all this had to do with the python, and that they intended, for their part to bite whenever they felt like it. The python immediately set upon them, chased them into the water, and there, of course, the poison was dissolved and washed away."

The Wart waited to see if there was any more of this story, but there was not. The voice of *T. Natrix* had been getting slower and sleepier towards the end of it, for the afternoon was advancing and the wind was beginning to fall cold. The sing-song had seemed to get more and more wrapped up in its subject, if you can follow the idea, until it seemed that the story was telling itself while the serpent only drowsed – though it was not possible to tell whether he was really asleep, because snakes have no eyelids to close.

"Thank you," said the Wart, "I think that was a good story."

"Dream about it," whispered *T. Natrix* sleepily, "while you hibernate."

"I will."

"Goodnight," said the snake.

"Goodnight."

The funny thing was that the Wart really did feel sleepy. Whether it was the voice of the snake, or the cold, or the influence of the story, in two minutes he was dreaming himself, in a reptilian drama. He was old, as old as the veins of the earth which were serpents like him, and Aesculapius with a beard as white as glaciers was lulling him to sleep. He was teaching him wisdom, the ancient wisdom, by which the old snakes can walk with three hundred feet at once upon the same world in which their grandchildren the birds have learnt to fly; he was singing to him the song of all the Waters:

> *In the great sea the stars swing over*
> *The eternal whirlpool flows.*
> *Rest, rest, wild head, in the old bosom*
> *Which neither feels nor knows.*

> *She only rocks us, cradled in heaven,*
> *The reptile and the rose.*
> *Her waters which bore us will receive us.*
> *Goodnight and sweet repose.*

In the end it took Merlyn twenty shouts, in his high human voice, to wake the sleeping serpent up in time for tea.

CHAPTER FOURTEEN

IN THE AUTUMN everybody was preparing for the winter. At night they spent most of the time rescuing daddy-long-legs from their candles and rushlights. In the daytime the cows were turned into the high stubble and weeds which have been left by the harvest sickles, while the pigs were driven into the purlieus of the forest where boys beat the trees to supply them with acorns. Everybody was at a different job. From the granary there proceeded an invariable thumping of flails; in the strip fields the slow and enormously heavy wooden ploughs sailed up and down all day for the rye and the wheat, while the sowers swung rhythmically along, with their hoffers round their necks, casting right hand for left foot and vice versa. Foraging parties came lumbering in with their spike-wheeled carts full of bracken, remarking wisely that they must:

> Get whome with ee breakes ere all summer be gone
> For tethered up cattle to sit down upon.

while others dragged in timber for the castle fires. The forest rang in the sharp air with the sound of beetle and wedge.

Everybody was happy. The villeins were slaves if you chose to look at it in one way, but, if you chose to look at it in another, they were just the same farm labourers as starve on thirty shillings a week today. Only neither the villein nor the farm labourer did starve. It has never been an economic proposition for an owner of cattle to starve his cows, so why should an owner of slaves starve them? The truth is that nowadays the farm labourer is ready to accept so little money because he does not have to throw his soul in with the bargain, as he would have to do in a town, and just the same freedom of spirit has obtained in the country since Sir Ector. The villeins were labourers; they lived in the same one-roomed hut with their families, few chickens, litter of pigs, or cow possibly called Crumbocke: most dreadful and insanitary! But they liked it. They were healthy, quite free of an air with no factory smoke in it, and, which was most of all, their heart's interest was bound up with their skill in labour. They knew that Sir Ector loved and was proud of them. They were more valuable to him than even his cattle, and, as he valued his cattle more than anything else except his children, this was saying a good deal. He walked and worked among them, thought of their welfare, and could tell the good workmen from the bad. He was the eternal farmer, in fact; one of those people who seem to be employing labour at thirty shillings a week, but is actually paying half as much again in voluntary overtime, providing a cottage free or at nominal rent, and possibly making an extra present of his milk and eggs and home-brewed beer.

Sir Ector now moved through all these activities with a brow of thunder. When an old lady who was sitting in a hedge on one of the strips of wheat, in order to scare away the rooks and pigeons, suddenly rose up beside him with an unearthly screech, he jumped a foot in the air. He was in a nervous state.

"Dang it," said Sir Ector. Then, considering the subject more attentively, he added in a loud, indignant voice, "Hell's bells and buckets of blood!" He took the letter out of his pocket and read it again.

The Overlord of the Castle of Forest Sauvage was not only a farmer. He was a military captain, of course, who was prepared to organize and lead the defence of his estate, and he was a sportsman who occasionally took a day's joustin' when he could spare the time; but he was more than these. Sir Ector was an M.F.H. – or rather a Master of stag and other hounds – and he hunted his own pack himself. Clumsy, Trowneer, Phoebe, Colle, Gerland, Talbot, Luath, Luffra, Apollon, Orthros, Bran, Gelert, Bounce, Boy, Lion, Bungey, Toby, Diamond and Cavall were not pet dogs: they were the Forest Sauvage Hounds, no subscription, two days a week, huntsman the Master.

This is what the letter said, if we translate it out of Latin:

Chapter Fourteen

The King to Sir Ector, etc.

We send you William Twyti, our huntsman, and his
fellows to hunt in the Forest Sauvage with our boar-
hounds (canibus nostris porkericis) in order that they
may capture two or three boars. You are to cause the
flesh they capture to be salted and kept in good
condition, but the skins you are to cause to be
bleached which they give you, as the said William shall
tell you. And we command you to provide necessaries
for them as long as they shall be with you by our
command, and the cost, etc., shall be accounted, etc.

Witnessed at the Tower of London, 20 November,
in the twelfth year of our reign.

UTHER PENDRAGON

12 Uther

Now the forest belonged to the King, and he had every right
to send his hounds to hunt in it. Also he maintained a large
number of hungry mouths, what with his court and his army,
so that it was natural that he would want as many dead boars,
bucks, roes, etc., to be salted down as possible.

He was perfectly in the right. All this did not take away
from the fact that Sir Ector regarded the forest as *his* forest,
however, and resented the intrusion of the royal hounds – as
if his own would not do just as well; the King had only to send
for a couple of boars and he would have been only too glad
to supply them himself. He feared that his coverts would be
disturbed by a lot of wild royal retainers – never know what

these city chaps will be up to next – and that the King's huntsman, this fellow Twyti, would sneer at his humble hunting establishment, unsettle the hunt servants and perhaps even try to interfere with his own kennel management. In fact, Sir Ector was shy. Then there was another thing. Where the devil were the royal hounds to be kept? Was he, Sir Ector, to turn his own hounds into the street, in order to put the King's hounds in his kennels? "Hell's bells and buckets of blood!" repeated the unhappy Master. It was as bad as paying tythes.

Sir Ector put the accursed letter in his pocket and stumped off up the ploughing. The villeins, seeing him go, remarked cheerfully, "Our wold measter be on the gad again seemingly."

It was a confounded piece of tyranny, that's what it was. It happened every year, but it still was that. He always solved the kennel problem in the same way, but it still worried him. He would have to invite his neighbours to the meet specially, so as to look as impressive as possible under the royal huntsman's eyes, and this would mean sendin' messengers through the forest to Sir Grummore, etc. Then he would have to show sport. The King had written early, so that evidently he intended to send the fellow at the very beginnin' of the season. The season did not begin till the 25th of December. Probably the chap would insist on one of those damned Boxin' Day meets, all show-off and no business, with hundreds of foot people all hollerin' and headin' the boar and trampin' down the seeds and spoilin' sport generally. How the devil was one to know in November where the best boars would be on

Boxin' Day? What with sounders and gorgeaunts and hogsteers, you never knew where you were. And another thing. A hound that was going to be used next summer for the proper hart huntin' was always entered at Xmas to the boar. It was the very beginnin' of its education, which led up through hares and what-nots to its real quarry, and this meant that the fellow Twyti would be bringin' down a lot of raw puppies which would be nothin' but a plague to everybody. "Dang it!" said Sir Ector, and stamped upon a piece of mud.

He stood gloomily for a moment, watching his two boys trying to catch the last leaves in the chase. They had not gone out with that intention, and did not really, even in those distant days, believe that every leaf you caught would mean a happy month next year. Only, as the west wind tore the golden rags away, they looked extremely fascinating and were difficult to catch. For the mere sport of catching them, of shouting and laughing and feeling giddy as they looked up, and of darting about to trap the creatures which were certainly alive in the cunning with which they slipped away, the two boys were prancing about like young fauns in the ruin of the year.

The only chap, reflected Sir Ector, who could really be useful in showin' the king's huntsman proper sport was that fellow Robin Hood. Robin Wood, they seemed to be callin' him now; some new-fangled idea, no doubt. But Wood or Hood, he was the chap to know where a fine tush was to be found. Been feastin' on the creatures for months now, he wouldn't be surprised, even if they were out of season.

But you couldn't very well ask a fellow to hunt up a few

beasts of venery for you, and then not invite him to the meet. While, if you did invite him to the meet, what would the King's huntsman and the neighbours say at havin' an outlaw for a fellow guest? Not that this Robin Wood wasn't a good fellow; he was a damn good fellow, and a good neighbour too. He had often tipped Sir Ector the wink when a raiding party was on its way from the marches, and never molested him or his farming in any way. What did it matter if he did chase himself a bit of venison now and then? There was forty square miles of this forest, they said, and enough for all. Leave well alone, that was Sir Ector's motto. But that didn't alter the neighbours.

Another thing was the riot. It was all very well for these crack hunts in practically artificial forests like those at Windsor, where the King hunted, but it was quite a different thing in the Forest Sauvage. Suppose His Majesty's famous hounds was to go runnin' riot after a unicorn or something? Everybody knew that you could never catch a unicorn without a young virgin for bait (in which case the unicorn meekly laid its white head and mother-of-pearl horn in her lap) and so the puppies would go chargin' off into the forest for leagues and leagues, and never catch it, and get lost, and then what would Sir Ector say to his sovereign? it wasn't only unicorns. There was this Beast Glatisant that everybody had heard so much about. If you had the head of a serpent, the body of a leopard, the haunches of a lion, and were footed like a hart, and especially if you made a noise like thirty couples of hounds qustin', it stood to reason that you would account for an excessive number of royal puppies before they pulled you down. Serve them right too. And what would King Pellinore say if Master William Twyti did succeed in killing his beast? Then there were the small dragons which lived under stones and hissed like kettles; dangerous varmints very. Or suppose they were to come across one of the really big dragons? The boy Wart had been talkin' for months about nothin' except some dragon called Atlantic something-or-other which was killed by a chap called St Georgius. Suppose they was to run into one of them? Why, the boy said it was a hundred and fifteen feet long.

Sir Ector considered the prospect moodily for some time, then began to feel better. It would be a jolly good thing, he concluded, if Master Twyti and his beastly dogs did meet Atlantic what-you-may-call-it, yes, and get eaten up by it too, every one.

Cheered by this vision, he turned round at the edge of the ploughing and stumped off home. At the hedge where the old lady lay waiting to scare rooks he was lucky enough to spot some approaching pigeons before she was aware of him or them, and let out such a screech that he felt amply repaid for his own jump by seeing hers. It was going to be a good evening after all. "Goodnight to you," said Sir Ector affably, when the old lady recovered herself enough to drop him a curtsey.

He felt so much restored by this that he dropped in on the vicar, halfway up the village street, and invited him to dinner in the hall. Then he climbed up to the solar, which was his special chamber, and sat down heavily to write a submissive message to King Uther in the two or three hours which remained to him before the meal. It would take him quite that time, what with sharpening quill pens, using too much sand to blot with, going to the top of the stairs to ask the butler how to spell things, and starting again if he made a mess.

Sir Ector sat in the solar, while the wintering sunlight threw broad orange beams across his bald head. He scratched and pluttered away, and laboriously bit the end of his pen, and the enormous castle room darkened about him. It was a room as big as the main hall over which it stood, and it could afford to have large southern windows because it was on the second storey. There were two fireplaces, in which the ashy logs of wood turned from grey to red as the sunlight retreated. Round these, some favourite hounds lay snuffling in their dreams, or scratching themselves for fleas, or gnawing mutton bones which they had scrounged from the kitchens. The peregrine falcon stood hooded on the perch in the corner, a motionless idol dreaming of other skies.

If you were to go now to view the solar of Castle Sauvage, you would find it empty of furniture; but the sun would still stream in at those stone windows two feet thick, and, as it barred the mullions, it would catch the warmth of sandstone from them: the amber light of age. If you went to the nearest curiosity shop, you might find some clever copies of the furniture which it was supposed to contain. These would be oak chests and cupboards with Gothic panelling and strange faces of men or angels – or devils – carved darkly upon them, black, bees-waxed, worm-eaten and shiny: gloomy testimonies of the old life in their coffin-like solidity. But the furniture in the solar was not like that. The devils' heads were there and the linen-fold panelling, but the wood was five or six centuries younger. So, in the warm-looking light of sunset, it was not only the millions which had an amber glow. All the spare, strong chests in the room (they were converted for sitting by laying bright carpets upon them) were the young, the golden oak, and the cheeks of the devils and cherubim shone as if they had just been given a good soaping.

CHAPTER FIFTEEN

IT WAS CHRISTMAS night, the eve of the Boxing Day Meet. You must remember that this was in the old Merry England, when the rosy barons ate with their fingers, and had peacocks served before them with all their tail feathers streaming, or boars' heads with the tusks stuck in again; when there was no unemployment because there were too few people to be unemployed; when the forests rang with knights walloping each other on the helm, and the unicorns in the wintry moonlight stamped with their silver feet and snorted their noble breaths of blue upon the frozen air. These marvels were great and comfortable ones, but in the old England there was a greater still. The weather behaved itself.

In the spring all the little flowers came out obediently in the meads, and the dew sparkled, and the birds sang; in the summer it was beautifully hot for no less than four months, and, if it did rain just enough for agricultural purposes, they managed to arrange it so that it rained while you were in bed; in the autumn the leaves flamed and rattled before the west winds, tempering their sad adieu with glory; and in the winter, which was confined by statute to two months, the snow lay evenly, three feet thick, but never turned into slush.

It was Christmas night in the Castle of the Forest Sauvage, and all around the castle the snow lay as it ought to lie. It hung heavily on the battlements, like extremely thick icing on a very good cake, and in a few convenient places it modestly turned itself into the clearest icicles of the greatest possible length. It hung on the boughs of the forest trees in rounded lumps, even better than apple-blossom, and occasionally slid off the roofs of the village when it saw a chance of falling upon some amusing character and giving pleasure to all. The boys made snowballs with it, but never put stones in them to hurt each other, and the dogs, when they were taken out to scombre, bit it and tolled in it and looked surprised but delighted when they vanished into the bigger drifts. There was skating on the moat, which roared all day with the gliding steel, while hot chestnuts and spiced mead were served on the bank to all and sundry. The owls hooted. The cooks put out all the crumbs they could for the small birds. The villagers brought out their red mufflers. Sir Ector's face shone redder even than these. And reddest of all shone the cottage fires all down the main street of an evening, while the winds howled outside and the old English wolves wandered about slavering in an appropriate manner, or sometimes peeping in at the keyholes with their blood-red eyes.

It was Christmas night and all the proper things had been done. The whole village had come to dinner in the hall. There had been boar's head and venison and pork and beef and mutton and capons; but no turkey, on account of this bird not having yet been invented. There had been plum pudding and snap-dragon, with blue fire on the tips of one's fingers, and as much mead as anybody could drink. Sir Ector's health had been drunk with "Best respects, Measter," or with "Best compliments of the Season, my lords and ladies, and many of them." There had been mummers to play the exciting dramatic presentation of a story in which St George and a Saracen and a very funny Doctor did some surprising things, also carol-singers who rendered "Adeste Fideles" and "I Sing of a Maiden," in high, clear tenor voices. After that, those children who had not been sick over their dinner played Hoodman Blind and other appropriate games, while the young men and maidens danced Morris dances in the middle, the tables having been cleared away. The old folks sat round the walls holding glasses of mead in their hands and feeling thankful that they were past all such capers, hoppings and skippings, while those children who had been sick sat with them, and soon went to sleep, the small heads leaning against their shoulders. At the high table Sir Ector sat with his knightly guests, who had come for the morrow's hunting, smiling and nodding and drinking burgundy or sherries sack or malmsey wine.

After a bit, silence was prayed for Sir Grummore. He stood

up and sang his old school song, amidst great applause, but forgot most of it and had to make a humming noise in his moustache. The King Pellinore was nudged to his feet and sang bashfully:

> *Oh, Ay was born a Pellinore in famous Lincolnshire.*
> *Full well Ay chased the Questing Beast for more*
> > *than seventeen year.*
> *Till Ay took up with Sir Grummore here*
> *In the season of the year.*
> *(Since when) 'tis my delight*
> *On a feather bed night*
> *To sleep at home, my dear.*

"You see," explained King Pellinore blushing, as he sat down with everybody whacking him on the back, "old Grummore invited me home, what, after we had been having a splendid joust together, and since then Ay've been letting my beastly Beast go and hang itself on the wall, what?"

"Well done," they all told him. "You live your own life while you've got it."

William Twyti was called for, who had arrived on the previous evening, and the famous huntsman stood up with a perfectly straight face, and his crooked eye fixed upon Sir Ector, to sing:

> *D'ye ken William Twyti*
> > *With his jerkin so dagged?*

D'ye ken William Twyti
  Who never yet lagged?
Yes, I ken William Twyti
  An he ought to be gagged
With his hounds and his horn in the morning.

"Bravo!" cried Sir Ector. "Did you hear that, eh? Said he ought to be gagged, my deah fellah. Blest if I didn't think he was going to boast when he began. Splendid chaps these huntsmen, eh? Pass Master Twyti the malmsey with my compliments."

The boys lay curled under the benches near the fire, Wart with Cavall in his arms. Cavall did not like the heat and the shouting and the smell of mead, and wanted to go away, but Wart held him tightly because he needed something to hug, and Cavall had to stay with him perforce, panting over a long pink tongue.

"Now, Ralph Passelewe," cried Sir Ector, and all his villeins cried "Ralph Passelewe." "Good wold Ralph." "Who killed the cow, Ralph?" "Pray silence for Master Passelewe that couldn't help it."

At this the most lovely old man got up at the very furthest and humblest end of the hall, as he had got up on all similar occasions for the past half-century. He was no less than eighty-seven years of age, almost blind, almost dumb, almost deaf, but still able and willing and happy to quaver out the same old song which he had sung for the pleasure of the Forest Sauvage since before Sir Ector was bound up in a kind of a tight linen

puttee in his cradle. They could not hear him at the high table
– he was much too far away in Time to be able to reach across
a room – but everybody knew what the cracked old voice was
singing, and everybody loved it. This is what he sang:

> *Whe – an/Wold King – Cole/was a /wakkin-doon-t'street,*
> *H – e/saw -a-lovely laid-y a/steppin-in-a-puddle. /*
> *She – e/lifted hup-er-skeat/*
> *For to/*
> *Hop acrost ter middle, /*
> *An ee/saw her/an-kel.*
> *Wasn't that a fuddle?/*
> *Ee could'ernt elp it, /ee Ad to.*

There were about twenty verses of this song, in which Wold
King Cole helplessly saw more and more things that he ought
not to have seen, and everybody cheered at the end of each
verse until, at the conclusion, old Ralph was overwhelmed
with congratulations and sat down smiling dimly to a
replenished mug of mead.

It was now Sir Ector's turn to wind up the proceedings.
He stood up importantly and delivered the following speech:

"Friends, tenants and otherwise. Unaccustomed as I am to
public speakin' – "

There was a faint cheer at this, for everybody recognized
the speech which Sir Ector had made for the last twenty years,
and welcomed it like a brother.

"Unaccustomed as I am to public speakin', it is my pleasant

duty – I might say my *very* pleasant duty – to welcome all and sundry to this our homely feast. It has bin a good year, and I say it without fear of contradiction, in pasture and plough. We all know how Crumbocke of Forest Sauvage won the first prize at Cardoyle Cattle Show for the second time, and one more year will win the cup outright. More power to the Forest Sauvage. As we sit down tonight, I notice some faces now gone from amongst us and some which have added to the family circle. Such matters are in the hands of an almighty Providence, to which we all feel thankful. We ourselves have been first created and then spared to enjoy the rejoicin's of this pleasant evening. I think we are all grateful for the blessin's which have been showered upon us. Tonight we welcome in our midst the famous King Pellinore, whose labours in riddin' our forest of the redoubtable Questin' Beast are known to us all. God bless King Pellinore. (Hear, hear.) Also Sir Grummore Grummursum, a sportsman, though I say it to his face, who will stick to his mount as long as his Quest will stand up in front of him. (Hooray!) Finally, last but not least, we are honoured by a visit from His Majesty's most famous huntsman, Master William Twyti, who will, I feel sure, show us such sport tomorrow that we will rub our eyes and wish that a royal pack of hounds could always be huntin' in the Forest which we all love so well. (View-halloo and several recheats blown in imitation.) Thank you, my dear friends, for your spontaneous welcome to these gentlemen. They will, I know, accept it in the true and warm-hearted spirit in which it is offered. And now it is time that I should bring my brief remarks to a close. Another year has almost sped and it is time that we should be lookin' forward to the challengin' future. What about the Cattle Show next year? Friends, I can only wish you a very Merry Christmas, and, after Reverent Sidebottom has said our grace for us, we shall conclude with a singin' of the National Anthem."

The cheers which broke out at the end of Sir Ector's speech were only just prevented, by several hush-es, from drowning the last part of the vicar's grace in Latin, and then everybody stood up loyally in the firelight and sang:

> *God save King Pendragon,*
> *May his reign long drag on,*
>   *God save the King.*
> *Send him most glorious,*
> *Great and uproarious,*
> *Horrible and hoarious,*
>   *God save our King.*

The last notes died away, the hall emptied of its rejoicing humanity. Lanterns flickered outside, in the village street, as everybody went home in bands for fear of the moonlit wolves, and the Castle of the Forest Sauvage slept peacefully and lightless, in the strange silence of the holy snow.

Chapter Sixteen

THE WART GOT up very early the next morning. He made a determined effort the moment he woke up, threw off the great bearskin rug under which he slept, and plunged his body into the biting air. He dressed furiously, trembling, skipping about to keep warm, and hissing blue breaths to himself as if he were grooming a horse. He broke the ice in a basin and dipped his face in it with a grimace like eating something sour, said A-a-ah, and rubbed his stinging cheeks vigorously with a towel. Then he felt quite warm again and scampered off to the emergency kennels to watch the King's huntsman making his last arrangements.

Master William Twyti turned out in daylight to be a shrivelled, harassed-looking man, with an expression of deep melancholy on his face. All his life he had been forced to pursue various animals for the royal table, and, when he had caught them, to cut them up into the various joints. He was more than half a butcher. He had to know what parts the hounds should eat, and what parts should be given to his various assistants. He had to cut everything up handsomely, leaving two vertebrae on the tail to make the chine look attractive, and almost ever since he could remember he had been either pursuing a hart or cutting it up into joints. He was not particularly fond of doing this. The harts and the hinds in their herds, the boars in their singulars, the skulks of foxes, the richesses of martens, the bevies of roes, the cetes of badgers and the routs of wolves; all came to him more or less as something which you either skinned or flayed and then took home to the cook. You could talk to him about os and argos, suet and grease, croteys, fewmets and fiants, but he only looked polite. He knew that you were showing off your knowledge of these words, which were to him a business. You could talk about a mighty boar which had nearly slashed you last winter, but he only stared at you with his distant eyes: He had been slashed sixteen times by mighty boars, and his legs had white weals of shiny flesh that stretched right up to his ribs. While you talked, he got on with whatever part of his profession he had in hand. There was only one thing which could move Master William Twyti. Summer or winter, snow or shine, he was running or galloping after boars and harts, and all the time his soul was somewhere else. Mention a *hare* to Master Twyti and, although he would still go on galloping after the wretched hart which seemed to be his destiny, he would gallop with one eye over his shoulder yearning for puss. It was the only thing he ever talked about. He was always being sent to one castle or another, all over England, and when he was there the local servants would fête him and keep his glass filled and ask him about his greatest hunts. He would answer distractedly in monosyllables. But if anybody mentioned a huske of hares he was all attention, and then he would thump his glass upon the table and discourse upon the marvels of this astonishing beast, declaring that you could never blow a menee for it, because the same hare could at one time be male and another time female, while it carried grease and croteyed and gnawed, which things no beast in the earth did except it.

Wart watched the great man in silence for some time, then went indoors to see if there was any hope of breakfast. He found that there was, for the whole castle was suffering from the same sort of nervous excitement which had got him out of bed so early, and even Merlyn had dressed himself in a pair of running shorts to see the fun.

Boar-hunting was fun. It was nothing like badger-digging or covert-shooting or fox-hunting today. Perhaps the nearest thing to it would be ferreting for rabbits: except that you used dogs instead of ferrets, had a boar that quite easily might kill you, instead of a rabbit, and carried a boar-spear upon which your life depended instead of a gun. They did not usually hunt the boar on horseback. Perhaps the reason for this was that the boar season happened in the two winter months, when the old English snow would be liable to ball in your horse's hoofs and render galloping too dangerous. The result was that you were yourself on foot, armed only with steel, against an adversary who weighed a good deal more than you did and who could unseam you from the nave to the chaps, and set your head upon his battlements. There was only one rule in boar-hunting. It was: Hold on. If the boar charged you, you had to drop on one knee and present your boar-spear in his direction. You held the butt of it with your right hand on the ground to take the shock, while you stretched your left arm to its fullest extent and held the spear tightly with it, as high up as possible. You kept the point towards the charging boar. The spear was as sharp as a razor, and it had a cross-piece about eighteen inches away from the point. This cross-piece or horizontal bar prevented the spear from going more than eighteen inches into his chest. Without the cross-piece, a charging boar would have been capable of rushing right up the spear, even if it did go through him, and getting at you like that. But with the cross-piece he was held away from you at a spear's length, with eighteen inches of steel inside him. It was in this situation that you had to hold on.

He weighed between ten and twenty score, and his one object in life was to heave and weave and sidestep, until he could get at you and champ you into chops, while your one object was not to let go of the spear, clasped tight under your arm, until somebody had come to finish him off. If only you could keep hold of your end of the spear, while the other end was stuck in him, you knew that there was at least a spear's length between you, however much he ran you round the forest. You may be able to understand, if you think this over, why all the sportsmen of the castle got up early for the Boxing

Day Meet, and ate their breakfast with a certain amount of suppressed feeling.

"Ah," said Sir Grummore, gnawing a pork chop which he held in his fingers, "down in time for breakfast, hey?"

"Yes, I am," said the Wart.

"Fine huntin' mornin'," said Sir Grummore. "Got your spear sharp, hey?"

"Yes, I have, thank you," said the Wart. He went over to the sideboard to get a chop for himself.

"Come on, Pellinore," said Sir Ector. "Have a few of these chickens. You're eatin' nothin' this mornin'."

King Pellinore said, "Ay don't think Ay will, thank you all the same. Ay don't think Ay feel quite the thing, this morning, what?"

Sir Grummore took his nose out of his chop, and inquired sharply, "Nerves?"

"Oh, no," cried King Pellinore. "Oh, no, really not that, what? Ay think Ay must have taken something last night that disagreed with me."

"Nonsense, my dear fellah," said Sir Ector, "here, you just have a few chickens to keep your strength up."

He helped the unfortunate King to two or three capons, and the latter sat down miserably at the end of the table, trying to swallow down a few bits of them.

"Need them," said Sir Grummore meaningly, "by the end of the day, I daresay."

"Do you think so?" asked King Pellinore anxiously.

"Know so," said Sir Grummore, and winked at his host.

The Wart, however, noticed that both Sir Ector and Sir Grummore were eating with rather exaggerated gusto. He did not himself feel that he could manage more than one chop, and, as for Kay, he had stayed away from the breakfast-room altogether.

When breakfast was over, and Master Twyti had been consulted, the Boxing Day cavalcade moved off to the Meet. Perhaps the hounds would have seemed rather a mixed pack to the Master of the Quorn today. There were half a dozen black and white alaunts, which looked like greyhounds with the heads of bull-terriers or worse. These, which were the proper hounds for boars, wore muzzles on account of their ferocity. The gaze-hounds of which there were two taken just in case, were in reality nothing but greyhounds according to modern language, while the lymers were a sort of mixture between the bloodhound and the red setter of today. The latter had collars on, and were led with straps. The brachets were just like beagles, and trotted along with the master in the way that beagles always have trotted, and a charming way it is.

With the hounds went the foot people. Merlin, in his running shorts, looked rather like Lord Baden-Powell, only, of course, the latter has not got a beard. Sir Ector was dressed in "sensible" leather clothes – it was not considered sporting to hunt in armour – and he walked beside Master Twyti with that bothered and important expression which has always been worn by masters of hounds. Sir Grummore, just behind, was puffing rather and asking everybody whether they had sharpened their spears. King Pellinore had dropped back right among the villagers, feeling that there was safety in numbers. And all the villagers were there, every male soul on the estate from Hob the austringer down to old Wat with no nose, all carrying spears or pitchforks or old scythe blades or stout poles. Even some of the young women who were courting had come out, with baskets of provisions for their men. It was a regular Boxing Day Meet.

At the edge of the forest the last follower joined up. He was a tall and distinguished-looking person dressed in green, and he carried a seven-foot bow.

"Good morning, Master," he said pleasantly to Sir Ector.

"Ah, yes," said Sir Ector. "Yes, yes, good mornin', eh? Yes, good mornin'."

Then he led the gentleman in green aside and said in a loud whisper that could be heard by everybody, "For heaven's sake, my dear fellow, do be careful. This is the King's own huntsman, and those two other chaps are King Pellinore and Sir Grummore. Now do be a good chap, my dear fellow, and don't say anything controversial, will you, old boy, there's a good chap?"

"Certainly I won't," said the green man reassuringly. "But I think you had better introduce me to them."

Sir Ector blushed deeply and called out: "Ah, Grummore, come over here a minute, will you? I want to introduce a friend of mine, old chap, a chap called Wood, old chap – Wood with a W, you know, not an H. Yes, and this is King Pellinore. Master Wood – King Pellinore."

"Hail," said King Pellinore, who had not quite got out of the habit when nervous.

"How do," said Sir Grummore. "No relation to Robin Hood, I suppose?"

"Oh, not in the least," interrupted Sir Ector hastily. "Double you, double owe, dee, you know, like the stuff they make furniture out of − furniture, you know, and spears, and − well − spears, you know, and furniture."

"How do you do," said Robin.

"Hail," said King Pellinore.

"Well," said Sir Grummore. "it's funny you should both wear green."

"Yes, it is funny, isn't it?" said Sir Ector anxiously. "He wears it in mournin' for an aunt of his, who died by fallin' out of a tree."

"Beg pardon, I'm sure," said Sir Grummore, grieved at having touched upon this tender subject; and all was well.

"Now, then, Mr Wood," said Sir Ector when he had recovered himself. "Where shall we go for our first draw?"

As soon as this question had been put, Master Twyti was fetched into the conversation, and a brief confabulation followed in which all sorts of techinical terms like "lesses" were bandied about. Then there was a long walk in the wintry forest, and the fun began.

Wart had lost the rather panickly feeling which had taken hold of his stomach when he was breaking his fast. The exercise and the snow-wind had breathed him, so that his eyes sparkled almost as brilliantly as the frost crystals in the white winter sunlight and his blood raced with the excitement of the chase. He watched the lymerer who held the two bloodhound-dogs on their leashes, and saw the dogs straining more and more as the boar's lair was approached. He saw how, one by one and ending with the gaze-hounds who did not hunt by scent, the various hounds became uneasy and began to whimper with desire. He noticed Robin pause and pick up some lesses, which he handed to Master Twyti, and then the whole cavalcade came to a halt. They had reached the dangerous spot.

Boar-hunting was like cub-hunting to this extent, that the boar was attempted to be held up. The object of the hunt was to kill him as quickly as possible. Wart took up his position in the circle round the monster's lair, and knelt down on one knee in the snow, with the handle of his spear couched on the ground, ready for emergencies. He felt the hush which fell upon the company and saw Master Twyti wave silently to the lymerer to uncouple his hounds. The two lymers plunged immediately into the covert which the hunters surrounded. They ran mute.

There were five long minutes during which nothing happened. The hearts beat thunderously in the circle, and a small vein on the side of each neck throbbed in harmony with each heart. The heads turned quickly from side to side, as each man assured himself of his neighbours, and the breath of life steamed away on the north wind most sweetly, as each realized how beautiful life was, which a reeking tusk might, in a few seconds, rape away from one or another of them if things went wrong.

The boar did not this time express his fury with his voice. There was no uproar in the covert or yelping from the lymers.

Only, about a hundred yards away from the Wart, there was suddenly a black creature standing on the edge of the clearing. It did not seem to be a boar particularly, not in the first seconds that it stood there. It had come too quickly to appear to be anything. It was charging Sir Grummore before the Wart had recognized what it was.

The black thing rushed over the white snow, throwing up little puffs of it. Sir Grummore, also looking black against the snow, turned a quick somersault in a rather large puff. A kind of grunt, but no noise of falling, came clearly on the north wind, and then the boar was gone. When it was gone, but not before, the Wart knew certain things about it: things which he had not had time to notice while the boar was there. He remembered the rank mane of bristles standing upright on its razor back, one flash of a sour tush, the staring ribs, the head held low, and a red flame from a piggy eye.

Sir Grummore got up, dusting snow out of himself unhurt, blaming his spear: a few drops of blood were to be seen frothing on the white earth. Master Twyti put his horn to his lips. The alaunts were uncoupled as the exciting notes of the menee began to ring through the forest, and then the whole scene began to move. The lymers which had reared the boar – the proper word for dislodging – were allowed to pursue him to make them keen on their work: the brachets gave musical tongue: the alaunts galloped baying through the drifts; everybody began to shout and run.

"Avoy, avoy!" cried the foot people. "Shahou, shahou! Avaunt, sire, avaunt."

"Swef, swef!" cried Master Twyti anxiously. "Now, now, gentlemen, give the hounds room *if* you please."

"Ay say, Ay say!" cried King Pellinore. "Did anybody see which way he went? What an exciting day, what? Sa sa cy avaunt, sa cy avaunt, sa cy avaunt!"

"Hold hard, Pellinore." cried Sir Ector. " 'Ware hounds, 'ware hounds. Can't catch him yourself, you know. Il est hault-t-il est hault!"

And "Til est ho," echoed the foot people. "Tilly-ho," sang the trees. "Tally-ho," murmured the distant snowdrifts as the heavy branches disturbed by the vibrations, slid noiseless puffs of sparkling powder on to the muffled earth.

The Wart found himself running with Master Twyti.

It was like beagling in a way, except that it was beagling in a forest where it was sometimes difficult even to move. Everything depended on the music of the hounds and the various notes which the huntsman could blow to tell where he was and what he was doing. Without these the whole field would have been lost in two minutes; and even with them about half of it was lost in three.

Wart stuck to Twyti like a burr. He could move as quickly as the huntsman because, although the latter possessed the experience of a lifetime, he himself was smaller to get through obstacles and had, moreover, been taught by Maid Marian. He noticed that Robin kept up too, but soon the grunting of Sir Ector and the baa-ing of King Pellinore was left behind. Sir Grummore had given in early, having had most of the breath knocked out of him by the boar, and stood far in the rear declaring that his spear could no longer be quite sharp. Kay had stayed with him, so that he should not get lost. The foot people had been early mislaid because they did not understand the notes of the horn. Merlyn had torn his shorts and stopped to try and mend them again by magic. The sergeant had thrown out his chest so far in crying Tally-ho and telling everybody which way they ought to run that he had soon lost all sense of place, and was leading a disconsolate party of villagers, in Indian file, at the double, with knees up, in the wrong direction. Hob was still in the running.

"Swef, swef," panted the huntsman again, addressing the Wart as if he had been a hound. "Not so fast, Master, they are going off the line."

Even as he spoke, Wart noticed that the hound music was weaker and more querulous.

"Stop," said Robin, "or we may tumble over him."

The music died away.

"Swef, swef!" shouted Master Twyti at the top of his voice. "Sto arere, so howe, so howe!" He swung his baldrick in front of him and, lifting the horn to his lips, began to blow a recheat.

There was a single note from one of the lymers.

"Hoo arere," cried the huntsman.

The lymer's note grew in confidence, faltered, then rose the full bay.

"Hoo arere! Here, how, amy. Hark to Beaumont the valiant! Ho moy, ho moy, hole, hole, hole, hole!"

The lymer was taken up by the tenor bells of the braches.

The noise grew to a crescendo of excitement as the bloodthirsty thunder of the alaunts pealed through the lesser notes.

"They have him," said Twyti briefly, and the three humans began to run again, while the huntsman blew encouragement with Trou-rou-root.

In a small bushment the grimly boar stood at bay. He had got his hind quarters into the nook of a tree blown down by a gale, in an impregnable position. He stood on the defensive with his upper jaw writhed back in a snarl. The blood of Sir Grummore's gash welled fatly among the bristles of his shoulder and down his leg, while the foam of his chops dropped on the blushing snow and melted it. His small eyes darted in every direction. The hounds stood round, yelling at his hateful mask, and Beaumont, with his back broken, writhed at his feet. He paid no further attention to the living hound, for it could do no harm. He was black, flaming and bloody.

"So-ho," said the huntsman softly.

He advanced upon the murderer with his spear held out in front of him, and the hounds encouraged by their master, stepped forward with him pace by pace.

The scene changed as suddenly as a house of cards falling down. The boar was not at bay any more, but charging Master Twyti. As it charged the alaunts closed in, seizing it fiercely by shoulder or throat or leg, so that what surged down on the huntsman was not one boar but a bundle of animals. He dared not use his spear for fear of hurting the dogs. The bundle rolled forward remorselessly, as if the hounds did not impede it at all. Twyti began to reverse his spear, to keep the charge off with its butt end, but even as he reversed it the tussle was upon him. He sprang back, tripped over a root, and the battle closed on top. The Wart pranced round the edge, waving his own spear in an agony, but there was nowhere he dared to thrust it in. Robin dropped his spear, drew his falchion in the same movement, stepped into the huddle of snarls, and calmly picked an alaunt up by the leg. The dog did not let go, but there was space where its body had been. Into this space the falchion went slowly, once, twice, thrice. The whole superstructure stumbled, recovered itself, stumbled again, and sank down ponderously on its left side. The hunt was over.

Master William Twyti drew one leg slowly from under the boar, stood up, took hold of his knee with his right hand, moved it inquiringly in various directions, nodded to himself and stretched his back straight. Then he picked up his spear without saying anything and limped over towards Beaumont. He knelt down beside him and took his head on his lap. He stroked Beaumont's head and said, "Hark to Beaumont. Softly Beaumont, *mon ami*. Oyez à Beaumont the valiant, Swef, *le douce* Beaumont, swef, swef." Beaumont licked his hand but could not wag his tail. The huntsman nodded to Robin, who was standing behind, and held the hound's eyes with his own. He said, "Good dog, Beaumont the valiant, sleep now, old friend Beaumont, good old dog." Then Robin's falchion let Beaumont out of this world, to run free with Orion and to roll among the stars.

The Wart did not like to watch Master Twyti for a moment or two. The strange, little leathery man stood up without saying anything and whipped the hounds off the corpse of the boar as he was accustomed to do. He put his horn to his lips and blew the four long notes of the mort without a quaver. But he was blowing the notes for something else, and he startled the Wart because he seemed to be crying.

The mort brought most of the stragglers up in due time. Hob was there already and Sir Ector came up next, whacking the brambles aside with his boar-spear, puffing importantly and shouting, "Well done, Twyti. Splendid hunt, very. That's the way to chase a beast of venery, I will say. What does he weigh?" The others dribbled in by batches, King Pellinore bounding along and crying out, "Tally-ho! tally-ho! tally-ho!" in ignorance that the hunt was done. When informed of this fact, he stopped and said "Tally-ho, what?" in a feeble voice, then relapsed into silence. Even the sergeant's Indian file arrived in the end, still doubling with knees up, and were halted in the clearing while the sergeant explained to them with great satisfaction that if it had not been for him, all would have been lost. Merlyn appeared, holding up his running shorts, having failed in his magic. Sir Grummore came stumping along with Kay, saying that it had been one of the finest points he had ever seen run, although he had not seen it, and then the butcher's business of the "undoing" was proceeded with apace.

Over this there was a bit of excitement. King Pellinore, who had really been scarcely himself all day, made the fatal mistake of asking when the hounds were going to be given their quarry? Now, as everybody knows, a quarry is a reward of entrails, etc., which is given to the hounds *on the hide of the dead beast (sur le quir)*, and, as everybody else knows, a slain boar is not skinned. It is disembowelled without the hide being taken off, and, since there can be no hide, there can be no quarry. We all know that the hounds are rewarded with a *fouail*, a mixture of bowels and bread cooked over a fire, and, of course, poor King Pellinore had used the wrong word.

So King Pellinore's trousers were taken down amid loud huzzas, and the protesting monarch was bent over the dead beast and given a hearty smack with a sword blade by Sir Ector. King Pellinore then said, "Ay do think you are all a lot of beastly cads," and wandered off mumbling into the forest.

The boar was undone, the hounds rewarded, and the foot people, standing about in chattering groups because they would have got wet if they had sat down in the snow, ate the provisions which the young women had brought in baskets. A small barrel of wine which had been thoughtfully provided by Sir Ector was broached, and a good drink was had by all. The boar's feet were tied together, a pole was slipped between its legs, and two men hoisted it upon their shoulders. William Twyti stood back, and courteously blew the *prise*.

It was at this moment that King Pellinore reappeared. Even before he came into view they could hear him crashing in the undergrowth and calling out, "Ay say, Ay say! Come here at once! A most dreadful thing has happened!" He appeared dramatically upon the edge of the clearing, just as a disturbed branch, whose burden was too heavy, emptied a couple of hundredweight of snow upon his head. King Pellinore paid no attention. He climbed out of the snow heap as if he had not noticed it, still calling out "Ay say! Ay say!"

"What is it, Pellinore?" shouted Sir Ector.

"Oh, come quick," cried the King and, turning round distracted, he vanished again into the forest.

"Is he all right?" inquired Sir Ector, "do you suppose?"

"Excitable character," said Sir Grummore. "Very."

"Better follow up and see what he's doin'."

The procession moved off sedately in King Pellinore's direction, following his erratic course by the fresh tracks in the snow.

The spectacle which they came across was one for which they were not prepared. In the middle of a dead gorse bush King Pellinore was sitting, with tears streaming down his face. In his lap there was an enormous snake's head, which he was patting. At the other end of the snake's head there was a long, lean, yellow body with spots on it. At the end of the body there were some lion's legs which ended in the slots of a hart.

"There, there," King Pellinore was saying. "Ay didn't mean to leave you altogether. It was only because Ay wanted to sleep in a feather bed, just for a bit. Ay was coming back, honestly Ay was. Oh, please don't die, Beast, and leave me without any fewmets."

When he saw Sir Ector, the King took command of the situation. Desperation had given him authority.

"Now, then, Ector," he exclaimed. "Don't stand there like

a ninny. Fetch that barrel of wine along at once."

They brought the barrel and poured out a generous tot for the Questing Beast.

"Poor creature," said King Pellinore indignantly. "It's pined away, positively pined away, just because there was nobody to take an interest in it. How Ay could have stayed all that while with Sir Grummore and never given my old beast a thought Ay really don't know. Look at its ribs, Ay ask you. Like the hoops of a barrel. And lying out in the snow all by itself, almost without the will to live. Come on, Beast, you see if you can't get down another gulp of this. It will do you good.

"Mollocking about in a feather bed," added the remorseful monarch, glaring at Sir Grummore, "like a – like a kidney!"

"But how did you – how did you find it?" faltered Sir Grummore.

"Ay *happened* on it. And small thanks to you. Running about like a lot of nincompoops and smacking each other with swords. Ay happened on it in this gorse bush here, with snow all over its poor back and tears in its eyes and nobody to care for it in the wide world. It's what comes of not leading a regular life. Before, it was all right. We got up at the same time, and quested for regular hours, and went to bed at half-past ten. Now look at it. It's gone to pieces altogether, and it will be your fault if it dies. You and your hummocky bed."

"But, Pellinore," said Sir Grummore.

"Shut your mouth," replied the King at once. "Don't stand there bleating like a fool, man. Do something. Fetch another pole so that we can carry old Glatisant home. Now, then,

Ector, haven't you got any sense? We must just carry him home and put him in front of the kitchen fire. Send somebody on to make some bread and milk. And you, Twyti, or whatever you choose to call yourself, stop fiddling with that trumpet of yours and run ahead to get some blankets warmed.

"When we get home," concluded King Pellinore, "the first thing will be to give it a nourishing meal, and then, if it's all right in the morning, Ay'll give it a couple of hours' start and then hey-ho for the old life once again. What about that, Glatisant, hey? You'll tak' the high road and Ay'll tak' the low road, what? Come along, Robin Hood, or whoever you are — you may think Ay don't know, but Ay do — stop leaning on your bow with that look of negligent woodcraft. Pull yourself together, man, and get that muscle-bound sergeant to help you carry her. Now then, lift her easy. Come along, you chuckle-heads, and mind you don't trip. Feather beds and quarry, indeed; a lot of childish nonsense. Go on, advance, proceed, step forward, march! Feather brains, Ay call it, that's what *Ay* do.

"And as for you, Grummore," added the King, even after he had concluded, "you can just roll yourself up in your feather bed and stifle in it."

CHAPTER SEVENTEEN

"I THINK IT is time," said Merlyn looking at him over the top of his spectacles one afternoon, "that you had another dose of education. That is, as Time goes."

It was an afternoon in early spring and everything outside the window looked most beautiful. The winter mantle had gone, taking with it Sir Grummore, Master Twyti, King Pellinore and the Questing Beast, the latter having revived under the influence of kindliness and bread and milk. It had bounded off into the snow with every sign of gratitude, to be followed two hours later by the excited King, and the watchers from the battlements had observed it confusing its snowy footprints most ingeniously, as it reached the edge of the chase — it was running backwards, bounding twenty foot sideways, rubbing out its marks with its tail, climbing along horizontal branches, and performing many other tricks with evident enjoyment. They had also seen King Pellinore, who had dutifully kept his eyes shut and counted ten thousand while this was going on, becoming quite confused when he arrived at the difficult spot, and finally galloping off in the wrong direction with his brachet trailing behind him.

It was a lovely afternoon. Outside the schoolroom window the larches of the distant forest had already assumed the fullness of their dazzling green, the earth twinkled and swelled with a million drops, and every bird in the world had come home to court and sing. The village folk were forth in their gardens every evening, planting garden beans, and it seemed that, what with these emergencies and those of the slugs (coincidentally with the beans), the buds, the lambs, and the birds, every living thing had conspired to come out.

"What would you like to be?" asked Merlyn.

Wart looked out of the window, listening to the thrush's twice-done song of dew.

He said, "I have been a bird once, but it was only in the mews at night, and I never got a chance to fly. Even if one ought not to do one's education, twice, don't you think I could be a bird so as to learn about that?"

He had been bitten with the craze for birds which bites all sensible people in the spring, and which sometimes even leads to such excesses as birds' nesting, etc.

"I can see no reason why you shouldn't," said the magician. "Why not try it at night?"

"But they will all be asleep at night."

"All the better chance of inspecting them without their

flying away. You could go with Archimedes this evening, and he would tell you about them."

"Would you do that, Archimedes?"

"I should love to," said the owl. "I was feeling like a little saunter myself."

"Do you know," asked the Wart, thinking of the thrush, "why birds sing, or how? Is it a language?"

"Of course it's a language. It isn't a big language like human speech, but it's large."

"Gilbert White," said Merlyn, "remarks, or will remark, however you like to put it, that 'the language of birds is very ancient, and, like other ancient modes of speech, little is said, but much is intended.' He also says somewhere that 'the rooks, in the breeding season, attempt sometimes, in the gaiety of their hearts, to sing – but with no great success.' "

"I love rooks," said the Wart. "It's funny, but I think they are my favourite bird."

"Why?" asked Archimedes.

"Well, I like them. I like their sauce."

"Neglectful parents," quoted Merlyn, who was in a scholarly mood, "and saucy, perverse children."

"It is true," said Archimedes reflectively, "that all the Corvidae possess a distorted sense of humour."

Wart explained.

"I love the way they enjoy flying. They don't just fly, like other birds, but they fly for fun. It is lovely when they hoist home to bed in a flock at night, all cheering and making rude remarks and pouncing on each other in a vulgar way. They turn over on their backs sometimes and tumble out of the air, just to be ridiculous, or else because they have forgotten they are flying and have coarsely begun to scratch themselves for fleas, without thinking about it."

"They are intelligent birds," said Archimedes, "in spite of their humour. They are one of the birds that have parliaments, you know, and a social system."

"Do you mean that they have laws?"

"Certainly they have laws. They meet in the autumn, in a field, to talk them over."

"What sort of laws?"

"Oh, well, laws about the defence of the rookery, and marriage, and so forth. You are not allowed to marry outside the rookery, and, if you do become quite lost to all sense of decency, and bring back a sable virgin from a neighbouring settlement, then everybody pulls your nest to pieces as fast as you can build it up. They make you go into the suburbs, you know, and that is why every rookery has out-lying nests all round it, several trees away."

"Another thing I like about them," said the Wart, "is their Go. They may be thieves and practical jokers, and they do quarrel and bully each other in a squawky way, but they have got the courage to mob their enemies. I should think it takes some courage to mob a hawk, even if there is a pack of you. And even while they are doing it they clown."

"They are mobs," said Archimedes loftily. "You have said the word."

"Well, they are larky mobs, anyway," said the Wart, "and I

like them!"

"What is your favourite bird?" asked Merlyn politely, to keep the peace.

Archimedes thought this over for some time, and then said, "Well, it's a large question, you know. It's rather like asking you what is your favourite book. On the whole, however, I think that I must prefer the pigeon."

"To eat?"

"I was leaving that side of it out," said the owl in civilized tones. "Actually the pigeon is the favourite dish of all raptors if they are big enough to take her, but I was thinking of nothing but domestic habits."

"Describe them."

"The pigeon," said Archimedes, "is a kind of Quaker. She dresses in grey. A dutiful child, a constant lover, and a wise parent, she knows like all philosophers that the hand of every man is against her. She has learnt throughout the centuries to specialize in escape. No pigeon has ever committed an act of aggression nor turned upon her persecutors; but no bird, likewise, is so skilful in eluding them. She has learnt to drop out of a tree on the opposite side to man, and to fly so that there is a hedge between them. No other bird can estimate a range so well. Vigilant, powdery, odorous and loose-feathered so that dogs object to take them in their mouths, armoured against pellets by the closeness of these feathers, the pigeons coo to one another with true love, nourish their cunningly hidden children with true solicitude, and flee from the aggressor with true philosophy, a race of peace lovers continually caravaning away from the destructive Indian in covered waggons. They are loving individualists surviving against the forces of massacre only by wisdom in escape.

"Did you know," added Archimedes, "that a pair of pigeons always roosts head to tail, so that they can keep a look-out in both directions?"

"I know our tame pigeons do," said the Wart. "What I like about wood-pigeons is the clap of their wings, and how they soar up and close their wings and sink, during their courting flights, so that they fly rather like woodpeckers."

"It isn't very like woodpeckers," said Merlyn.

"No, it isn't," admitted the Wart.

"And what is your favourite bird?" asked Archimedes, feeling that his master ought to be allowed a say.

Merlyn put his fingers together like Sherlock Holmes and replied immediately, "I prefer the chaffinch. My friend Linnaeus calls him *coelebs* or bachelor bird. The flocks have the sense to separate during the winter, so that all the males are in one flock and all the females in the other. For the winter months at any rate, there is perfect peace."

"The conversation," observed Archimedes, "arose out of whether birds could talk."

"Another friend of mine," said Merlyn immediately, in his most learned voice, "maintains, or will maintain, that the questions of the language of birds arises out of imitation. Aristotle, you know, also attributes *tragedy* to imitation."

Archimedes sighed heavily, and remarked in prophetic tones, "You had better get it off your chest."

"It's like this," said Merlyn. "The kestrel drops upon a mouse, and the poor mouse, transfixed with those needle talons, cries out in agony his one squeal of K-e-e-e! Next time the kestrel sees a mouse, his own soul cries out Kee in imitation. Another kestrel, perhaps his mate, comes to that cry, and after a few million years all the kestrels are calling each other with their individual notes of Kee-kee-kee."

"You can't make the whole story out of one bird," said the Wart.

"I don't want to. The hawks scream like their prey; the mallards croak like the frogs they eat, the shrikes also, like those creatures in distress; the blackbirds and thrushes click like the snail shells they hammer to pieces; the various finches make the noise of cracking seeds, and the woodpecker imitates the tapping on wood which he makes to get the insects that he eats."

"But all birds do not give a single note!"

"No, of course not. The call note arises out of imitation, and then the various bird songs are developed by repeating the single call note and descanting upon it."

"I see," said Archimedes coldly. "And what about me?"

"Well, you know quite well," said Merlyn, "that the shrew-mouse you pounce upon squeals out Kweek! That is why the young of your species call Kee-wick."

"And the old?" inquired Archimedes sarcastically.

"Hooroo, Hooroo," cried Merlyn, refusing to be damped. "It's obvious, my dear fellow After their first winter, that's the wind in the hollow trees where they prefer to sleep."

"I see," said Archimedes, more coolly than ever. "This time, we note, it is not a question of prey at all."

"Oh, come along," replied Merlyn. "There are other things besides the things you eat. Even a bird drinks sometimes, for instance, or bathes itself in water; it is the liquid notes of a river that we hear in a robin's song."

"It seems now," said Archimedes, "that it is no longer a question of what we eat, but also of what we drink or hear."

"And why not?"

The owl said resignedly, "Oh, well."

"I think it is an interesting idea," said the Wart, to encourage his tutor. "But how does a language come out of these imitations?"

"They repeat them at first," said Merlyn, "and then they vary them. You don't seem to realize what a lot of meaning there resides in the tone and the speed of voice. Suppose I were to say 'What a nice day,' just like that. You would answer, 'Yes, so it is.' But if I were to say, 'What a *nice* day,' in caressing tones, you might think I was a nice person. But then again, if I were to say, 'What a nice day,' quite breathless, you might look about you to see what had put me in a fright. It is like this that the birds have developed their language."

"Would you mind telling us," said Archimedes, "since you know so much about it, how many various things we birds are able to express by altering the tempo and emphasis of the elaborations of our call-notes?"

"But a large number of things. You can cry Kee-wick in tender accents, if you are in love, or Kee-wick angrily in challenge or in hate: you can cry it on a rising scale as a call-note, if you don't know where your partner is, or to attract their attention away if strangers are straying near your nest: if you go near the old nest in the winter-time you may cry Kee-wick lovingly, a conditioned reflex from the pleasures which you once enjoyed within it, and if I come near to you in a startling way you may cry out Keewick-keewick-keewick, in loud alarm."

"When we come to conditioned reflexes," remarked Archimedes sourly, "I prefer to look for a mouse."

"So you may. And when you find it I daresay you will make another sound characteristic of owls, though not often mentioned in books of ornithology. I refer to the sound 'Tock' or 'Tck' which human beings call a smacking of the lips."

"And what sound is that supposed to imitate?"

"Obviously, the breaking of mousy bones."

"You are a cunning master," said Archimedes admiringly, "and as far as a poor owl is concerned you will just have to get away with it. All I can tell you from my own personal experience is that it is not like that at all. A tit can tell you not only that it is in danger, but what kind of danger it is in. It can say, 'Look out for the cat,' or 'Look out for the hawk,' or 'Look out for the tawny owl,' as plainly as A.B.C."

"I don't deny it," said Merlyn. "I am only telling you the beginnings of language. Suppose you try to tell me the song of any single bird which I can't attribute originally to imitation?"

"The night-jar," said the Wart.

"The buzzing of the wings of beetles," replied his tutor at once.

"The nightingale," cried Archimedes desperately.

"Ah," said Merlyn, leaning back in his comfortable chair. "Now we are to imitate the soul-song of our beloved Proserpine, as she stirs to wake in all her liquid self."

"Tereu," said the Wart softly.

"Pieu," added the owl quietly.

"Music!" concluded the necromancer in ecstasy, quite unable to make the smallest beginnings of an imitation.

"Hallo," said Kay, opening the door of the afternoon schoolroom. "I'm sorry I'm late for the geography lesson. I was trying to get a few small birds with my cross-bow. Look, I have killed a thrush."

CHAPTER EIGHTEEN

THE WART LAY awake as he had been instructed to do. He was to wait until Kay was asleep, and then Archimedes would come for him with Merlyn's magic. He lay under the great bearskin and stared out of the window at the stars of spring, no longer frosty and metallic, but as if they had been new-washed and had swollen with the moisture. It was a lovely evening, without rain or cloud. The sky between the stars was of the deepest and the fullest velvet. Framed in the thick western window, Aldebaran and Betelgeuse were racing Sirius over the horizon, the hunting dog-star looked to his master Orion, who had only just heaved himself above the rim. In at the window came also the unfolding scent of benighted flowers, for the currants, the wild cherries, the plums and the hawthorn were already in bloom, and no less than five nightingales were holding a contest of beauty among the bowery, the looming trees.

Wart lay on his back with his bearskin half off him and his hands clasped behind his head. It was too beautiful to sleep, too temperate for the rug. He watched out at the stars in a kind of trance. Soon it would be the summer again, when he could sleep on the battlements and watch these stars hovering as close as moths above his face – and, in the Milky Way at least, with something of the mothy pollen. They would be at the same time so distant that unutterable thoughts of space and eternity would baffle themselves in his sighing breast, and he would imagine to himself how he was falling upwards higher and higher amongst them, never reaching, never ending, leaving and losing everything in the tranquil speed of space.

He was fast asleep when Archimedes came for him.

"Eat this," said Archimedes, and handed him a dead mouse.

The Wart felt so strange that he took the furry atomy without protest, and popped it into his mouth without any feelings that it was going to be horrid. So he was not surprised when it turned out to be excellent, with a fruity taste like eating a peach with the skin on, though naturally the skin was not so nice as the mouse.

"Now, we had better fly," said the owl. "Just flip to the window-sill here, to get accustomed to yourself before we take off."

Wart jumped for the sill and automatically gave himself an extra kick with his wings, just as a high jumper swings his arms. He landed on the sill with rather a thump, as owls are apt to do, did not stop himself in time, and toppled straight out of the window. "This," he thought to himself cheerfully, "is where I break my neck." It was curious, but he was not taking life at all seriously. He felt the castle walls streaking past him, and the ground and the moat swimming up. He kicked with his wings, and the ground sank again, like water in a leaking well. In a second that kick of his wings had lost its effect, and the ground was welling up again. He kicked again. It was extraordinarily queer, going forward like this with the earth ebbing and flowing beneath him, in the utter silence of his down-fringed feathers.

"For heaven's sake," panted Archimedes, bobbing up and down in the dark air beside him, "do stop flying like a woodpecker. Anybody would take you for a little owl, if the brutes had been invented. What you are doing is to give yourself flying speed with one flick of your wings. You then rise on that flick until you have lost flying speed and begin to stall. Then you give another just as you are beginning to drop out of the air, and do a switchback. It's extremely confusing to keep up with you."

"Well," said the Wart recklessly, "if I stop doing this I shall just go bump altogether."

"Idiot," said the owl. "Waver your wings all the time, like me, instead of doing these solitary bounds."

The Wart did what he was told, and was surprised to find that the ridiculous earth became stable again and moved underneath him without tilting, in a regular pour. He did not feel himself to be moving at all.

"That's better."

"How curious everything looks," observed the Wart with some wonder, now that he had time to look about him.

And, indeed, the world did look curious. In some ways the best description of it would be to say that it looked a little like a photographer's negative, for he was seeing one ray beyond the spectrum which is visible to human beings. An infra-red camera will take photographs in the dark, when we cannot see, and it will also take photographs in daylight. The owls are the same, for it is quite untrue that they can only see at night. They see in the day just as well, only they happen to possess the advantage of seeing pretty well at night also, and so they naturally prefer to do their hunting then, when other creatures are more at their mercy. To the Wart the green trees would have looked whitish in the daytime, as if they were covered with apple blossom, and now, at night, everything had the same kind of different look. It was like flying in a twilight which had reduced everything to shades of the same colour, and, as in the twilight, there was a considerable amount of gloom.

"Do you like it?" asked the owl.

"I like it very much. Do you know, when I was a fish there were parts of the water which were colder or warmer than other parts, and now it is the same in the air."

"The temperature of both," said Archimedes instructively, "depends upon the vegetation of the bottom. Woods or weeds, they make it warm above them."

"Well," said the Wart. "I can see why the reptiles who had given up being fishes decided to become birds. It certainly is fun."

Chapter Eighteen

"You are beginning to fit things together," remarked Archimedes. "Do you mind if we sit down?"

"How does one?"

"You must stall. That means you must launch yourself upwards until you lose flying speed, and then, just as you feel yourself beginning to tumble – why, you sit down. Haven't you noticed how birds usually fly upwards to perch? They don't come straight down on the branch, but dive below it and then rise. At the top of their rise they stall and sit down."

"But birds land on the ground too. And what about mallards on the water? They can't rise to sit on that."

"Well, it's perfectly possible to land on flat things, but more difficult. You have to glide in at stalling speed all the way, and then increase your wind resistance by cupping your wings, dropping your feet, tail, etc. You may have noticed that few birds do it really gracefully. Look how a crow thumps down and how the mallard splashes. The spoon-winged birds like heron and plover seem to do it best. As a matter of fact, we owls aren't so bad at it ourselves."

"And the long-winged birds like swifts, I suppose they are the worst, for they can't rise from a flat surface at all?"

"The reasons are different," said Archimedes, "yet the fact is true. But need we talk on the wing? I am getting quite tired."

"So am I."

"Owls usually prefer to sit down every few hundred yards."

The Wart copied Archimedes in zooming up towards the

branch which they had selected. He began to fall just as they were above it, clutched it with his furry feet at the last moment, swayed backwards and forwards twice, and found that he had landed successfully. He folded up his wings.

While the Wart was still admiring the view, his friend proceeded to give him a longish lecture upon flight in birds. He told how, although the swift was so fine a flyer that he could sleep on the wing all night, and although the Wart himself had claimed to admire the way in which rooks enjoyed their flights, the real aeronaut of the lower strata (which cut out the swift) was the plover. He explained how plovers indulged in aerobatics, and would actually do such stunts as spins, stall turns and even rolls for the mere grace of the thing. They were the only birds which made a practice of slipping off height to land. Wart paid little or no attention to the lecture, but got his eyes accustomed to the strange tones of light instead, and watched Archimedes out of the corner of one of them. For Archimedes, while he was talking, was absent-mindedly spying for his dinner. This spying was an odd performance.

You know how a spinning top which is beginning to lose its spin slowly describes circles with its highest point before falling down. The leg of the top remains in the same place, but the apex makes circles which get bigger and bigger towards the end. This is what Archimedes was absent-mindedly doing. His feet remained stationary, but he moved the upper part of his body round and round, like somebody trying to see from behind a fat lady at a cinema, and uncertain which side of her gave the best view. As he could also turn his head almost completely round on his shoulders, you may imagine that his antics were worth watching.

"What are you doing?" asked the Wart.

But, even as he asked, Archimedes was gone. First there had been an owl talking about plover, and then there was no owl. Only, far below the Wart, there was a thump and a rattle of leaves, as the aerial torpedo went smack into the middle of a bush, quite regardless of obstructions.

In a minute the owl was sitting beside him again on the branch, thoughtfully breaking up a dead sparrow.

"May I do that?" asked the Wart, inclined to be bloodthirsty.

"As a matter of fact," said Archimedes, after waiting to crop his mouthful, "you may not. That magic mouse which turned you into an owl will be quite enough for you – after all, you've been eating as a human all day – and no owl kills for pleasure. It simply isn't done. Besides, I am supposed to be taking you for your education, and, as soon as I have finished my snack here, that is what we shall have to do."

"Where are you going to take me?"

Archimedes finished his sparrow, wiped his beak politely on the bough, and turned his tender eyes full upon the Wart. These great, round eyes had, as a famous writer has expressed it, a bloom of light upon them like the purple bloom of powder on a grape.

"I am going to take you," said he slowly, "where no human being has ever been, to see my dear mother Athene, the goddess of wisdom."

★ ★ ★

It was a long and terrible journey, passing beyond the midnight country of sorrow and the sun-drained wastes of solitude into the undiscovered country of Kennaquhair, whose latitude is 91 degrees north and longitude 181 degrees west. Here, in the luminous hollow of a tree stump that had been blasted by lightning and whittled clean by the winds of knowledge, they alighted on the outstretched hands of the goddess. Athene was invisible, or at least the Wart never remembered having seen her afterwards. At the time he did not notice that she was invisible – it only struck him when he woke up next morning – because he was aware of her without seeing her. He was aware that her unthinkable beauty was neither that of age nor of youth. That her eyes were the only things you thought of looking at, and that to be her was terrible, whereas to be with her was the only joy. If you can understand this, she was in herself so unhappy that words only melt in such temperatures, but towards other people she was the spirit of invincible mercy and protection. She lived, of course, beyond sorrow and solitude, and, if you follow me, the suffering which had brought her there had left her with a kind of supernatural *good manners*.

She was the conqueror.

Archimedes kissed her tenderly. He was not over-awed by her, but saluted her almost with pity, as if he were a man of the world visiting his sister, a nun who did not understand how to get on in his world, or perhaps a prosperous banker who had always tried to be reasonably decent, meeting the man whose destiny it was to be nailed up and left to die of sunstroke, agony and exhaustion, in order to save the prosperous bankers.

Even Archimedes did not understand her.

She knew this.

"Hail, mother," said Archimedes. "I have brought you a young human, who is to learn things, by decree."

When the Wart came to think about it afterwards, he realized that he had not only never seen the goddess but that he had also never heard her speak. The owl spoke, and he spoke; but the words of Athene did not come out of a mouth.

"This part," said Archimedes with a sort of purr, "is at the rate of thirty years in a minute. It is one of our owl's dreams, you know, such as we gain our wisdom from in the sighing of the night."

Athene did not speak, but she held the Wart in the hollow of her kind hand, and he knew that he was to look in front of him.

He saw the world with his own eyes now, no longer using the strange spectrum which he had experienced since he came out with Archimedes, and no doubt this was done in order to make things easier for him. They needed to be made easier, for it was now his business to watch a world in which a year passed in two seconds. It was a world of trees.

"We dream of this," explained Archimedes, "when we perch on a tree in the winds of winter, or sleep in its hollow in the rains of spring."

Sometimes nowadays you can see a cinema film of a flower, for instance, in which one exposure has been taken every hour. In it you see the petals expand and throb open or shut for day or night, until the whole story is over and the seeds have been thrown out upon the wind. There was a woodland now in front of the Wart, and in it an oak sapling which grew, flourished and shed its leaves into nakedness, all in the time during which you could slowly count three. A whole year had passed in that time, with all its human joys and sorrows.

"This," said Athene, or at any rate it is what she seemed to be saying, in the most glorious of voices, "is called the Dream of the Trees."

People don't think of trees as alive. We never see them moving unless the wind disturbs them, and then it is not their movement but the wind's. The Wart saw now that trees are living, and do move. He saw all the forest, like seaweed on the ocean's floor, how the branches rose and groped about and waved, how they panted forth their leaves like breathing (and indeed they were breathing) and, what is still more extraordinary, how they talked.

If you should be at a cinema when the talking apparatus breaks down, you may have the experience of hearing it start again too slowly. Then you will hear the words which would be real words at a proper speed now droning out unintelligibly in long roars and sighs, which give no meaning to the human brain. The same thing happens with a gramophone whose disc is not revolving fast.

So it is with humans. We cannot hear the trees talking, except as a vague noise of roaring and hushing which we attribute to the wind in the leaves, because they talk too slowly for us. These noises are really the syllables and vowels of the trees.

"You may speak for yourselves," said Athene.

Oak spoke first, as became the noblest of all. He stood throbbing his leaves in the twilight, to which Time had mixed down day and night; stretching out his great muscular branches; yawning, as if it were, like a noble giant of the earth who cracks his limbs in the morning when he wakes.

"Ah," said the oak. "It's good to be alive. Look at my biceps, will you? Do you see how the other trees are afraid of Gravity, afraid that he will break their branches off? They point them up in the air, or down at the ground, so as to give the old earth-giant his least purchase upon them. Now I am ready to challenge Gravity, and I can stretch my branches straight out in a line parallel to the earth. He may swing on them for all I care, but, bless you, they won't break. Do you know how long I live? A thousand years is my expectation. Three hundred years to grow, three hundred years to live, and three hundred years to die. And when I am dead, what of that? They make me into timber, into ships and house beams that will be good for another thousand. My leaves come the last and go the last. I am a conservative, I am; and out of my apples they make ink, whose words may live as long as me, even as me, the oak."

Ash said softly, "I am the Venus of the forest. I am pliable."

"My dear Madam," said a rather society box, in smirking, urban, scholastic, eighteenth-century accents, "a decoction of boxwood promotes the growth of hair, while an oil distilled from its shavings is a cure for haemorrhoids, toothache, epilepsy, and stomach worms. So, at least, we are told."

"If it comes to being sarcastic," replied a homely hazel, who was a good fellow at heart, although he was inclined to snap, "may I mention that hazel chips will clear turbid wine in twenty-four hours, and twigs of hazel twisted together will serve for yeast in brewing? You may be a sort of Lord Chesterfield, but at least you will have to yield to me in the matter of genteel tipsy-fication practised by the elegant gentlemen of your century."

"As far as drink goes," said an impossibly female ivy, who was always clinging to her husband, putting her oar in, and making his life a misery, "ground ivy is used for clarifying beer."

She simpered when she said the word "beer" in the most unpleasant way. She was a sour creature in any light.

"I don't know why we are talking about drink," said a dignified beech. "But if we are talking about it I may as well mention that Virgil's drinking bowl, *divini opus Alcimedontis*, was turned out of my wood."

"Great men," remarked a close-grained svelt lime, "are always going back to the trees. Grinling Gibbons would never carve his nets and baskets out of anything but me."

"And Salvatore Rosa," said a chestnut, "was always painting me."

"Corot," said a willow, sighing, "was fond of me."

"How your humans do spin about," remarked a crafty elm coldly. "What a speed they live at. It is rather good sport trying to spot them, and then to drop an old bough on their heads if you get them directly underneath. But of course you have to stand very still and give no signs of dropping it till the actual moment. The cream of the joke is that they make the coffins out of me afterwards."

"You always were a treacherous fellow," replied an old yew. "What's the point of it? Surely it's better to help than to hinder? Now Oak here, and a few others of us, we take pride in keeping faith. We like to be steadfast. Everybody prizes me because, like Alder, I scorn to rot in water. My gateposts are more durable than iron, for they do not even rust."

"Yes," chimed in some cypresses, sycamores and others. "Live and let live, that's the best motto. We and our sisters are always pleased to see the grass growing under our shade."

"On the contrary, " said a fir who always killed the grass beneath him, and a nervous aspen joined in. "Kill or be killed, that's the way to get on.

"But please don't talk of killing," added the aspen. "The cross was made out of me, and I have trembled ever since. I only kill, you know, because I am frightened. It is a terrible thing always to be afraid."

A cedar decided to cheer her up. "Oh, come," he remarked, twinkling his dusky spines. "What's the point of all this argument and boasting about your powers? It seems to me that you all take life too seriously. Look at my old friend Sequoia here, who has had the humorous idea of constructing himself a very hard-looking bark out of soft blotting-paper, so that you can punch him without hurting yourself. If it comes to that, look at me. What is my mission in life? You may think it a humble one, considering my size, but I find it amusing. I am antipathetic to fleas."

All the trees laughed at this — it resulted in a splendid summer that year — and decided to go on with their dance. It was a sort of Indian dance, in which they moved their bodies but not their feet, and a very graceful one it was. The Wart watched while the whole troop of them rippled their twigs like serpents, or made slow ritual gestures about their heads and bodies with the larger boughs. He saw how they grew big and lusty in their dancing, how they threw their arms out towards heaven in an ecstasy of being alive. The younger trees tired first. The little fruit trees stopped waving, hung their weary heads for a moment, then fell down on the ground. The big ones moved more slowly, faltered and fell one by one; till only Oak was left. He stood with his chin sunk upon his chest, kept upright by his mighty will, thinking of the lovely dance which now was over. He sighed and looked upwards to Athene, stretched out his bare arms sorrowfully to her, to ask her why, and then he also fell on sleep.

"The next dream," said Athene, "is called the Dream of the Stones."

"It is the last dream she will give you," added Archimedes, "and this one goes at two million years a second. You will have to keep your eyes skinned."

Wart saw a darkness in front of him, with lights in it. The dark was so dark that it was like lampblack, and the lights so light that the coldest blue fire of diamonds could not touch them. The harsh contrast between them made his eyes ache. He was looking at Sirius, actually, just as he had been looking at him a few hours before, but it took him quite a time before he realized that he was looking at a star at all. There was none of the mellow velvet which he had been accustomed to see through the earth's atmosphere, but only this fierce emptiness of black and white, and, beside this fact, the constellations were in different positions. It was a few thousand million years ago and all the shapes of the evening have altered since then.

The nearest star, which looked the biggest for that reason, burnt with a roar of terrible gases, and another star was coming towards it. You could see them surging on their endless paths into eternity, marking their aimed but aimless courses across the universe with straight lines of remembered fire – like the meteors with which the Creator sometimes stitched together the weak seams of our dome, the bright darning-needles suddenly darted in and out of the velvet by a finger on the other side.

As the two stars came closer together a huge mountain of flame was dragged out by attraction from each. When they were at their closest point the top of this mountain broke off from the smaller star and streamed through the emptiness towards the bigger. Some of it reached its destination; but the bigger star was proceeding quickly on its way, and some of it was left behind. This part hung in space, lost to both its parents and its seducer, a whirling cigar of fire. Its mists of flame began to crystallize as they cooled to turn into drops, as water does when it is cooled from steam. The drops took up a circular path of their own, spinning round the star from which they had been dragged.

The Wart found himself closer to the third drop. Its haze of incandescent worms crawled in and out of it, formed into funnels and whirlpools, crept over its round surface, sometimes leapt out into space, curled over, and rained back. They were flames. The light died down from far beyond white to blue, to red, to a dim brown. It became a ball of steam. Out of this steam a smaller ball shot out. The first ball shrank and was a globe of boiling water.

The water began to cool but the fires still burnt inside it. They convulsed the surface of the water, threw up great continents and islands of the interior rock. The centuries were passing so quickly that even these continents seemed to bubble like porridge, as the volcanoes and mountains and earthquakes came and went. The unbridled furnace within was still unstable, and, till quite late in the dream, the globe did not always spin on the same axis, but lurched over sideways as some stress gave way inside. The lurches destroyed continents and made more.

The Wart found himself closer still. He was actually on the globe and facing an enormous cliff. At two million years a second, the cliff's mountain moved. It was alive as the trees had been, and roared most dreadfully. It fell, it folded on itself, it shoved itself along the surface of the globe, pushing a bow wave of its own folds for miles. Its great rock split and powdered, pouring stone torrents into the heaving sea. The sea itself grew tired of the mountain, made it to sink down and to be covered. Another convulsion threw up the remains again, streaming.

Round the foot of the chastened mountain there lay its powder and its pebbles, great rocks worn smooth by the sea. The rocks themselves broke and were scattered, the sea always rolling and rolling them together between its hands until the tiny fragments were often as round as their mother had been, the globe.

A green scum formed over the sinking mountain, a haze of colour which was still sometimes dipped under the water or lifted high above it, as the earth undulated. The trees came, but their voices were quite drowned by the slower howling of the mineral world, which twitched through millennia like a dog's skin in sleep.

"Hold fast," was what the rocks thundered. "Hold, cohere."

But all the time they were broken apart, thrown down, and their hold broken. There was nothing to be seen of the mountain except a flat green plain which had some pebbles on it. They were bits of the cliff which he had first watched.

The dream, like the one before it, lasted about half an hour. In the last three minutes of the dream some fishes, dragons and such-like ran hurriedly about. A dragon swallowed one of the pebbles, but spat it out.

In the ultimate twinkling of an eye, far tinier in time than the last millimetre on a six-foot rule, there came a man. He split up the one pebble which remained of all that mountain with blows; then made an arrow-head of it, and slew his brother.

★ ★ ★

"Well, Wart," said Kay in an exasperated voice. "Do you want all the rug? And why do you heave and mutter so? You were snoring too."

"I don't snore," replied the Wart indignantly.

"You do."

"I don't."

"You do. You snore like a volcano."

"I don't."

"You do."

"I don't. And you snore worse."

"No, I don't."

"Yes, you do."

"How can I snore worse if you don't snore at all?"

By the time they had thrashed this out, they were nearly late for breakfast. They dressed hurriedly and ran out into the spring.

CHAPTER NINETEEN

IN THE EVENINGS, except in the very height of summer, they used to meet in the solar after the last meal of the day. There the parson, Reverent Sidebottom, or if he were busy over his sermon then Merlyn himself, would read to them out of some learned book of tales, to calm their spirits. It was glorious in the winter, while the big logs roared in the fire – the beech blue-flamy and relentless, the elm showy and soon gone, the holly bright, or the pine with his smoking scents – while the dogs dreamed of conquest, or the boys imagined those sweet maidens letting down their golden hair so that their rescuers might save them out of towers. But almost at any time of the year it was as good.

The book they usually used was *Gesta Romanorum*, whose fascinating tales began with such provoking sentences as "There was a certain King who had a singular partiality for little dogs that barked loudly," or "A certain nobleman had a white cow, to which he was extremely partial: he assigned two reasons for this, first because she was spotlessly white, and next, because…"

The boys, and for that matter the men, would sit as quiet as church mice while the marvels of the story were unfolded, and, when the unpredictable narrative had come to an end, they would look towards Reverent Sidebottom (or Merlyn – who was not so good at it) to have the story explained. Reverent Sidebottom would draw a deep breath and plunge into his task, explaining how the certain King was really Christ, and the barking dogs zealous preachers, or how the white cow was the soul and her milk represented prayer and supplication. Sometimes, indeed generally, the unfortunate vicar was hard put to it to find a moral, but nobody ever doubted that his explanations were the right ones; and anyway most of his listeners were soon asleep.

It was a fine summer night, the last night which would give any excuse for fires, and Reverent Sidebottom was reading out his tale. Wart lay snoozing among the lean ribs of the gaze-hounds: Sir Ector sipped his wine with his eyes brooding on the logs which lit the evening: Kay played chess with himself rather badly: and Merlyn, with his long beard saffron in the firelight, sat cross-legged knitting, beside the Wart.

"'There was once discovered at Rome,'" read Reverent Sidebottom through his nose "'an uncorrupted body, taller than the wall of the city, on which the following words were inscribed — "Pallas, the son of Evander, whom the lance of a crooked soldier slew, is interred here." A candle burnt at his head which neither water nor wind could extinguish, until air was admitted through a hole made with the point of a needle beneath the flame. The wound of which this giant had died was four and a half feet long. Having been killed after the overthrow of Troy, he remained in his tomb two thousand two hundred and forty years.'"

"Have you ever seen a giant?" asked Merlyn softly, so as not to interrupt the reading. "No, I remember you haven't. Just catch hold of my hand a moment, and shut your eyes."

The vicar was droning on about the gigantic son of Evander, Sir Ector was staring into the fire, and Kay was making a slight click as he moved one of the chessmen, but the Wart and Merlyn were immediately standing hand in hand in an unknown forest.

"This is the Forest of the Burbly Water," said Merlyn, "and we are going to visit the giant Galapas. Now listen. You are invisible at the moment, because you are holding my hand. I am able to keep myself invisible by an exercise of willpower — an exceedingly exhausting job it is — and I can keep you invisible so long as you hold on to me. It takes twice as much willpower, but there. If, however, you let go of me even for a moment, during that moment you will become visible, and, if you do it in the presence of Galapas, he will munch you up in two bites. So hold on."

"Very well," said the Wart.

"Don't say 'Very well'. It isn't very well at all. On the

contrary, it is very ill indeed. And another thing. The whole of this beastly wood is dotted with pitfalls and I shall be grateful if you will look where you are going."

"What sort of pitfalls?"

"He digs a lot of pits about ten feet deep, with smooth clay walls, and covers them over with dead branches, pine needles and suchlike. Then, if people walk about, they tumble into them, and he goes round with his bow every morning to finish them off. When he has shot them dead, he climbs in and collects them for dinner. He can hoist himself out of a ten-foot pit quite easily."

"Very well," said the Wart again, and corrected himself to, "I will be careful."

Being invisible is not so pleasant as it sounds. After a few minutes of it you forget where you last left your hands and legs – or at least you can only guess to within three or four inches – and the result is that it is by no means easy to make your way through a brambly wood. You can see the brambles all right, but where exactly you are in relation to them becomes more confusing. The only guide to your legs, for the feeling in them soon becomes complicated, is by looking for your footprints – these you can see in the neatly flattened grass below you – and as for your arms and hands, it becomes hopeless unless you concentrate your mind to remember where you put them last. You can generally tell where your body is, either by the unnatural bend of a thorn branch, or by the pain of one of its thorns, or by the strange feeling of *centralness* which all human beings have, because we keep our souls in the region of our liver.

Chapter Nineteen

"Hold on," said Merlyn, "and for glory's sake don't trip up."

They proceeded to tread their tipsy way through the forest, staring carefully at the earth in front of them in case it should give way, and stopping very often when an extra large bramble fastened itself in their flesh. When Merlyn was stuck with a bramble, he swore, and when he swore he lost some of his concentration and they both became dimly visible, like Autumn mist. The rabbits up-wind of them stood on their hind legs at this, and exclaimed, "Good gracious!"

"What are we going to do?" asked the Wart.

"Well," said Merlyn. "Here we are at the Burbly Water. You can see the giant's castle on the opposite bank, and we shall have to swim across. It may be difficult to walk when you are invisible, but to swim is perfectly impossible, even with years of practice. You are always getting your nose under water. So I shall have to let go of you until we have swum across in our own time. Don't forget to meet me quickly on the other side."

The Wart went down into the warm starlit water, which ran musically like a real salmon stream, and struck out for the other side. He swam fast, across and down river, with a kind of natural dog-stroke, and he had to go about a quarter of a mile below his landing-place along the bank before Merlyn also came out to meet him, dripping. Merlyn swam the breast-stroke, very slowly and with great precision, watching ahead of him over the bow wave of his beard, with that faintly anxious expression of a faithful retriever.

"Now," said Merlyn, "catch hold again, and we will see what Galapas is about."

They walked invisible across the sward, where many unhappy-looking gardeners with iron collars round their necks were mowing, weeding and sweeping by torchlight, although it was so late, in what had begun to be a garden. They were slaves.

"Talk in whispers," said Merlyn, "if you have to talk."

There was a brick wall in front of them, with fruit trees nailed along it, and this they were forced to climb. They did so by the usual methods of bending over, climbing on each other's backs, giving a hand up from on top, and so forth, but every time that the Wart was compelled to let go of his magician for a moment he became visible. It was like an early cinematograph flickering very badly, or one of those magic lanterns where you put in slide after slide. A slave gardener, looking at that part of the wall, sadly tapped himself on the head and went away into a shrubbery to be sick.

"Hush," whispered Merlyn from the top of the wall, and they looked down upon the giant in person, as he took his evening ease by candlelight upon the bowling green.

"But he's not big at all," whispered the Wart disappointedly.

"He is ten feet high," hissed Merlyn, "and that is *extremely* big for a giant. I chose the best one I knew. Even Goliath was only six cubits and a span – or nine feet four inches. If you don't like him you can go home."

"I'm sorry. I didn't mean to be ungrateful, Merlyn, only I thought they were sixty feet long and that sort of thing."

"Sixty feet," sniffed the necromancer.

The giant had heard something at the top of the wall, and looked up towards them, remarking in a rumbling tone, "How the bats squeak at night!" Then he poured himself out another hornful of madeira and tossed it off in one draught.

Merlyn lowered his voice and explained. "People find the teeth and bones of creatures like your friend *Atlantosaurus*, and then they tell stories about human giants. One of them found a tooth weighing two hundred ounces. It's dragons, not giants, that grow really big."

"But can't humans grow big too?"

"I don't understand it myself, but it is something about the composition of their bones. If a human was to grow sixty feet high, he would simply snap his bones with the weight of their own gravity. The biggest real giant was Eleazer, and he was only ten feet and a half."

"Well," said the Wart. "I must say it is rather a disappointment.

"I don't mean being brought to see him," he added hastily, "but that they don't grow like I thought. Still, I suppose ten feet is quite big when you come to think of it."

"It is twice as high as you are," said Merlyn. "You would just come up to his navel, and he could pitch you up to a corn rick about as high as you can throw a sheaf."

They had become interested in this discussion, so that they got less and less careful of their voices, and now the giant rose up out of his easy chair. He came towards them with a three-gallon bottle of wine in his hand, and stared earnestly at the wall on which they were sitting. Then he threw the bottle at the wall rather to their left, said in an angry voice, "Beastly screech owls!" and proceeded to stump off into the castle.

"Follow him," cried Merlyn quickly.

They scrambled down off the wall, joined hands, and hurried after the giant by the garden door.

In the beginning the downstairs parts were reasonably civilized, with green baize doors behind which butlers and footmen — though with iron collars round their necks — were polishing silver and finishing off the decanters. Later on there were strong-rooms with ancient safes in them, that contained the various gold cups, epergnes and other trophies won at jousts and horse-races by the giant. Next there were dismal cellars with cobwebs over the wine bins, and dreary-looking rats peeping thoughtfully at the bodiless footprints in the dust, and several corpses of human beings hanging up in the game cupboards until they should be ready to eat. It was like the place for adults only in the Chamber of Horrors at Madame Tussaud's.

At the very bottom of the castle they came upon the dungeons. Here the chalky walls dripped with greasy moisture, and there were pathetic messages and graffiti scratched upon the stone. "Pray for poor Priscilla," said one, and another said, "Oh, if I had only paid for my dog licence honestly, I should never have come to this pass." There was a picture of a man hanging from a gallows, with arms and legs sticking out like those of a Guy Fawkes in all directions, and another of a demon with horns. A fifth carving said, "Midnight Sun for the two-thirty," while the sixth said, "Oh, yeah?" and a seventh exclaimed, "Alas, that I should have forgotten to feed my poor canary: now I am in the same dread doom." A message which had been scratched out said, "Beastly old Galapas loves Madame Mim, the dirty hound," and somebody else had written, "Repent and be saved, for the Kingdom of Hell is at hand." There were kisses, dates, pious ejaculations, mottoes such as "Waste not, want not," and "Good-night, ladies," also hearts with arrows in them, skulls and crossbones, pictures of pigs drawn with the eyes shut, and pathetic messages such as, "Don't forget to take the potatoes off at half-past twelve," "The key is under the geranium," "Revenge me on stinking Galapas, by whom I am foully slain," or merely "Mazawatee Mead for Night Starvation." It was a grimly place.

"Ha!" cried Galapas, stopping outside one of his cells. "Are you going to give me back my patent unbreakable helm, or make me another one?"

"It's not your helm," answered a feeble voice. "I invented it, and I patented it, and you can go sing for another one, you beast."

"No dinner tomorrow," said Galapas cruelly, and went on to the next cell.

"What about that publicity?" asked the giant. "Are you going to say that the Queen of Sheba made an unprovoked attack upon me and that I took her country in self-defence?"

"No, I'm not," said the journalist in the cell.

"Rubber truncheons for you," said Galapas, "in the morning."

"Where have you hidden my elastic stays?" thundered the giant at the third cell.

"I shan't tell you," said the cell.

"If you don't tell me," said Galapas, "I shall have your feet burnt."

"You can do what you like."

"Oh, come on," pleaded the giant. "My tummy hangs down without them. If you will tell me where you put them I will make you a general, and you shall go hunting in Poland in a fur cap. Or you can have a pet lion, or a comic beard, and you can fly to America with an Armada. Would you like to marry any of my daughters?"

"I think all you propositions are foul," said the cell. "You had better have a public trial of me for propaganda."

"You are just a mean, horrible bully," said the giant, and went on to the next cell.

"Now then," said Galapas. "What about that ransom, you dirty English pig?"

"Ay'm not a pig," said the cell, "and Ay'm not dirty, or Ay wasn't until I fell into that beastly pit. Now Ay've got pine needles all down my back. What have you done with my toothbrush, you giant, and where have you put my poor little brachet, what?"

"Never mind your brachet and your toothbrush" shouted Galapas, "what about that ransom, you idiot, or are you too steeped in British sottishness to understand anything at all?"

"Ay want to brush my teeth," answered King Pellinore obstinately. "They feel funny, if you understand what I mean, and it makes me feel not very well."

"*Uomo bestiale*," cried the giant. "Have you no finer feelings?"

"No," said King Pellinore. "Ay don't think Ay have. Ay want to brush my teeth, and Ay am getting cramp through sitting all the time on this bench, or whatever you call it."

"Unbelievable sot," screamed the master of the castle. "Where is your soul, you shopkeeper? Do you think of nothing but your teeth?"

"Ay think a lot of things, old boy," said King Pellinore. "Ay think of how nice it would be to have a poached egg, what?"

"Well, you shan't have a poached egg, you shall just stay there until you pay my ransom. How do you suppose I am to run my business if I don't have my ransoms? What about my concentration camps, and my thousand-dollar wreaths at funerals? Do you suppose that all this is run on nothing? Why, I had to send a wreath for King Cwythno Garanhir which consisted of a Welsh harp forty feet long, made entirely out of orchids. It said, 'Melodious Angels Sing Thee to Thy Rest'."

"Ay think that was a very good wreath," said King Pellinore admiringly. "But couldn't Ay have my toothbrush, what? Dash it all, really, it isn't much compared with a wreath like that. Or is it?"

"Imbecile," exclaimed the giant, and moved on to the next cell.

"We shall have to rescue him," whispered the Wart. "It is poor old King Pellinore, and he must have fallen into one of those traps you were telling me about, while he was after the Questing Beast."

"Let him stay," said Merlyn. "A chap who doesn't know enough to keep himself out of the clutches of one of these giants isn't worth troubling about."

"Perhaps he was thinking about something else," whispered the Wart.

"Well, he shouldn't have been," hissed the magician. "Giants like this do absolutely no harm in the long run, and you can keep them quite quiet by the smallest considerations, such as giving them back their stays. Anybody knows that. If he has got himself into trouble with Galapas, let him stay in it. Let him pay the ransom.

"I know for a fact," said the Wart, "that he hasn't got the money. He can't even afford to buy himself a feather bed."

"Then he should be polite," said Merlyn doubtfully.

"He is trying to be," said the Wart. "He doesn't understand very much. Oh, please, King Pellinore is a friend of mine and I don't like to see him in these forbidding cells without a single helper."

"Whatever can we do?" cried Merlyn angrily. "The cells are firmly locked."

There was really nothing to do, but the magician's louder cry had altered matters into a crisis. Forgetting to be silent as well as invisible, Merlyn had spoken too loudly for the safety of his expedition.

"Who's there?" shrieked Galapas, wheeling round at the fifth cell.

"It's nothing," cried Merlyn. "Only a mouse."

The giant Galapas whipped out his mighty sword, and stared backwards down the narrow passage with his torch held high above his head. "Nonsense," he pronounced. "Mouses don't talk in human speech."

"Eek," said Merlyn, hoping that this would do.

"You can't fool me," said Galapas. "Now I shall come for

you with my shining blade, and I shall see what you are, by yea or by nay."

He came down towards them, holding the blue glittering edge in front of him, and his fat eyes were brutal and piggish in the torchlight. You can imagine that it was not very pleasant having a person who weighed thirty-five stone looking for you in a narrow passage, with a sword as long as yourself, in the hopes of sticking it in your liver.

"Don't be silly," said Merlyn. "It is only a mouse, or two mice. You ought to know better."

"It is an invisible magician," said Galapas. "And as for invisible magicians, I slit them up, see? I shed their bowels upon the earth, see? I rip them and tear them, see, so that their invisible guts fall out upon the earth. Now, where are you, magician, so that I may slice and zip?"

"We are behind you," said Merlyn anxiously. "Look in that further corner behind your back."

"Yes," said Galapas grimly, "except for your voice."

"Hold on," cried Merlyn, but the Wart in the confusion had slipped his hand.

"A visible magician," remarked the giant, "this time. But only a small one. We shall see whether the sword goes in with a slide."

"Catch hold, you idiot," cried Merlyn frantically, and with several fumblings they were hand in hand.

"Gone again," said Galapas, and swiped with his sword towards where they had been. It struck blue sparks from the stones.

Merlyn put his invisible mouth right up to the Wart's

invisible ear, and whispered. "Lie flat in the passage. We will press ourselves one to each side, and hope that he will go beyond us."

This worked; but the Wart, in wriggling along the floor, lost contact with his protector once again. He groped everywhere but could not find him, and of course he was now visible again, like any other person.

"Ha!" cried Galapas. "The same small one, equally visible."

He made a swipe into the darkness, but Merlyn had snatched his pupil's hand again, and just dragged him out of danger.

"Mysterious chaps," said the giant. "The best thing would be to go snip-snap along the floor.

"That's the way they cut up spinach, you know," added the giant, "or anything you have to chop small."

Merlyn and the Wart crouched hand in hand at the furthest corner of the corridor, while the horrible giant Galapas slowly minced his way towards them, laughing from the bottom of his thunderous belly, and not sparing a single inch of the ground. Click, click, went his razor sword upon the brutal stones, and there seemed to be no hope of rescue. He was behind them now and had cut them off.

"Goodbye," whispered the Wart. "It was worth it."

"Goodbye," said Merlyn. "I don't think it was at all."

"You may well say Goodbye," sneered the giant, "for soon this choppy blade will rip you."

"My dear friends," shouted King Pellinore out of his cell, "don't you say Goodbye at all. Ay think Ay can hear something coming, and while there is life there is hope."

"Yah," cried the imprisoned inventor, also coming to their

help. He feebly rattled the bars of his cell. "You leave those persons alone, you grincing giant, or I won't make you an unbreakable helmet, ever."

"What about your stays?" exclaimed the next cell fiercely, to distract his attention. "Fatty!"

"I am not fat," shouted Galapas, stopping halfway down the passage.

"Yes you are," replied the cell. "Fatty!"

"Fatty!" shouted all the prisoners together. "Fat old Galapas.

"Fat old Galapas cried for his mummy
He couldn't find his stays and down fell his tummy!"

"All right," said the giant, looking perfectly blue in the face. "All right, my beauties. I'll just finish these two off and then it will be truncheons for supper."

"Truncheons yourself," they answered. "You leave those two alone."

"Truncheons," was all the giant said. "Truncheons and a few little thumbscrews to finish up with. Now then, where are we?"

There was a distant noise, a kind of barking; and King Pellinore, who had been listening at his barred window while this was going on, began to jump and hop.

"It's it!" he shouted in high delight. "It's it."

"What's it?" they asked him.

"It!" explained the King. "It, itself."

While he was explaining, the noise had come nearer and

now was clamouring just outside the dungeon door, behind the giant. It was a pack of hounds.

"Wouff!" cried the door, while the giant and all his victims stood transfixed.

"Wouff!" cried the door again, and the hinges creaked.

"Wouff!" cried the door for the third time, and the hinges broke.

"Wow!" cried the giant Galapas, as the door crashed to the stone flags with a tremendous slap, and the Beast Glatisant bounded into the corridor.

"Let go of me, you awful animal," cried the giant, as the Questing Beast fixed its teeth into the seat of his pants.

"Help! help!" squealed the giant, as the monster ran him out of the broken door.

"Good old Beast!" yelled King Pellinore, from behind his bars. "Look at that, Ay ask you! Good old Beast. Leu, leu, leu, leu! Fetch him along then, old lady: bring him on then, bring him on. Good old girl, bring him on: bring him on then, bring him on.

"Dead, dead," added King Pellinore rather prematurely. "Bring him on dead, then: bring him on dead. There you are then, good old girl. Hie lost! Hie lost! Leu, leu, leu, leu! What do you know about that, for a retriever entirely self-trained?"

"Hourouff," barked the Questing Beast in the far distance. "Hourouff, hourouff." And they could just hear the giant Galapas running round and round the circular stairs towards the highest turret in his castle.

Merlyn and Wart hurriedly opened all the cell doors with

the keys which the giant had dropped – though the Beast would no doubt have been able to break them down if he had not – and the pathetic prisoners came out blinking in the torchlight. They were thin and bleached like mushrooms, but their spirits were not broken.

"Well," they said. "Isn't this a bit of all right?"

"No more thumbscrews for supper."

"No more dungeons, no more stench," said the inventor. "No more sitting on this hard bench."

"Ay wonder where he can have put my toothbrush?"

"That's a splendid animal of yours, Pellinore. We owe her all our lives."

"Three cheers for Glatisant!"

"And the brachet must be somewhere about."

"Oh, come along, my dear fellow. You can clean your teeth some other time, with a stick or something, when we get out. The thing to do is to set free all the slaves and to run away before the Beast lets him out of the tower."

"As far as that goes, we can pinch the epergnes on the way out."

"Lordy, I shan't be sorry to see a nice fire again. That place fair gives me the rheumatics."

"Let's burn all his truncheons, and write what we think of him on the walls."

"Good old Glatisant!"

"Three cheers for Pellinore!"

"Three cheers for everybody else!"

"Huzza! Huzza! Huzza!"

Merlyn and the Wart slipped away invisibly from the rejoicings. They left the slaves thronging out of the castle while King Pellinore carefully unlocked the iron rings from their necks with a few appropriate words, as if he were distributing the prizes on speech day. Glatisant was still making a noise like thirty couple of hounds questing, outside the tower door, and Galapas, with all the furniture piled against the door, was leaning out of the tower window shouting for the fire brigade. The occupant of cell No. 3 was busily collecting the Ascot Gold Cup and other trophies out of the giant's safe, while the publicity man was having a splendid time with a bonfire of truncheons, thumbscrews and anything else that looked as if it would melt the instruments of torture. Across the corridor of the now abandoned dungeons the inventor was carving a rude message with hammer and chisel, and this said, "Sucks to Galapas". The firelight and the cheering, and King Pellinore's encouraging remarks, such as "Britons never shall be slaves," or "I hope you will never forget the lessons you have learnt while you were with us here," or "I shall always be glad to hear from any Old Slaves, how they get on in life," or "Try to make it a rule always to clean your teeth twice a day," combined to make the leave-taking a festive one, from which the two invisible visitors were sorry to depart. But time was precious, as Merlyn said, and they hurried off towards the Burbly Water.

Considering the things that had happened, there must have been something queer about Time, as well as its preciousness, for when the Wart opened his eyes in the solar, Kay was still clicking his chessmen and Sir Ector still staring into flames.

"Well," said Sir Ector, "what about the giant?"

Merlyn looked up from his knitting, and the Wart opened a startled mouth to speak, but the question had been addressed to the vicar.

Reverent Sidebottom closed his book about Pallas, the son of Evander, rolled his eyeballs wildly, clutched his thin beard, gasped for breath, shut his eyes, and exclaimed hurriedly, "My beloved, the giant is Adam, who was formed free from all corruption. The wound from which he died is transgression of the divine command."

Then he blew out his cheeks, let go of his beard and glanced triumphantly at Merlyn.

"Very good," said Merlyn. "Especially that bit about remaining uncorrupted. But what about the candle and the needle?"

The vicar closed his eyes again, as if in pain, and all waited in silence for the explanation.

After they had waited for several minutes, Wart said, "If I were a knight in armour, and met a giant, I should smite off both his legs by the knees, saying, 'Now art thou better of a size to deal with an thou were,' and after that I should swish off his head."

"Hush," said Sir Ector. "Never mind about that."

"The candle," said the vicar wanly, "is eternal punishment, extinguished by means of a needle — that is by the passion of Christ."

"Very good indeed," said Merlyn, patting him on the back.

The fire burnt merrily, as if it were a bonfire which some

slaves were dancing round, and one of the gaze-hounds next to the Wart now went "Hourouff, hourouff" in its sleep, so that it sounded like a pack of thirty couple of hounds questing in the distance, very far away beyond the night-lit woods.

CHAPTER TWENTY

IT WAS HAYMAKING again, and Merlyn had been with them a year. The wind had been, and the snow, and the rain, and the sun once more. The boys looked longer in the leg, but otherwise everything was the same.

Six other years passed by.

Sometime Sir Grummore came on a visit: sometimes King Pellinore could be descried galloping over the purlieus after the Beast, or with the Beast after him if they happened to have got muddled up. Cully lost the vertical stripes of his first year's plumage and became greyer, grimmer, madder, and distinguished by smart horizontal bars where the long stripes had been. The merlins were released every winter and the new ones caught again next year. Hob's hair went white. The sergeant-at-arms developed a pot-belly and nearly died of shame, but continued to cry out One-Two, in a huskier voice, upon every possible occasion. Nobody else seemed to change at all, except the boys.

They grew longer. They ran like wild colts as before, and visited Robin when they had a mind to, and had innumerable adventures too lengthy to be recorded.

Merlyn's extra tuition went on just the same: for in those days even the grown-ups were so childish that they saw nothing uninteresting in being turned into snakes or owls, or in going invisibly to visit giants. The only difference was that now, in their fencing lessons, Kay and Wart were an easy match for the pot-bellied sergeant, and paid him back accidentally for many of the buffets which he had once given them. They had more and more proper weapons given to them, when they had reached their teens, until in the end they had full suits of armour and bows nearly six feet long, which would fire the real cloth-yard shaft. You were not supposed to use a bow longer than your own height, for it was considered that by doing so you were expending unnecessary energy, rather like using an elephant-gun to shoot an *ovis ammon* with. At any rate, modest men were careful not to over-bow themselves. It was a form of boasting.

As the years went by, Kay became more difficult. He always used a bow too big for him, and did not shoot very accurately with it either. He lost his temper and challenged nearly every body to have a fight, and in those few cases where he did actually have the fight, he was invariably beaten. Also he became sarcastic. He made the sergeant miserable by nagging about his stomach, and went on at the Wart about his father and mother when Sir Ector was not about. He did not seem to want to do this. It was as if he disliked it, but could not help it.

The Wart continued to be stupid, fond of Kay, and interested in birds.

Merlyn looked younger every year; which was only natural, because he was younger.

Archimedes got married, and brought up several handsome families of quilly youngsters in the tower-room.

Sir Ector got sciatica; three trees were struck by lightning; Master Twyti came every Christmas without altering a hair; Goat lost all his teeth and could eat nothing but slops, but miraculously lived on; Master Passelewe remembered a new verse about Old King Cole.

The years passed regularly and the old English snow lay as it was expected to lie – sometimes with a robin redbreast in one corner of the picture, a church bell or lighted window in the other – and in the end it was nearly time for Kay's initiation as a full-blown knight. Proportionately as the day became nearer, the two boys drifted apart: for Kay did not care to associate with the Wart any longer on the same terms, because he would need to be more dignified as a knight, and could not afford to have his squire on intimate terms with him. The Wart, who would have to be the squire, followed him about disconsolately as long as he was allowed to do so, and then went off full miserably to amuse himself alone, as best he might.

He went to the kitchen.

"Well, I am a Cinderella now," he said to himself. "Even if I had the best of it for some mysterious reason, up to the present time, in our education, now I must pay for my past pleasures and for seeing all those delightful dragons, witches, unicorns, camelopards and suchlike, by being a mere second-rate squire and holding Kay's extra spears for him while he hoves by some well or other and jousts with all comers. Never mind, I have had a good time while it lasted, and it is not such bad fun being a Cinderella, when you can do it in a kitchen which has a fireplace big enough to roast an ox."

And the Wart looked round the busy kitchen, which was coloured by the flames till it looked much like hell, with sorrowful affection.

The education of any civilized gentleman in those days used to go through three stages, page, squire, knight, and at any rate the Wart had been through the first two of these. It was rather like being the son of a modern gentleman who has made his money out of trade, for your father started you on the bottom rung even then, in your education of manners. As a page, Wart had learnt to lay the tables with three cloths and a carpet, and to bring meat from the kitchen, and to serve Sir Ector or his guests on bended knee, with one clean towel over his shoulder, one for each visitor, and one to wipe out the basins. He had been taught all the noble arts of servility, and, from the earliest time that he could remember, there had lain pleasantly in the end of his nose the various scents of mint – used to freshen the water in the ewers – or of basil, camomile, fennel, hyssop and lavender – which he had been taught to strew upon the rushy floors – or of the angelica, saffron, aniseed, and tarragon, which were used to spice the savouries which he had to carry. So he was accustomed to the kitchen, quite apart from the fact that everybody who lived in the castle was a friend of his, who might be visited on any occasion.

Wart sat in the enormous firelight and looked about him with pleasure. He looked upon the long spits which he had often turned when he was smaller, sitting behind an old straw target soaked in water, so that he might not be roasted himself, and upon the ladles and spoons whose handles could be measured in yards, with which he had been accustomed to baste the meat. He watched with water in his mouth the arrangements for the evening meal – a boar's head with a lemon in its jaws, and split almond whiskers, which would be served with a fanfare of trumpets; a kind of pork pie with sour apple juice, peppered custard, and several birds' legs, or spiced leaves, sticking out of the top to show what was in it; and a most luscious-looking frumenty. He said to himself with a sigh, "It is not so bad being a servant after all."

"Still sighing?" asked Merlyn who had turned up from somewhere, "like you were that day we went to watch King Pellinore's joust?"

"Oh, no," said the Wart. "Or rather, oh yes, and for the same reason. But I don't really mind. I am sure I shall make a better squire than old Kay would. Look at the saffron going into that frumenty: it just matches the firelight on the hams in the chimney."

"It is lovely," said Merlyn. "Only fools want to be great."

"Kay won't tell me," said the Wart, "what happens when you are made a knight. He says it is too sacred. What does happen?"

"Oh, just a lot of fuss. You will have to undress him and put him into a bath hung with rich hangings, and then two experienced knights will turn up – probably Sir Ector will get hold of old Sir Grummore and King Pellinore – and they will both sit on the edge of the bath and give him a long lecture about the ideals of chivalry. When they have done, they will pour some of the bath water over him and sign him with the cross, and then you will have to conduct him into a clean bed to get dry. Then you dress him up as a hermit and take him off to the chapel, and there he stays awake all night, watching his armour and saying prayers. People say it's lonely and terrible for him in this vigil, but it isn't at all really, because the vicar and the man who sees to the candles and an armed guard, and probably you as well, as his esquire, will have to sit up with him at the same time. In the morning you lead him off to bed to have a good sleep, as soon as he has confessed and heard Mass and offered a candle with a piece of money stuck into it as near the lighted end as possible, and then, when all are rested, you dress him up again in his very best clothes for dinner. Before dinner you lead him into the hall, with his spurs and sword all ready, and King Pellinore puts on the first spur, and Sir Grummore puts on the second, and then Sir Ector girds on the sword and kisses him and smacks him on the shoulder and says, 'Be thou a good knight.' "

"Is that all?"

"No. You go to the chapel again then, and Kay offers his sword to the vicar, and the vicar gives it back to him, and after that our good cook over there meets him at the door and claims his spurs as a reward, and says 'I shall keep these spurs for you, and if at any time you don't behave like a true knight should do, why, I shall pop them in the soup.' "

"That is the end?"

"Yes, except for the dinner."

"If I were to be made a knight," said the Wart, staring dreamily into the fire, "I should insist upon my doing my vigil all by myself, as Hob does with his hawks, and I should pray to God to let me encounter all the evil in the world in my own person, so that if I conquered there should be none left, while if I were defeated, it would be I who would suffer for it."

"That would be extremely presumptuous of you," said Merlyn, "and you would be conquered, and you would suffer for it."

"I shouldn't mind."

"Wouldn't you? Wait till it happens and see."

"Why do people not think, when they are grown up, as I do when I am young?"

"Oh dear," said Merlyn. "You are making me feel confused. Suppose you wait till you are grown up and know the reason?"

"I don't think that is an answer at all," replied the Wart, pretty justly.

Merlyn wrung his hands.

"Well, anyway," he said. "Suppose they didn't let you stand against all the evil in the world?"

"I could ask," said the Wart.

"You could ask," repeated Merlyn.

He thrust the end of his beard into his mouth, stared tragically in the fire, and began to munch it fiercely.

CHAPTER TWENTY-ONE

THE DAY FOR the great ceremony drew near, the invitations to King Pellinore and Sir Grummore were sent out, and the Wart withdrew himself more and more into the kitchen. "Come on, Wart, old boy," said Sir Ector ruefully. "I didn't think you would take it so bad. It doesn't become you to do this sulkin'."

"I am not sulking," said the Wart. "I don't mind a bit and I am very glad that Kay is going to be a knight. Please don't think I am sulking."

"You are a good boy," said Sir Ector. "I know you're not sulkin' really, but do cheer up. Kay isn't such a bad stick, you know, in his way."

"Kay is a splendid chap," said the Wart. "Only I was not happy because he did not seem to want to go hawking, or anything, with me, any more."

"It's his youthfulness," said Sir Ector. "It will all clear up."

"I am sure it will," said the Wart. "It is only that he doesn't want me to go with him, just at the moment. And so, of course, I don't go.

"But I will go," added the Wart. "As soon as he commands me, I will do exactly what he says. Honestly, I think Kay is a good person, and I am not sulking a bit."

"You have a glass of this canary," said Sir Ector, "and go and see if old Merlyn can't start cheerin' you up."

"Sir Ector has given me a glass of canary," said the Wart, "and sent me to see if you can't cheer me up."

"Sir Ector," said Merlyn, "is a wise man."

"Well," said the Wart, "what about it?"

"The best thing for disturbances of the spirit," replied Merlyn, beginning to puff and blow, "is to learn. That is the only thing that never fails. You may grow old and trembling in your anatomies, you may lie awake at night listening to the disorder of your veins, you may miss your only love and lose your moneys to a monster, you may see the world about you devastated by evil lunatics, or know your honour trampled in the sewers of baser minds. There is only one thing for it then, – to learn. Learn why the world wags and what wags it. That is the only thing which the poor mind can never exhaust, never alienate, never be tortured by, never fear or distrust, and never dream of regretting. Learning is the thing for you. Look at what a lot of things there are to learn – pure science, the only purity there is. You can learn astronomy in a lifetime, natural history in three, literature in six. And then, after you have exhausted a milliard lifetimes in biology and medicine and theo-criticism and geography and history and economics, why, you can start to make a cartwheel out of the appropriate wood, or spend fifty years learning to begin to learn to beat your adversary at fencing. After that you can start again on mathematics, until it is time to learn to plough."

"Apart from all these things," said the Wart, "what do you suggest for me to do just now?"

"Let me see," said the magician, considering. "We have had a short six years of this, and in that time I think I am right in saying that you have been something in either animal, vegetable or mineral; something in earth, air, fire or water?"

"I don't know much," said the Wart, "about the animals and the earth."

"Then the best thing is, that you shall meet my friend the badger."

"I have never met a badger."

"Good," said Merlyn. "Except for dear old Archimedes, I think he is the most learned creature that I know. You will like him.

"By the way, Wart," added the magician, stopping in the middle of his spell, "there is one thing I ought to tell you. This is the last time I shall be able to turn you into anything. All the magic for that kind of thing has been used up, and this will be the end of your education. When Kay has been knighted my labours will be over. You will have to go away then, to be his squire in the wide world, and I shall go elsewhere. Do you think you have learnt anything?"

"I have learnt and been happy."

Chapter Twenty-One

"That's all right, then," said Merlyn. "Try to remember what you learnt."

He proceeded with the spell, pointed his wand of lignum vitae at the Little Bear, which had just begun to glow in the dimity as it hung by its tail from the North Star, and called out cheerfully, "Have a good time for the last night. Give love to Badger."

The call sounded from far away, and Wart found himself standing at the edge of a fallen bank in the Forest Sauvage, with a big black hole in front of him.

"Badger lives in there," he said to himself, "and I am supposed to go in and talk to him. But I won't. It was bad enough never to be a knight, but now my own tutor that I found on the only Quest I shall ever have is to be taken from me also, and there will be no more natural history or exciting duels with Madame Mim. Very well, I will have one more night of joy before I am condemned, and, as I am a wild beast now, I will be a wild beast, and there it is."

So he trundled off fiercely over the twilight snow, for it was winter.

If you are feeling desperate, a badger is a good thing to be. A relation of the bears, otters and wizzles, you are the nearest thing to a bear now left in England, and your skin is so thick that it makes no difference who bites you. As far as your own bite is concerned, there is something about the formation of your jaw which makes it almost impossible to be dislocated, and so, however much the thing you are biting twists about, there is no reason why you should ever let go. You are one of the few creatures which can munch up hedgehogs quite unconcernedly, just as you can munch up everything else from wasps' nests and roots to baby rabbits.

It so happened that a sleeping hedgehog was the first thing which came in the Wart's way.

"Hedge-pig," said the Wart, peering at his victim with blurred, short-sighted eyes, "I am going to munch you up."

The hedgehog, which had hidden its own bright little eye-buttons and long sensitive nose inside its curl, and which had ornamented its spikes with a not very tasteful arrangement of dead leaves, before going to bed for the winter in its grassy nest, woke up at this and squealed most lamentably.

"The more you squeal," said the Wart, "the more I shall gnash. It makes my blood boil within me."

"Ah, Mëaster Brock," cried the hedgehog, holding himself tight shut. "Good Mëaster Brock, shew mercy to a poor urchin and don't ee be tyrannical. Us be'nt no common tiggy, measter, for to be munched and mumbled. Have mercy, kind sir, on a harmless, flea-bitten crofter which can't tell his left hand nor his right."

"Hedge-pig," said the Wart remorselessly, "Forbear to whine, neither thrice nor once."

"Alas, my poor wife and children!"

"I bet you haven't got any. Come out of that, thou tramp, and prepare to meet thy doom."

"Mëaster Brock," implored the unfortunate pig, "come now, doant ee be okkered, sweet Mëaster Brock, my duck. Hearken to an urchin's prayer! Grant the dear boon of life to this most uncommon tiggy, lordly measter, and he shall sing to ee in numbers sweet or teach ee how to suck cow's milk in the pearly dew."

"Sing?" asked the Wart, stopping, quite taken aback.

"Aye, sing," cried the hedgehog. And it began hurriedly to sing in a very placating manner, but rather muffled because it dared not uncurl.

"Oh, Geneveve," it sang most mournfully into its tummy, "Sweet Geneveve,

> Ther days may come,
> Ther days may go
> But still the light of Mem'ry weaves
> Those gentle dreams
> Of long ago."

It also sang, without pausing for a moment between the songs: "Home Sweet Home" and "The Old Rustic Bridge by the Mill". Then, because it had finished all its repertoire, it drew a hurried but quavering breath, and began again on "Geneveve". After that, it sang "Home Sweet Home" and "The Old Rustic Bridge by the Mill".

"Come on," said the Wart. "You can stop that. I won't bite you."

"Clementious mëaster," whispered the hedge-pig humbly. "Us shall bless the saints and board of governors for ee and for they most kindly chops, so long as fleas skip nor urchins climb up chimneys."

Then, for fear that its brief relapse into prose might have hardened the tyrant's heart, it launched out breathlessly into "Geneveve", for the third time.

"Stop singing," said the Wart, "for heaven's sake. Uncurl. I won't do you any harm. Come, you silly little urchin, and tell me where you learnt these beautiful songs?"

"Uncurl is one word," answered the porpentine tremblingly – it did not feel in the least fretful at the moment, "but curling up is still another. If ee was to see my liddle naked nöase, mëaster, at this dispicuous moment, ee might feel a twitching in thy white toothsomes; and all's fear in love and war, that we do know. Let un sing to ee again, sweet Mëaster Brock, concerning thic there rustic mill?"

"I don't want to hear it any more. You sing it very well, but I don't want it again. Uncurl, you idiot, and tell me where you learnt to sing?"

"Us be'nt no common urchin," quavered the poor creature, staying curled up as tight as ever. "Us wor a tëuk when little by one of them there gentry, like, as it might be from the mother's breast. Ah, doant ee nip our tender vitals, lovely Mëaster Brock, for ee wor a proper gennelman, ee wor, and brought us up full comely on cow's milk an that, all supped out from a lordly dish. Ah, there, be'nt many urchins what a drunken tap water outer porcelain, that there be'nt."

"I don't know what you are talking about," said the Wart.

"Ee wor a gennelman," cried the hedgehog desperately, "like I tell ee. Es tëuk un when us wor liddle, an fed un when us hant no more. Ee wor a proper gennelman what fed un in ter parlour, like what no urchins hant been afore nor since; fed out from gennelman's porcelain, aye, and a dreary day it wor whenever us left un for nought but wilfulness, that thou may'st be sure."

"What was the name of this gentleman?"

"Ee wor a gennelman, ee wor. Ee hadden no proper nëame, like, not like you may remember, but ee wor a gennelman, that ee wor, an fed un out a porcelain."

"Was he called Merlyn?" asked the Wart curiously.

"Ah, that wor is nëame. A proper fine nëame it wor, but us never could lay a tongue to it by nary mëans. Ah, Mëarn ee called to iself, and fed un out a porcelain, like a proper fine gennelman."

"Oh, do uncurl," exclaimed the Wart. "I know the man who kept you, and I think I have seen you, yourself, when you were a baby in cotton wool. Come on, urchin, I'm sorry I frightened you. We are friends here, and I want to see your little grey wet twitching nose, just for old time's sake."

"Twitching nöase be one nëame," answered the hedgehog obstinately, "and a-twitching of that nöase be another, mëaster. Now you move along, kind Mëaster Brock, and leave a poor crofter to tëak is winter drowse. Let you think of beetles or honey, sweet baron, and flights of angels sing ee to thy rest."

"Nonsense," exclaimed the Wart. "I won't do you any harm, because I knew you when you were little."

"Ah, them badgers," said the poor thing to its tummy, "they go a-barrowing about with no harm in their hearts, Lor bless em, but doant they fair give you a nip without a noticing of it, and Lor bless ee, what is a retired mun to do? It's that there

skin of theirs, that's which it be, which from earliest childer
they've been a nipping of among each other, and also of their
ma's, without a-feeling of anything among theirselves, so
natural they nips elsewhere like the sëame. Now my poor
gennelman, Mëaster Mëarn, they was allars a-rushing arter his
ankels, with their yik-yik-yik, when they wanted to be fed
like, those what ee kept from liddles – and, holy church, how
ee would scrëam! Aye, tis a mollocky thing to dëal with they
badgers, that us may be sure.

"Doant see nothing," added the hedgehog, before the Wart
could protest. "Blunder along like to one of they ambling
hearth rugs, on the outsides of their girt feet. Get in their way
for a moment, just out of fortune like, without nary wicked
intention and tis snip-snap, just like that, out of self defence for
the hungry blind, and then where are you?

"Only plëace us can do for un," continued the urchin, "is
to hit un onter nöase. A killee's heel they nëame un in ter
scriptures. Hit one of they girt trollops on ter nöase, bim-bam,
like that ere, and the sharp life is fair outer him ere ee can
snuffle. Tis a fair knock-out, that it is.

"But how can a pore urchin dump un on ter nöase?"
concluded the lecturer mournfully, "when ee hant got
nothing to dump with, nor way to hold un? And then they
comes about ee and asks ee for to uncurl!"

"You needn't uncurl," said the Wart resignedly. "I am sorry I
woke you up, chap, and I'm sorry I frightened you. I think you
are a charming hedgehog, and meeting you has made me feel
more cheerful again. You just go to sleep like you were when I

met you, and I shall go off to look for my friend badger, as I was told to do. Goodnight, urchin, and good luck in the snow."

"Goodnight, it may be," muttered the pig grumpily. "And then again it mayernt. First it's uncurl and then it's curl. One thing one moment, and another thing ter next. Hey–ho, tis a turvey world; but Goodnight Ladies is my motter, come hail, come snow, and so us shall be continued in our next."

With these words the humble animal curled himself up still more snugly than before, gave several squeaky grunts, and was far away in a dream-world so much deeper than our human dreams as a whole winter's sleep is longer than the mercy of a single night.

"Well," thought the Wart, "he certainly gets over his trouble pretty quickly. Fancy going to sleep again as quick as that. I daresay he was never more than half-awake all the time, and will think it was only a dream when he gets up properly in the spring."

He watched the dirty little ball of leaves and grass and fleas for a moment, curled up tightly inside its hole, then grunted and moved off towards the badger's sett, following his own oblong footmarks backwards in the snow.

"So Merlyn sent you to me," said the badger, "to finish off your education. Well, I can only teach you two things, to dig, and to love your home. These are the true end of philosophy."

"Would you show me your home?"

"Certainly," said the badger, "though, of course, I don't use it all. It's a rambling old place, much too big for a single man.

I suppose some parts of it may be a thousand years old. There are about four families of us in it, here and there, take it by and large, from cellar to attics, and sometimes we don't meet for months. A crazy old place, I suppose it must seem to you modern people, but there, it's cosy."

He went ambling off down the corridors, rolling from leg to leg with that queer badger paddle, his white mask with its black stripes looked ghostly in the gloom.

"It's along that passage," he said, "if you want to wash your hands."

Badgers are not like foxes. They have a special midden where they put out their used bones and rubbish, proper earth closets, and bedrooms whose bedding they turn out frequently, to keep it clean. The Wart was enchanted with all he saw. He admired the Great Hall most, for this was the central room of the whole fortification — it was difficult to know whether to think of it as a fortification or as a palace — and all the various suites and bolt holes radiated outwards from it. It was a bit cobwebby, owing to being a sort of common room instead of being looked after by one particular family, but it was decidedly solemn. Badger called it the Combination Room. All round the panelled walls there were ancient paintings of departed badgers, famous in their day for scholarship or godliness, lit up from above by shaded glow-worms. There were stately chairs with the badger arms stamped in gold upon their Spanish leather seats — the leather was coming off — and a portrait of the Founder over the fireplace. The chairs were arranged in a semicircle round the fire, and there were mahogany fans with which everybody could shield their faces from the flames, and a kind of tilting-board by means of which the decanters could be slid back from the bottom of the semicircle to the top. Some black gowns hung in the passage outside, and all was extremely ancient.

"I'm a bachelor at the moment," said the badger apologetically, when they got back to his own snug room with the flowered wallpaper, "so I'm afraid there is only one chair. You will have to sit on the bed. Make yourself at home, my dear, while I brew some punch, and tell me how things are going on in the wide world."

"Oh, they go on much the same. Merlyn is very well, and Kay is to be made a knight next week."

"An interesting ceremony," commented the badger, stirring the spirits with a big spoon.

"What enormous arms you have got," remarked the Wart, watching him. "So have I, for that matter." And he looked down at his own bandy-legged muscles. He was really just a tight chest holding together a pair of forearms, mighty as thighs.

"It's to dig with," said the badger complacently. "Mole and I, I suppose you would have to dig pretty quick to match with us."

"I met a hedgehog outside," said the Wart.

"Did you now? They say nowadays that hedgehogs can carry swine fever and foot and mouth disease."

"I thought he was rather nice."

"They do have a sort of pathetic appeal," said the badger sadly, "but I'm afraid I generally just munch them up. There is something irresistible about pork crackling.

"The Egyptians," he added, and by this he meant the gypsies, "are fond of them for eating, too."

"Mine wouldn't uncurl."

"You should have pushed him into some water," said the badger, "and then he'd have shown you his poor legs quick enough. Come, the punch is ready. Sit you down by the fire and take your ease."

"It's nice to sit here with the snow and wind outside."

"It is nice. Let us drink good luck to Kay in his knighthood."

"Good luck, to Kay, then."

"Good luck."

"Well," said the badger, setting down his glass again with a sigh. "Now what could have possessed Merlyn to send you to me?"

"He was talking about learning," said the Wart.

"Ah, well, if it's learning you are after, you have come to the right shop. But don't you find learning rather dull?"

"Sometimes I do," said the Wart, "and sometimes I don't. On the whole I can bear a good deal of learning if it's about natural history."

"I am writing a treatise just now," said the badger, coughing diffidently to show that he was absolutely set upon explaining it, "which is to point out why Man has become the master of all the animals. Perhaps you would like to hear that?

"It's for my D.Litt., you know," added the badger hastily, before Wart could protest. He got so few chances of reading his treatises to anybody, that he could not bear to let this priceless opportunity slip by.

"Thank you very much," said the Wart.

"It will be good for you, you know," explained the badger in a humble tone. "It's just the thing to top off your education. Study birds and fish and animals: then finish off with Man. How fortunate you came. Now where the devil did I put that manuscript?"

The old gentleman hurriedly scratched about with his great claws until he had turned up a dirty old bundle of papers, one corner of which had been used for lighting something. Then he sat down in his leather armchair, which had a deep depression in the middle of it; put on his velvet smoking-cap, with the tassel; and produced a pair of tarantula spectacles, which he balanced on the end of his nose.

"Hem," said the badger.

He immediately became completely paralysed with shyness, and sat blushing at his papers, unable to begin.

"Go on," said the Wart.

"It's not very good," explained the badger coyly. "It's just a rough draft, you know. I shall alter a lot before I send it in."

"I am sure it must be interesting," said the Wart.

"Oh, no, it isn't a bit interesting. It's just an odd thing I threw off in an odd half-hour, just to pass the odd time, you know. But still, this is how it begins.

"Hem!" said the badger. Then he put on an impossible high falsetto voice and began to read as fast as possible.

"People often ask as an idle question whether the process of evolution began with the chicken or the egg. Was there an egg out of which the first chicken came, or did a chicken lay the first egg? I am in a position to state that the first thing created was the egg.

"When God had manufactured all the eggs out of which the fishes and the serpents and the birds and the mammals and even the duck-billed platypus would eventually emerge, he called the embryos before him, and saw that they were good.

"Perhaps I ought to explain," added the badger, lowering his papers nervously and looking at the Wart over the top of them, "that *all embryos look very much the same*. They are what you are before you are born, and, whether you are going to be a tadpole or a peacock or a camelopard or a man, when you are an embryo you just look like a peculiarly repulsive and helpless human being. I continue as follows:

"The embryos stood up in front of God, with their feeble hands clasped politely over their tummies and their heavy heads hanging down respectfully, and God addressed them.

"He said: 'Now, you embryos, here you are, all looking exactly the same, and We are going to give you the choice of what you are going to be. When you grow up you will get bigger anyway, but We are pleased to grant you another gift as well. You may alter any parts of yourselves into anything which you think would be useful to you in after life. For instance, at the moment you can't dig. Anybody who would like to turn his hands into a pair of spades or garden forks is allowed to do so. Or, to put it another way, at present you can only use your mouths for eating with. Anybody who would like to use his mouth as an offensive weapon, can change it by asking, and be a corkindrill or a sabre-toothed tiger. Now then, step up and choose your tools, but remember that what you choose you will grow into, and will have to stick to.'

"All the embryos thought the matter over politely, and then, one by one, they stepped up before the eternal throne. They were allowed two or three specializations, so that some chose to use their arms as flying machines and their mouths as weapons, or crackers, or drillers, or spoons, while other selected to use their bodies as boats and their hands as oars. We badgers thought very hard and decided to ask three boons. We wanted to change our skins for shields, our mouths for weapons, and our arms for garden forks. These boons were granted to us. Everybody specialized in one way or another, and some of us in very queer ones. For instance, one of the lizards decided to swap his whole body for blotting-paper, and one of the toads who lived in the Antipodes decided simply to be a water-bottle.

"The asking and granting took up two long days – they were the fifth and sixth, so far as I remember – and at the very end of the sixth day, just before it was time to knock off for Sunday, they had got through all the little embryos except one. This embryo was Man.

" 'Well, Our little man,' said God. 'You have waited till the last, and slept on your decision, and We are sure you have been thinking hard all the time. What can We do for you?'

" 'Please God,' said the embryo, 'I think that You made me in the shape which I now have for reasons best known to Yourselves, and that it would be rude to change. If I am to have my choice I will stay just as I am. I will not alter any of the parts which You gave to me, for other and doubtless inferior tools, and I will stay a defenceless embryo all my life, doing my best to make unto myself a few feeble implements out of the wood, iron and other materials which You have seen fit to put before me. If I want a boat I will endeavour to construct it out of trees, and if I want to fly I will put together a chariot to do it for me. Probably I have been very silly in refusing to take advantage of Your kind offer, but I have done my best to think it over carefully, and now hope that the feeble decision of this small innocent will find favour with Yourselves.'

" 'Well done,' exclaimed the Creator in delighted tones. 'Here, all you embryos, come here with your beaks and what-nots to look upon Our first Man. He is the only one who has guessed Our riddle, out of all of you, and We have great pleasure in conferring upon him the Order of Dominion over the Fowls of the Air, and the Beasts of the Earth, and the Fishes of the Sea. Now let the rest of you get along, and love and multiply, for it is time to knock off for the weekend. As for you, Man, you will be a naked tool all your life, though a user of tools: you will look like an embryo till they bury you, but all others will be embryos before your might; eternally undeveloped, you will always remain *potential* in Our image, able to see some of Our sorrows and to feel some of Our joys. We are partly sorry for you, Man, and partly happy, but always proud. Run along then, Man, and do your best. And listen, Man, before you go…'

" 'Well?' asked Adam, turning back from his dismissal.

" 'We were only going to say,' said God shyly, twisting Their hands together. 'Well, We were just going to say, God bless you.' "

CHAPTER TWENTY-TWO

KING PELLINORE ARRIVED for the important weekend in a high state of flurry.

"Ay say," he exclaimed. "Do you know? Have you heard? Is it a secret, what?"

"Is what a secret, what?" they asked him.

"Why, the King," cried His Majesty. "You know, about the King?"

"What's the matter with the King?" inquired Sir Ector. "You don't say he's comin' down to hunt with those damned hounds of his or anythin' like that?"

"He's dead," cried King Pellinore tragically. "He's dead, poor fellah, and can't hunt any more."

Sir Grummore stood up respectfully and took off his helm.

"The King is dead," he said. "Long live the King."

Everybody else felt they ought to stand up too, and the

boys' nurse burst into tears.

"There, there," she sobbed. "His loyal highness dead and gone, and him such a respectful gentleman. Many's the illuminated picture I've cut out of him, from the Illustrated Missals, aye, and stuck up over the mantel. From the time when he was in swaddling bands, right through them world towers till he was a-visiting the dispersed areas as the world's Prince Charming, there wasn't a picture of 'im but I had it out, aye, and give 'im a last thought o' night."

"Compose yourself, Nannie," said Sir Ector.

"It's solemn, isn't it?" said King Pellinore, "what?"

"A solemn moment," said Sir Grummore. "The King is dead. Long live the King."

"We ought to pull down the blinds," said Kay, who was always a stickler for good form, "or half-mast the banners."

"That's right," said Sir Ector. "Somebody go and tell the sergeant-at-arms."

It was obviously the Wart's duty to execute this command, for he was now the junior of all the noblemen present, and so he ran out cheerfully to find the sergeant. Soon those who were left in the solar could hear a voice crying out, "Nah then, one-two, special mourning fer is lite majesty, lower awai on the command Two!" and then the flapping of all the standards, banners, pennons, pennoncelles, banderols, guidons, streamers and cognisances which made gay the snowy turrets of the Forest Sauvage.

"How did you hear?" asked Sir Ector.

"Ay was just pricking through the purlieus of the forest

after that Beast, you know, when Ay met with a solemn friar of orders grey, and he told me. It's the very latest news."

"Poor old Pendragon," said Sir Ector.

"The King is dead," said Sir Grummore solemnly, "long live the King."

"It's all very well for you to keep on mentioning that, my dear Grummore," exclaimed King Pellinore petulantly, "but who is this King, what, that is to live so long, what, accordin' to you?"

"Well, his heir," said Sir Grummore, rather taken aback.

"Our blessed monarch," said the Nurse tearfully, "never had no hair. Anybody that studied the loyal family knowed that."

"Good gracious!" exclaimed Sir Ector. "But he must have had a next-of-kin?"

"That's just it," cried King Pellinore in high excitement: "That's the excitin' part about it, what? No hair and no next-of-skin, and who's to succeed to the throne? That's what my friar was so excited about, what, what? What?"

"Do you mean to tell me," exclaimed Sir Grummore indignantly, "that there ain't no King of England?"

"Not a scrap of one," cried King Pellinore, feeling most important. "And there have been signs and wonders of no mean might."

"I think it's a scandal," said Sir Grummore. "God knows what the dear old country is comin' to. It's these Bolsheviks, no doubt."

"What sort of signs and wonders?" asked Sir Ector.

"Well, there has appeared a sort of sword in a stone, what, in a sort of church. Not in the church, if you see what Ay mean, and not in the stone, but that sort of thing, what, like you might say."

"I don't know what the Church is coming to," said Sir Grummore.

"It's in an anvil," explained the King.

"The church?"

"No, the sword."

"But I thought you said the sword was in the stone?"

"No," said King Pellinore. "The stone is outside the church."

"Look here, Pellinore," said Sir Ector. "You have a bit of a rest, old boy, and start again. Here, drink up this horn of mead and take it easy."

"The sword," said King Pellinore, "is stuck through an anvil which stands on a stone. It goes right through the anvil and into the stone. The anvil is stuck to the stone. The stone stands outside a church. Give me some more mead."

"I don't think that's much of a wonder," remarked Sir Grummore, "what I wonder at is that they should allow such things to happen. But you can't tell nowadays, what with all these socialists."

"My dear fellah," cried Pellinore, getting excited again, "it's not where the stone is, that Ay'm trying to tell you, but what is written on it, what, where it is."

"What?"

"Why, on its pommel."

"Come on, Pellinore," said Sir Ector. "You just sit quite still with your face to the wall for a minute, and then tell us what you are talkin' about. Take it easy, old fruit. No need for hurryin'. You sit still and look at the wall, there's a good chap, and talk as slow as you can."

"There are words written on this sword in this stone outside this church," cried King Pellinore piteously, "and these words are as follows. Oh, do try to listen to me, you two, instead of interruptin' all the time about nothin', for it makes a man's head go ever so."

"What are these words?" asked Kay.

"These words say this," said King Pellinore, "so far as Ay can understand from that old friar of orders grey."

"Go on, do," said Kay, for the King had come to a halt.

"Go on," said Sir Ector, "what do these words on this sword in this anvil in this stone outside this church, say?"

"Some red propaganda, no doubt," remarked Sir Grummore.

King Pellinore closed his eyes tight, extended his arms in both directions, and announced in capital letters, "Whoso Pulleth Out This Sword of this Stone and Anvil is Rightwise King Born of All England."

"Who said that?" asked Sir Grummore.

"But the sword said it, like Ay tell you."

"Talkative weapon," remarked Grummore sceptically.

"It is written on it," cried the King angrily. "Written on it in letters of gold."

"Why didn't you pull it out then?" asked Sir Grummore.

"But Ay tell you that Ay wasn't there. All this that Ay am telling you was told to me by the friar Ay was telling you of, like Ay tell you."

"Has this sword with this inscription been pulled out?" inquired Sir Ector.

"No," whispered King Pellinore dramatically. "That's where the whole excitement comes in. They can't pull this sword out at all, although they have all been tryin' like fun, and so they have had to proclaim a tournament all over England, for New Year's Day, so that the man who comes to the tournament and pulls out the sword can be King of England for ever, what, Ay say?"

"Oh, Father," cried Kay. "The man who pulls that sword out of the stone will be the King of England. Can't we go to this tournament, Father, and have a shot?"

"Couldn't think of it," said Sir Ector.

"Long way to London," said Sir Grummore, shaking his head.

"My father went there once," said King Pellinore.

Kay said, "Oh, surely we could go? When I am knighted I shall have to go to a tournament somewhere, and this one happens at just the right date. All the best people will be there, and we should see the famous knights and great kings. It doesn't matter about the sword, of course, but think of the tournament, probably the greatest there has ever been in England, and all the things we should see and do. Dear Father, let me go to this tourney, if you love me, so that I may bear away the prize of all, in my maiden fight."

Chapter Twenty-Two

"But Kay," said Sir Ector. "I have never been to London."

"All the more reason to go. I believe that anybody who doesn't go for a tournament like this, will be proving that he has no noble blood in his veins. Think what people will say about us, if we don't go and have a shot at that sword. They will say that Sir Ector's family was too vulgar and knew it had no chance."

"We all know the family has no chance," said Sir Ector, "that is, for the sword."

"Lot of people in London," remarked Sir Grummore, with a mild surmise. "So they say."

He took a deep breath and goggled at his host with eyes like marbles.

"And shops," added King Pellinore suddenly, also beginning to breathe heavily.

"Dang it!" cried Sir Ector, bumping his horn mug on the table so that it spilled. "Let's all go to London, then, and see the new King!"

They rose up as one man.

"Why shouldn't Ay be as good a man as my father?" exclaimed King Pellinore.

"Dash it all," cried Sir Grummore. "After all, damn it all, it is the capital."

"Hurray!" shouted Kay.

"Lord have mercy," said the nurse.

At this moment the Wart came in with Merlyn, and everybody was too excited to notice that, if he had not now been grown up, he would have been on the verge of tears.

"Oh, Wart," cried Kay, forgetting for the moment that he was only addressing his squire, and slipping back into the familiarity of their boyhood. "What do you think? We are all going to London for a great tournament on New Year's Day!"

"Are we?"

"Yes, and you will carry my shield and spears for the jousts, and I shall win the palm off everybody and be a great knight!"

"Well, I am glad we are going," said the Wart, "for Merlyn is leaving us too."

"Oh, we shan't need Merlyn."

"He is leaving us," repeated the Wart.

"Leavin' us?" asked Sir Ector. "I thought it was we that were leavin'?"

"He is going away from the Forest Sauvage."

Sir Ector said, "Oh, come now, Merlyn, what's all this about? I don't understand all this a bit."

"I have come to say Goodbye, Sir Ector," said the old magician. "Tomorrow my pupil Kay will be knighted, and the next week my other pupil will go away as his squire. I have outlived my usefulness here, and it is time to go."

"Now, now, don't say that," said Sir Ector. "I think you're a jolly useful chap whatever happens. You just stay here and teach me, or be the librarian or something. Don't you leave an old man alone, after the children have flown."

"We shall all meet again," said Merlyn. "There is no cause to be sad."

"Don't go," said Kay.

"I must go," replied their tutor. "We have had a good time

336

while we were young, but it is in the nature of Time to fly. There are many things in other parts of the kingdom which I ought to be attending to just now: and it is a specially busy time for me. Come, Archimedes, say Goodbye to the company."

"Goodbye," said Archimedes tenderly to the Wart.

"Goodbye," said the Wart without looking up at all.

"But you can't go," cried Sir Ector, "not without a month's notice."

"Can't I?" replied Merlyn, taking up the position always assumed by philosophers who propose to dematerialize. He stood on his toes, while Archimedes held tight to his shoulder: began to spin on them slowly like a top: spun faster and faster till he was only a blur of greyish light: and in a few seconds there was no one there at all.

"Goodbye, Wart," cried two faint voices outside the solar window.

"Goodbye," said the Wart for the last time; and the poor fellow went quickly out of the room.

CHAPTER TWENTY-THREE

THE KNIGHTING TOOK place in a whirl of preparations. Kay's sumptuous bath had to be set up in the box-room, between two towel-horses and an old box of selected games which contained a worn-out straw dart-board – it was called a flechette in those days – because all the other rooms were full of packing. The nurse spent the whole time constructing new warm pants for everybody, on the principle that the climate of any place outside the Forest Sauvage must be treacherous to the extreme, and, as for the sergeant, he polished all the armour till it was quite brittle and sharpened the swords till they were almost worn away.

At last it was time to set out.

Perhaps, if you happen not to have lived in the old England of the twelfth century, or whenever it was, and in a remote castle on the borders of the Marches at that, you will find it difficult to imagine the wonders of their journey.

The road, or track, ran most of the time along the high ridges of the hills or downs, and they could look down on either side of them upon the desolate marches where the snowy reeds sighed, and the ice crackled, and the duck in the red sunsets quacked loud on the winter air. The whole country was like that. Perhaps there would be a moory marsh on one side of the ridge, and a forest of thirty thousand acres on the other, with all the great branches weighted in white. They could sometimes see a wisp of smoke among the trees, or a huddle of buildings far out among the impassable reeds, and twice they came to quite respectable towns which had several inns to boast of; but on the whole it was an England without civilization. The better roads were cleared of cover for a bow-shot on either side of them, lest the traveller should be slain by hidden thieves.

They slept where they could, sometimes in the hut of some cottager who was prepared to welcome them, sometimes in the castle of a brother knight who invited them to refresh themselves, sometimes in the firelight and fleas of a dirty little hovel with a bush tied to a pole outside it – this was the sign-board used at that time by inns – and once or twice on the open ground, all huddled together for warmth between their grazing chargers. Wherever they went and whenever they slept, the east wind whistled in the reeds, and the geese went over high in the starlight, honking at the stars.

London was full to the brim. If Sir Ector had not been lucky enough to own a little land in Pie Street, on which there stood a respectable inn, they would have been hard put to it to find a lodging. But he did own it, and as a matter of fact drew most of his dividends from this source, so that they were able to get three beds between the five of them. They thought themselves fortunate.

On the first day of the tournament, Sir Kay managed to get them on the way to the lists at least an hour before the jousts could possibly begin. He had lain awake all night, imagining how he was going to beat the best barons in England, and he had not been able to eat his breakfast. Now he rode at the front of the cavalcade, with pale cheeks, and Wart wished there was something he could do to calm him down.

For country people who only knew the dismantled tilting ground of Sir Ector's castle, the scene which now met their eyes was really ravishing. It was a huge green pit in the earth, about as big as the arena at a football match. It lay about ten feet lower than the surrounding country, with sloping banks, and all the snow had been swept off it. It had been kept warm with straw, which had been cleared off that morning, and now all the close-mown grass sparkled green in the white landscape. Round the arena there was a world of colour so dazzling and moving and twinkling as to make you blink your eyes. The wooden grandstands were painted in scarlet and white. The silk pavilions of famous people, pitched on every side, were azure and green and saffron and chequered. The pennons and pennoncells which floated everywhere in the sharp wind were flapping with every colour of the rainbow, as they strained and slapped at their flagpoles, and the barrier down the middle of the arena itself was done in chessboard squares of black and white. Most of the combatants and their friends had not yet arrived, but you could see from those few who had arrived how the very people would turn the scene into a bank of flowers, and how the armour would flash, and the scalloped sleeves of the heralds jig in the wind, as they raised their brazen trumpets to their lips to shake the fleecy clouds of winter with joyances and fanfares.

"Good heavens!" cried Sir Kay. "I have left my sword at home."

"Can't joust without a sword," said Sir Grummore. "Quite irregular."

"Better go and fetch it," said Sir Ector. "You have time."

"My squire will do," said Sir Kay. "What a damned mistake to make. Here, squire, ride hard back to the inn and fetch my sword. You shall have a shilling if you fetch it in time."

The Wart went as pale as Sir Kay was, and looked as if he were going to strike him. Then he said, "It shall be done, Master," and turned his stupid little ambling palfrey against the stream of newcomers. He began to push his way towards their hostelry as best he might.

"To offer me money!" cried the Wart to himself. "To look down at this beastly little donkey-affair off his great charger and call me Squire! Oh, Merlyn, give me patience with the brute, and stop me from throwing his filthy shilling in his face."

When he got to the inn it was closed. Everybody had thronged out to see the famous tournament, and the entire household had followed after the mob. Those were lawless days and it was not safe to leave your house – or even to go to sleep in it – unless you were certain that it was impregnable. The wooden shutters bolted over the downstairs windows were two inches thick, and the doors were double-barred.

"Now what do I do," said the Wart, "to earn my shilling?"

He looked ruefully at the little blind inn, and began to laugh.

"Poor Kay," he said, "all that shilling stuff was only because he was scared and miserable, and now he has good cause to be. Well, he shall have a sword of some sort if I have to break into the Tower of London.

"How does one get hold of a sword?" he continued. "Where can I steal one? Could I waylay some knight, even if I am mounted on an ambling pad, and take his weapons by force? There must be some swordsmith or armourer in a great town like this, whose shop would be still open."

He turned his mount and cantered off along the street.

There was a quiet churchyard at the end of it, with a kind of square in front of the church door. In the middle of the square there was a heavy stone with an anvil on it, and a fine new sword was struck through the anvil.

"Well," said the Wart, "I suppose it's some sort of war memorial, but it will have to do. I am quite sure nobody would grudge Kay a war memorial, if they knew his desperate straits."

He tied his reins round a post of the lych-gate, strode up the gravel path, and took hold of the sword.

"Come, sword," he said. "I must cry your mercy and take you for a better cause.

"This is extraordinary," said the Wart. "I feel queer when I have hold of this sword, and I notice everything more clearly. Look at the beautiful gargoyles of this church, and of the monastery which it belongs to. See how splendidly all the famous banners in the aisle are waving. How nobly that yew holds up the red flakes of its timbers to worship God. How clean the snow is. I can smell something like fetherfew and sweet briar – and is that music I hear?"

It was music, whether of pan-pipes or of recorders, and the light in the churchyard was so clear, without being dazzling, that you could have picked a pin out twenty yards away.

"There is something in this place," said the Wart. "There are people here. Oh, people, what do you want?"

Nobody answered him, but the music was loud and the light beautiful.

"People," cried the Wart. "I must take this sword. It is not for me, but for Kay. I will bring it back."

There was still no answer, and Wart turned back to the sword. He saw the golden letters on it, which he did not read, and the jewels on its pommel, flashing in the lovely light.

"Come, sword," said the Wart.

He took hold of the handles with both hands, and strained against the stone. There was a melodious consort on the recorders, but nothing moved.

The Wart let go of the handles, when they were beginning to bite into the palms of his hands, and stepped back from the anvil, seeing stars.

"It is well fixed," said the Wart.

He took hold of it again and pulled with all his might. The music played more and more excitedly, and the lights all about the churchyard glowed like amethysts; but the sword still stuck.

"Oh, Merlyn," cried the Wart, "help me to get this sword."

There was a kind of rushing noise, and a long chord played along with it. All round the churchyard there were hundreds of old friends. They rose over the church wall all together, like the Punch and Judy ghosts of remembered days, and there were otters and nightingales and vulgar crows and hares and serpents and falcons and fishes and goats and dogs and dainty unicorns and newts and solitary wasps and goat-moth caterpillars and corkindrills and volcanoes and mighty trees and patient stones. They loomed round the church wall, the lovers and helpers of the Wart, and they all spoke solemnly in turn. Some of them had come from the banners in the church, where they were painted in heraldry, some from the waters and the sky and the fields about, but all, down to the smallest shrew mouse, had come to help on account of love. Wart felt his power grow.

"Remember my biceps," said the oak, "which can stretch out horizontally against Gravity, when all the other trees go up or down."

"Put your back into it," said a luce (or pike) off one of the heraldic banners, "like you did once when I was going to snap you up. Remember that all power springs from the nape of the neck."

"What about those forearms," asked a badger gravely, "that are held together by a chest? Come along, my dear embryo, and find your tool."

A merlin sitting on the top of the yew tree cried out, "Now then, Captain Wart, what is the first law of foot? I thought I once heard something about never letting go?"

"Don't work like a stalling woodpecker," urged a tawny owl affectionately. "Keep up a steady effort, my duck, and you will have it yet."

"Cohere," said a stone in the church wall.

A snake, slipping easily along the coping which bounded the holy earth, said, "Now then, Wart, if you were once able to walk with three hundred ribs at once, surely you can co-ordinate a few little muscles here and there? Make everything work together, as you have been learning to do ever since God let the amphibia crawl out of the sea. Fold your powers together, with the spirit of your mind, and it will come out like butter. Come along, *Homo sapiens*, for all we humble friends of yours are waiting to cheer."

The Wart walked up to the great sword for the third time. He put out his right hand softly and drew it out as gently as from a scabbard.

There was a lot of cheering, a noise like a hurdy-gurdy which went on and on. In the middle of this noise, after a very long time, he saw Kay and gave him the sword. The people at the tournament were making a frightful row.

"But this isn't my sword," said Sir Kay.

"It was the only one I could get," said the Wart. "The inn was locked."

"It is a nice-looking sword. Where did you get it?"

"I found it stuck in a stone, outside a church."

Sir Kay had been watching the tilting nervously, waiting for his turn. He had not paid much attention to his squire.

"That's a funny place to find a sword," he said.

"Yes, it was stuck through an anvil."

"What?" cried Sir Kay, suddenly rounding upon him. "Did you just say this sword was stuck in a stone?"

"It was," said the Wart. "It was a sort of war memorial."

Sir Kay stared at him for several seconds in amazement, opened his mouth, shut it again, licked his lips, then turned his back and plunged through the crowd. He was looking for Sir Ector, and the Wart followed after him.

"Father," cried Sir Kay, "come here a moment."

"Yes, my boy," said Sir Ector. "Splendid falls these professional chaps do manage. Why, what's the matter, Kay? You look as white as a sheet."

"Do you remember that sword which the King of England would pull out?"

"Yes."

"Well, here it is. I have it. It is in my hand. I pulled it out."

Sir Ector did not say anything silly. He looked at Kay and he looked at the Wart. Then he stared at Kay again, long and lovingly, and said, "We will go back to the church."

"Now then, Kay," he said, when they were at the church door. He looked at his first-born again, kindly, but straight between the eyes. "Here is the stone, and you have the sword. It will make you the King of England. You are my son that I am proud of, and always will be, whatever happens. Will you promise me that you took it out by your own might?"

Kay looked at his father. He also looked at the Wart and at the sword.

Then he handed the sword to the Wart quite quietly.

He said, "I am a liar. Wart pulled it out."

As far as the Wart was concerned, there was a time after this in which Sir Ector kept telling him to put the sword back into the stone – which he did – and in which Sir Ector and Kay then vainly tried to take it out. The Wart took it out for them, and stuck it back again once or twice. After this, there was another time which was more painful.

He saw that his dear guardian Sir Ector was looking quite old and powerless, and that he was kneeling down with difficulty on a gouty old knee.

"Sir," said poor old Sir Ector, without looking up, although he was speaking to his own boy.

"Please don't do this, Father," said the Wart, kneeling down also. "Let me help you up, Sir Ector, because you are making me unhappy."

"Nay, nay, my lord," said Sir Ector, with some very feeble old tears. "I was never your father nor of your blood, but I wote well ye are of an higher blood than I wend ye were."

"Plenty of people have told me you are not my father," said the Wart, "but it doesn't matter a bit."

"Sir," said Sir Ector humbly, "will ye be my good and gracious lord when ye are King?"

"Don't!" said the Wart.

"Sir," said Sir Ector, "I will ask no more of you but that you will make my son, your foster-brother, Sir Kay, seneschal of all your lands."

Kay was kneeling down too, and it was more than the Wart could bear.

"Oh, do stop," he cried. "Of course he can be seneschal, if I have got to be this King, and, oh, Father, don't kneel down there like that, because it breaks my heart. Please get up, Sir Ector, and don't make everything so horrible. Oh, dear, oh, dear, I wish I had never seen that filthy sword at all."

And the Wart also burst into tears.

CHAPTER TWENTY-FOUR

PERHAPS THERE OUGHT to be one more chapter about the coronation. The barons naturally kicked up a dreadful fuss, but as the Wart was preparing to go on putting the sword in the stone and pulling it out again till Doomsday, and as there was nobody else who could do the thing at all, in the end they had to give in. A few revolted, who were quelled later, but in the main the people of England were glad to settle down.

The coronation was a splendid memory, and, what was still more splendid, it was like a birthday or Christmas Day. Everybody sent presents to the Wart, for his prowess in having learnt to pull swords out of stones, and several burghers of the City of London asked him to help them in taking stoppers out of unruly bottles, unscrewing taps which had got stuck, and in other household emergencies which had got beyond their control. The Dog Boy and Wat clubbed together and sent him a mixture for the distemper, which contained quinine and was absolutely priceless. Goat sent him a watch-chain plaited out of his own beard. Cavall came quite simply and gave him his heart and soul. The Nurse of the Forest Sauvage sent a cough mixture, thirty dozen handkerchiefs all marked, and a pair of combinations with a double chest. The sergeant sent him his medals, to be preserved in the British Museum. Hob lay awake in agony all night, and sent off Cully with brand-new white leather jesses, silver varvels and silver bell. Robin and Marian went out on an expedition which took them six weeks, and sent a whole gown made out of the skins of pine martens. Little John added a yew bow, seven feet long, which he was quite unable to draw. An anonymous hedgehog sent four or five dirty leaves with some fleas on them. The Questing Beast and King Pellinore put their heads together and sent some of their most perfect fewmets, all wrapped up in the green leaves of spring in a golden horn with a red velvet baldrick. Sir Grummore sent a gross of spears, with the old school crest on all of them. The vicar chose a work called *De Clericali Disciplina*, attributed to Petrus Alphonsus, which would be read at nights and did not have to be explained. The cooks, tenants, villeins and retainers of the Castle of the Forest Sauvage, who were all given an angel each and sent up for the ceremony in a charabanc at Sir Ector's charge, brought an enormous silver model of cow Crumbocke, who had won the championship for the third time, and Ralph Passelewe to sing at the coronation banquet. Archimedes sent his own great-great-grandson, so that he could sit on the back of the King's throne at dinner, and make messes in the soup. The Lord Mayor and Aldermen of the City of London subscribed for a spacious aquarium-mews-cum-menagerie in which all the creatures were starved one day a week for the good of their stomachs, and here, for the fresh food, good bedding, constant attention, and every modern convenience, all the Wart's friends resorted in their old age, on wing and foot and fin, for the sunset of their happy lives. The citizens of London sent fifty million pounds, to keep the menagerie up, and the Ladies of Britain constructed a pair of black velvet carpet slippers with the Wart's initials embroidered on in gold. Kay sent his own record Scythian, with honest love. There were many other tasteful presents, from various barons, archbishops, princes, landgraves, tributary Kings, corporations, popes, sultans, royal commissions, urban district councils, czars, beys, mahatmas, and so forth, but the nicest present of all was sent most affectionately by his own guardian, Sir Ector. This present was a dunce's cap, rather like a pharoah's serpent, which you lit at the top end. The Wart lit it, and watched it grow. When the flame had quite gone out, Merlyn was standing before him in his magic hat.

"Well, Wart," said Merlyn, "here we are — or were — again. How nice you look in your crown. I was not allowed to tell you before, or since, but your father was, or will be, King Uther Pendragon, and it was I myself, disguised as a beggar, who first carried you to Sir Ector's castle, in your golden swaddling bands. I know all about your birth and parentage and who gave you your real name. I know the sorrows before you, and the joys, and how there will never again be anybody who dares to call you by the friendly name of Wart. In future it will be your glorious doom to take up the burden and to enjoy the nobility of your proper name: so now I shall crave the privilege of being the very first of your subjects to address you with it – as my dear liege lord, King Arthur."

"Will you stay with me for a long time?" asked the Wart, not understanding much of this.

"Yes, Wart," said Merlyn. "Or rather, as I should say (or is it have said?) Yes, King Arthur."

THE BEGINNING

Postscript

I remember that my father gave me *The Sword in the Stone* to read when I had measles – or chickenpox; and to me the interesting thing now is that it wasn't either a brand-new copy, *or* one from the public library. My father had evidently owned it for years, since it was a first edition (published in 1938) which had long since lost its dust jacket. He had written his name in it, and I have the copy by me as I'm writing now.

In 1938 my father was thirty-seven and an Oxford don. What was he doing buying – and carefully keeping – a children's book? The simple answer is that, in one sense, *The Sword in the Stone* isn't a children's book at all (none of the best children's books are really children's books; they've all been written because their authors needed to write them for themselves). T. H. White described it as "more or less a kind of wish-fulfilment of the things I should like to have happened when I was a boy". He added: "It seems impossible to determine whether it is for grown-ups or children."

If you read the biographical note at the front of this book, you will see that T. H. White had what seems to be a wonderful life. In fact, for a large part of it, White was lonely and melancholy. He lived mostly by himself, preferring remote cottages hidden away from the gaze of the world (like Merlyn in the third chapter of *The Sword in the Stone*). He was expert at a wide range of physical skills: among other things he could fly a plane, deep-sea dive, and hawk (he wrote a superb book about hawking called *The Goshawk*). He was also hugely knowledgeable about medieval history and literature. Though it all seems to come out of White's head, *The Sword in the Stone* is deeply indebted to the man to whom White dedicated it, Sir Thomas Malory (or "Maleore" as White has it, using the medieval spelling), whose *Morte d'Arthur* (or *Death of Arthur*) is a vast, rambling, fascinating collection of weird and wonderful stories about Arthur and the Knights of the Round Table and the sundry witches and wizards who made their lives so complicated.

But if *The Sword in the Stone* were just a reworking of Malory, it would be dull indeed. The book glows with life because White is writing about himself in two disguises: as the lonely young Wart, the un-needed orphan who has to take second place to the important boy in the household (the silly, bumptious, but in the end very likeable Kay); and also as the all-wise Merlyn, whose "magic" mostly comes from the fact that he *lives backwards* – so that he has experienced the future before everyone else gets to it. This surely is a metaphor for the grown-up White looking back on his childhood from the experience of adulthood; and it's also immensely touching – especially the moment when Wart tells Merlyn that they only met half an hour earlier, because for backwards-living Merlyn that means they're about to say goodbye for ever.

If you're reading this after you've already got to the end of the book, you don't need me to tell you how wonderful it is. Personally I've always loved the anachronisms – the things which are deliberately out of their time, like Sir Ector planning to send Kay to Eton (mind you, Eton College was founded so long ago that this may not be an anachronism at all). Some of it is shrewd political commentary on the times White lived in: we know from White's own drawings in the first edition (not included in this book) that the bullying giant Galapas, whom White has drawn with a swastika on his arm, is partly meant to stand for the fascist dictators Hitler and Mussolini, who were just rising to power when the book was written.

But best of all, I think, is the wistful, melancholy air which hangs over the whole book, so that it feels oddly like the ending of a story rather than, as White puts on the last page, "The Beginning" of Wart's reign as the Once and Future King. It's a middle-aged man looking back at an imaginary childhood when the summers were a blissfully hot riot of haymaking; when there were comic adults like King Pellinore wandering absent-mindedly in and out of the place; when there were wonderful meals to be eaten – there is as much marvellous writing about food in *The Sword in the Stone* as in *The Wind in the Willows*; and when delicious danger lurks round every corner. (White cut out Madame Mim when he revised the book for the completed *Once and Future King*; I've always been angry with him about this, so I revived her and turned her into the music-teaching witch Wilhemina Worlock in my own Mr Majeika books.)

No, I'm not surprised my father bought the book in 1938, even though his own childhood was long since past. I handed it on to my own children in turn, but I've stolen it back from them now, and I keep it on a very special shelf, which I reserve for the children's books that really *matter* to me. If I live to 2038, by which time I shall be ninety-two, I shall celebrate its centenary by reading it yet again – and thanking my father for handing it over to me, that day I had measles – or was it chickenpox?

HUMPHREY CARPENTER

ELIDOR
BY ALAN GARNER

Four children from a Manchester suburb are drawn into Elidor, a twilight world almost destroyed by fear and darkness. And Elidor's salvation remains in the children's power alone. A richly imagined, spine-chilling book.

THE WEIRDSTONE OF BRISINGAMEN AND
THE MOON OF GOMRATH
BY ALAN GARNER

Fierce, wild fantasies about the loss and recovery of a stone containing great power and strength. In the highly evocative landscape of Cheshire, an area rich in legend, Susan and Colin are captured by evil forces in a struggle that leaves the reader spellbound and breathless.

THE OWL SERVICE
BY ALAN GARNER
(Winner of the Carnegie Medal and the Guardian Award)

Ancient jealousies, hatreds and high passions are re-awakened and lived anew by three young people who become trapped in a seemingly endless re-enactment of a tragic Welsh legend.

RED SHIFT
BY ALAN GARNER

Red Shift is a daring exploration of a contemporary love story cut into by two violent fragments from the past. The result is one of the most profoundly imaginative, strange, controversial, and rewardingly demanding novels to have been published for children.

The Road to Irriyan
Louise Lawrence

'She was as huge as a condor, hovering over him on great black wings. Her eyes were merciless. Her hooked beak gaped and her talons spread as she prepared to strike...'

Woken from the long, herb-induced sleep by the encroaching presence of the Grimthane, Roderick, Craig and Carrie take to the vast underground caves and passages of the old city of the giants in their attempt to reach Irriyan and safety. Led by goblins and a dwarf, they are forced away from familiar territory by the vicious shape-changer, Merrigan, and must rush from the dwarfs' stronghold to escape the massive rock trolls. In desperate peril, Roderick acts selflessly to save Llandor.

A fantastic world of mystery and adventure. Part Two of Louise Lawrence's *Llandor* trilogy.

DEAR NOBODY
Berlie Doherty

Winner of the Carnegie Medal

October was the month when Helen would go
to music college, and Chris to university – now
October is the month their baby will be born.

Chris cannot think about the baby. He is just
desperate not to lose Helen.

Bur Helen turns to the unborn baby – her little
Nobody – for reassurance. Locked out from her
own mother's thoughts, Helen is determined
that she will never be a stranger to their child.

As they sort out their conflicting feelings, Helen
and Chris try to make sense of their future –
together or apart.

*"I have never read a book that evokes so vividly
how it feels to be a teenager in love."*
Daily Telegraph

Collins
An imprint of HarperCollins Publishers

S.E. HINTON

THE OUTSIDERS

The chillingly realistic story of the Socs and
the Greasers, rival teenage gangs, whose
hatred for each other leads to the mindless
violence of gang warfare.

RUMBLE FISH

Rusty James has a reputation for
toughness: he runs his own gang, and
attends school only when he has nothing
better to do. But his blind ambition to be
just like his glamorous older brother, the
Motorcycle Boy, leads to an explosive and
tragic climax.

THE CHRONICLES OF NARNIA

by C. S. LEWIS

C. S. Lewis's wit and wisdom, and his blend of excitement and adventure with fantasy, have made this magnificent series beloved of many generations of readers. The final book, *The Last Battle*, won the Carnegie Medal for 1956.

Each of the seven titles is a complete story in itself, but all take place in the magical land of Narnia. Guided by the noble Lion Aslan, the children learn that evil and treachery can only be overcome by courage, loyalty and great sacrifice.

The titles, in suggested reading order, are as follows:

The Magician's Nephew
The Lion, the Witch and the Wardrobe
The Horse and His Boy
Prince Caspian
The Voyage of the Dawn Treader
The Silver Chair
The Last Battle

Order Form

To order direct from the publishers, just make a list of the titles you want and fill in the form below:

Name ....

Address ....

....

....

Send to: Dept 6, HarperCollins Publishers Ltd, Westerhill Road, Bishopbriggs, Glasgow G64 2QT.

Please enclose a cheque or postal order to the value of the cover price, plus:

UK & BFPO: Add £1.00 for the first book, and 25p per copy for each additional book ordered.

Overseas and Eire: Add £2.95 service charge. Books will be sent by surface mail but quotes for airmail despatch will be given on request.

A 24-hour telephone ordering service is available to holders of Visa, MasterCard, Amex or Switch cards on 0141- 772 2281.

Collins
An *Imprint* of HarperCollins*Publishers*